ONCE UPON A MIRROR

C. M. MASON

For all who keep fairy tales alive.
May fairy tales continue to live on in the imaginations of all—young, old,
and those who believe.

An Everfell Fairy Tale

EVERFELL

BRIGHTFELL

FROST FELL

EMBERFELL

IRONFELL

GLIMMERFELL

HOLLOWREACH

SHADOWFELL

THE MUMMERS
FOREST

THE DARK FOREST

MYSTFELL

N
NW · NE
W · E
SW · SE
S

ONCE UPON A TIME . . .

TWENTY YEARS AGO

"When was the last time you saw your daughter?" The policeman's voice carried from the living room, into the entryway, and up the winding staircase.

Fun family pictures adorned the walls. Smiling faces at family events, a family portrait, and school pictures. Pictures of Nessa.

Charlie Grimm sat cross-legged, clutching the white spindles of the balcony overlooking the entryway. His face and forehead pressed against the wood. Indentations formed in his cheeks. His breath quickened, inhaling and exhaling as fast as possible. His eyes focused on the light spilling forth from the living room into the darkened hallway.

"Before school," Vanessa's mom said from the living room.

"And she was supposed to come right home afterward?" the policeman asked.

"Well . . ." Her mom stumbled over the words, her voice cracking. "Sometimes she'll go visit the Grimm's house, but she's always home before dinner."

Dinner.

Dinner was four hours ago. 6:30 p.m. sharp. It was Vanessa's unofficial curfew. Charlie's as well. Always end play, and be home for dinner at 6:30. They stuck to that rule. Always.

"The Grimms?" the policeman asked. "What relationship are they to the young girl—"

"Vanessa," her mom said, her voice high-pitched, as if speaking through tears. "Vanessa Davis."

"Vanessa," the policeman repeated.

"Sometimes she went by her nickname, Nessa," her mom added. She sniffled.

There was a brief pause, but the name echoed over and over in Charlie's mind.

Nessa.

He clasped his hand tighter around the wood of the round spindle. The whites of his knuckles showed.

"What relation are they to Nessa?" the policeman asked.

"We're friends of the family. Neighbors. We live a few houses down," Charlie's mom said. "Our son, Charlie, is friends with Nessa. They're basically inseparable. They've been that way since they were four or five."

"What's the age of your son?" the policeman asked.

"Thirteen," Charlie's dad said. "He turned thirteen a week ago."

Charlie held his breath.

"And the girl is the same age?" the policeman asked.

"Yes," Vanessa's dad replied. "Sort of. Her birthday is next week."

"So, she's twelve?" the policeman asked.

"Yes," Vanessa's dad said.

Charlie exhaled, tearing his forehead away from the spindles. He sat upright, his shoulders leaning back to gain a better vantage point down the hall. His eyes followed the beige carpet, similar to a trail of breadcrumbs, leading to Nessa's room.

Brightly colored stickers and drawings covered the brown bedroom door. Light peered through the crack of the slightly ajar door. A pink bedcover. Stuffed animals strewn about the bed. Posters of musicians on the wall.

Charlie gulped.

Charlie and Vanessa spent some of their time together in her room, listening to music. The latest pop-punk hits of the day played on the radio. She was fortunate to get a new iPod and shared one earbud, so they could listen to the songs together. Their preferred song of choice, "All the Small Things," played on repeat.

Nessa's short, flipped-out bob haircut swayed above her shoulders as the two of them danced and bounced across the room. Her black canvas and white rubber shoes flared through the air with every beat. With each kick, she avoided tripping on her baggy pants. A pair of thick, black leather bracelets wrapped around her wrists instead of a crown. A black band T-shirt over a white long-sleeved shirt was her royal gown. Nessa was a princess of punk rock, and the iPod was her kingdom.

Despite spending time in each other's rooms hanging out, that's not where they played. That was reserved for Charlie's basement—a special area known only to them. His parents knew they played down there. They had for years. But their parents didn't know why it was special.

They didn't know about the mirror.

"Is there anyone else in your home, Mr. and Mrs. Grimm?" the policeman asked.

"We have an older daughter," Charlie's mom said. "Julie. She's eighteen. A senior in high school."

"Was she at home this afternoon?" the policeman asked.

"No," Charlie's dad answered. "She was at volleyball practice."

"So, there was no one at home?" the policeman asked.

"No," Charlie's mom said.

A hush fell over the house. Only the sound of Charlie's heartbeat echoed in his ears. *Thump. Thump. Thump.*

"Has she ever threatened to run away or leave?" the policeman asked.

"No," her mother said. "She has a bit of a rebellious streak, but she never threatened to leave."

"Can I speak with the young boy?" the policeman asked. "He may know where she's hiding or have some additional information."

"We asked him," his mom said. "He said he didn't know where she was."

He did know. Charlie knew the answer. They wouldn't believe him, or far worse, they would take it away. Nessa would be lost forever. Trapped inside.

Every time they played, the mirror responded. It opened a gateway to another realm. A realm of magic and fairy tales and mythical creatures. A realm ruled by a kind king and queen. A funny wizard's apprentice. A wise wizard.

The mirror was a portal to a place of joy, laughter, and happiness.

They were supposed to meet there after school. Normally, they'd walk home from the school bus stop and enter the mirror together. They'd go on fantastical adventures. Gallant knights. Mythical beasts. Special envoys of royalty.

However, today was different. Charlie had a doctor's appointment and missed the last part of school. He wasn't there to walk home with Nessa from the school bus.

Vanessa was welcomed into their home. She knew exactly where the spare key was hidden in the back. She easily could have let herself inside and ventured through the mirror to wait for him.

Yeah. She entered the mirror to wait for me, Charlie thought.

Upon arriving at home, Charlie had rushed down the stairs to the basement. It smelled of mildew and was scattered with boxes and other items for storage. Mundane to the adults, but a place of wonder and whimsy to a child.

Charlie rushed over to the mirror, expecting Vanessa to be waiting for him. But she was nowhere to be found. The full-framed mirror, housed in ornate, carved dark wood, stood quietly waiting for the pair in the corner of the basement.

She must have already gone through. Yes. She already went through to the magical realm inside.

Atop the mirror was a round knob. A radiating sun was centered in the curve above the mirror glass. Unbeknownst to most, but Charlie knew instinctively how to activate the mirror.

The knob twisted and turned like a dial. With a series of clockwise and counterclockwise turns, the mirror activated. The glass turned into suspended water with an image of a castle room on the other side. Charlie and Nessa passed through as if walking through a waterfall, but they remained dry.

On the other side, they went on their fantastical adventures. Knights and derring-dos. The fairy tale stories of old. They were there on the other side. Every fairy tale told in childhood existed in this world . . . for the most part. A few liberties were taken, but they were there. Waiting.

Charlie and Nessa weren't only told the tales; they experienced them. Sword lessons. Horseback riding. Magical shows. All compliments of the kind king and queen of the kingdom of Glimmerfell.

However, earlier that day, the mirror didn't respond. Charlie turned the dial over and over in the proper manner, but nothing happened. He spun and spun the dial, but the mirror fell silent.

Why wouldn't it work for me? Charlie dipped his head.

"Where is the boy now?" the policeman asked.

"He was upstairs," his mom said. "Charlie!"

He froze, not wanting to move from his spot.

"Come here, Charlie!" his mom yelled.

"I'll go to him," the policeman said. "Sometimes it's easier to talk to children in a place they feel comfortable."

Charlie snapped to attention. His heart beat in his chest. He was grounded for certain. Three months at least. Maybe a year. Worse . . . the policeman might take him to jail. He recently turned thirteen. Practically an adult, no longer seen as a child. He was facing jail time for certain. Charlie clutched the white spindles, practicing for his sentence.

A figure emerged from the light of the living room. The shadows of the hall cloaked his face. Tall and stocky, he wore a dark uniform decorated with unknown gear of some kind. Charlie could only focus on the policeman's face in the living room entryway, glaring back at him.

"Hello, Charlie," the policeman said. "I'm Officer Ron with the Newbury Grove Police Department." Officer Ron approached the staircase in small steps. He placed his right hand on the wooden newel post.

He continued, "It's about your friend Vanessa. Can I ask you a few questions?"

Charlie pressed his face into the spindles, trying to hide and disappear behind the white bars. He was trapped, caged with nowhere to run. He had to tell them the truth or they would lock him up or worse . . .

They would take away the mirror.

She'd be trapped forever. If Charlie told the truth, Nessa would be trapped forever in Glimmerfell, living a life on the streets with no one to care for her. Would the King and Queen take her in? Would someone else?

A shiver ran down Charlie's back. A bead of sweat rolled down the side of his face. What other choice did he have? He had to tell them.

"Am I in trouble?" Charlie asked.

The officer shook his head. "No, Charlie," he said. "You're not in trouble."

Charlie gulped. "Do I have to come down there?"

"No, you can—you can stay there," Officer Ron replied. "We do need your help, though. Your friend Nessa is missing. We need to find her as quickly as we can. Would you know anything about where she might be?"

Charlie's chest rose and fell with each labored breath. His eyes intently focused on the officer waiting at the bottom of the steps. He squeezed the spindles harder. The ridges of the wood bore into his fingers.

"You can tell him, Charlie," his mom said. She stood in the entryway, along with his dad and Vanessa's parents.

"If you know anything about Nessa's whereabouts . . ." Vanessa's mom said. "Please. Please tell us."

"You promise I won't get into trouble?" Charlie asked.

"I promise," Officer Ron replied.

Charlie paused for a moment. He shifted his focus to his parents. "I need my parents to promise."

Charlie's dad maneuvered around the gathered group to stand in the middle of the hallway. His dad locked onto him, square in the eyes.

"Charlie, I promise you won't be in trouble," his dad said. "We need you to tell Officer Ron anything you might know about Vanessa's whereabouts right now. No matter where she is, I promise you won't be in trouble. Do you understand?"

Charlie nodded twice.

"Charlie, where is she?" Vanessa's mother asked in a hurried tone. She clutched a fist to her chest and held that arm with her other hand.

He released his death grip on the spindles. He pulled himself up using the white railing. Charlie gazed down at the audience before him as they waited for his answer.

The mirror was a secret—a secret only Vanessa and Charlie knew. A family heirloom passed down through generations. To his parents, it was an ordinary mirror. Nothing more. They held onto it out of familial generational guilt. A few times they had wanted to get rid of it, but Charlie protested. His parents saw it as nothing but a play item.

Now, he could lose it and Vanessa. Forever.

He licked his lips before speaking. "I know where Vanessa is," Charlie said in a hushed tone.

"Where is she?" Officer Ron said.

"Where's my Vanessa?" her mother asked, nearly stumbling over Officer Ron's words.

Charlie pulled his shoulders back. This was the time—the time his parents found out the truth.

"She's in the basement," Charlie said. "Our basement."

"Vanessa!" her mother yelled. "Vanessa, are you here?"

The crowd thundered down the wooden steps like a herd of wild beasts. The wooden steps creaked as they bore the weight of the concerned adults rushing into the musty darkness.

"Were you playing in the crawlspace?" Charlie's dad asked. "I told you kids to stay out of the crawlspace."

Charlie's dad pulled the draw string from an overhead light. The soft orange glow of the incandescent bulb illuminated the basement. Stacks of cardboard boxes and other plastic containers littered the space like castle walls. A bench in the corner scattered with an assortment of tools and other items for menial home repairs. Christmas, Halloween, and other holiday decorations packed into a corner waited for their seasons. The hint of mildew permeated the air.

"Vanessa," her mother called out. "Vanessa, this isn't funny."

"Vanessa. Get out here right now or you're grounded for a week," her father yelled.

The adults scattered to the four corners of the basement searching for her.

A pair of feet thundered down the steps. "Loser, what did you do now?" a voice asked.

Charlie turned and glared at his sister, Julie, standing near the end of the basement steps, still wearing the sweatpants and T-shirt from her volleyball practice.

"Julie, this isn't the time," Charlie's mom said. She pointed a finger at her—the universal parental sign to knock it off. "Go back upstairs."

"Fine," she said as she stomped her way back upstairs.

"Get the flashlight from the workbench," Charlie's dad said. "I think I see something in the crawlspace."

"Here. Use mine," Officer Ron said as he rushed to join Charlie's father. He shone the light into the small space above the cinderblocks on the back side of the basement.

"I don't see her," Officer Ron said. "I don't see anything. Wait . . . maybe something back there. Here, give me a hand."

The other adults tore into the boxes and plastic containers. They searched under every nook and cranny of the basement. They searched a few cabinets that had been placed down there.

Nothing. They found nothing.

"Where is she, Charlie?" his mother asked.

Charlie's eyes locked onto her real location. Where she was hidden. Where she was trapped.

Next to an old storage cabinet was the oval-shaped full-length mirror carved into a dark mahogany wood. A radiant sun dial was in the wood above the mirror. Two wooden legs kept it upright. This was their secret. Their secret place for adventure. For fun. And now everyone must know.

Charlie's mom approached him. She placed her hands on his shoulders. "Charlie, you need to tell us right now," his mother said. "Where is Vanessa hiding down here?"

Charlie gulped. "Promise I won't get in trouble?"

"I promise you. You won't be in trouble."

Charlie pointed to the mirror and said, "She's in there."

"She's in where?" Vanessa's mother asked.

"She's in the mirror," Charlie said.

"Charlie, this isn't one of your silly games or stories," his mother said. "This is serious."

Tears welled in Charlie's eyes. "I'm serious, Mom," he said. "I need you to believe me."

"Charlie, tell the truth," his father said in a stern voice. "Where is she?"

"She's in the mirror!" Charlie yelled. "And I can't get to her."

"What is he talking about?" Vanessa's dad asked.

Charlie rushed over to the mirror. "She's in here," he proclaimed. "Nessa is in the mirror. We can travel through this mirror to a magical realm. It has castles and knights and magic. Turning this dial activates the mirror."

Charlie turned the sun dial clockwise and counterclockwise a series of times.

"When I do that, it should open, and we can pass through. We've been going there for years. Years. Since we were like five. We were supposed to go through today after school. But I had my doctor's appointment. She must have gone through before I got home." His words trailed off. Tears fell down his face.

He continued, "Now, I can't get it to work again, and she's trapped inside."

Silence fell over the basement. The five adults stood in stunned silence. It could have been a moment, an hour, or a week. It was all the same to Charlie. Their eyes wandered back and forth between each other. Their mouths moved, but Charlie didn't hear what was being said. He only thought of Vanessa and how he couldn't get to her.

Charlie's mom broke the silence. "When will you grow up?" she shouted. "Charles Grimm, this isn't one of your little games. This is serious."

Vanessa's mother sobbed uncontrollably, consoled by Vanessa's father.

Officer Ron jogged up the steps. "I'll call in the missing person report. We'll get an Amber Alert out as soon as possible."

Charlie's mom helped Vanessa's parents up the steps.

Charlie's father approached in large steps. His chest puffed out and his head pulled back. He pointed a finger at Charlie, wagging it back and forth. "I want you to go upstairs and head to bed right now," he commanded. "We'll discuss this in the morning."

Charlie flared out his arms before smacking the sides of his legs. "But Dad, I'm telling you the truth." His voice cracked, pleading for anyone to believe him.

"I don't want to hear it. Playtime is over. You're thirteen. This is serious. Upstairs. Now!"

"But, Dad . . ." Charlie said.

"You're done," Charle's dad scolded. "You need to grow up."

Charlie slumped his head, curling in his lips. His fingers dragged across the mirror, hoping one final touch would activate it.

There was nothing. Only his defeated, dejected reflection.

Charlie sniffled, fighting the urge to bawl his eyes out as he climbed the steps. He knew where his friend was. Trapped in a magical realm. Hopefully safe. She must be scared. Maybe something happened on her end. Maybe she tried to get back and couldn't?

Charlie's dad pulled on the drawstring, shrouding the basement in darkness.

In that moment, Charlie vowed to never stop trying. To never let her down.

On that night, a girl vanished, and a young boy vowed to wait for her.

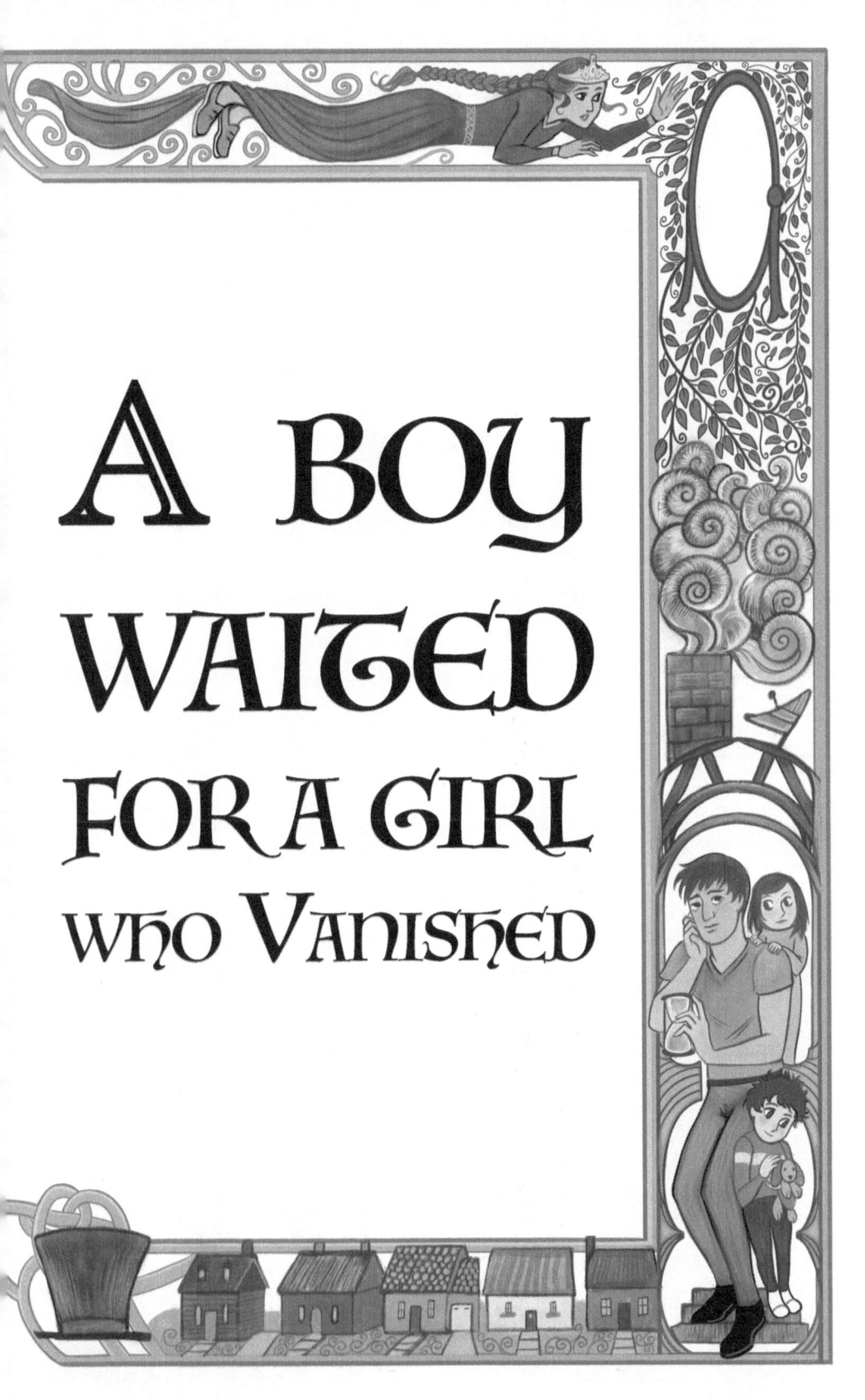

A BOY
WAITED
FOR A GIRL
WHO VANISHED

CHAPTER 1
ADULTING

C harlie Grimm stood on the precipice of a question that would determine the rest of his life. Well, not the rest of his life, but the outcome of the following week. Held in his hands were two options. If he chose correctly, he would be heralded as the savior of fun. If he chose incorrectly, he would be a scourge upon their impressionable young minds, detesting and lamenting their breakfast options for the upcoming week.

A choice had to be made: chocolate-flavored cereal or the one with marshmallows.

He turned the boxes over and examined which option his niece and nephew would enjoy for their upcoming visit. Being the cool uncle, Charlie had to make the correct choice. He had a reputation to uphold. The options weighed on his mind.

On one hand, chocolate. What kid didn't like chocolate? Chocolate for breakfast. He'd be seen as a true king among uncles.

But what of marshmallows? Colorful. Sugary. A mixture of shapes. All delightful things for six-year-olds.

The choice had to be perfect. The week had to be perfect. It wasn't the first time Charlie was babysitting his niece and nephew.

He had babysat them before, but only for a few hours. This was a whole week. It had to be special. Not for Charlie, but for the kids and the issues they were facing.

Adult issues.

Life could be cruel when you were young. Charlie knew it all too well and was determined not to let life be cruel to his niece and nephew. At least for the upcoming week. After all, they got a whole week off from school while staying with him. So the week was already off to a good start. At least, in Charlie's mind.

"Charlie Grimm?" a woman's voice asked. "Is that you?"

He turned his head toward the woman who had broken his concentration. "Depends on who's asking," Charlie said. "And why."

"It's Melissa. Melissa Hart from high school," she said. "You sat behind me in history class. You kept asking to see my notes."

"Oh, Melissa," Charlie said with a smile. "How have you been?"

"I'm going to be a mom," she said. Her eyes almost twinkled in the fluorescent lighting of Raskin's Neighborhood Market. She rubbed the small bump under her green top.

"Congratulations," Charlie said, lifting the cereal boxes to shoulder height.

"Thank you."

"First one?"

"Yeah. We're pretty excited."

Charlie chuckled. "Don't let Rumpelstiltskin know, or else he might try to trick you."

Melissa squinted her eyes and tilted her head as if taken aback by his playful comment.

"Because it's your firstborn," Charlie said. He waved his hands, filled with the cereal boxes, around in circles. "And Rumpelstiltskin will use a spinning wheel to turn straw into gold for it. Like in the story."

Melissa laughed. "Oh, right. That's right. You used to tell those stories all the time. I remember you were obsessed with fairy tales, claiming they were real."

Charlie averted his eyes, glancing into his cart full of goodies for the upcoming week. "Yeah," he said. "It sort of comes with the name, I guess. Grimm."

"Do you have any of your own?" Melissa asked.

"Umm . . . no. I do have a niece and a nephew. I'm going to be babysitting them for the week." He flipped his wrists around, holding the two boxes close to his chest for Melissa to see. "By the way, if you were six, which cereal would you like?"

She thought for a moment. "Why do I have to choose?"

"Well, I mean, there can only be one cereal chosen. Right?"

"We're adults. We can make the adult decision of having two cereals."

Charlie lowered the boxes. He paused for a moment.

"You're right," Charlie said as he flung both boxes into the grocery cart. "See, this is why I had to copy notes from you in history class. I'm . . . I'm not good at making choices like this."

"Well, I'm glad I could contribute to your niece and nephew having a great week." She pushed her cart down the aisle. "Take care, Charlie. I'll be on the lookout for old Rumpel. You keep those kids away from any witches."

Charlie grinned. "Will do."

He grabbed the cart and ventured deeper into Raskin's Neighborhood Market. He collected various items for the upcoming week. Quick fix items that kids enjoyed. Mac and cheese. Spaghetti. Chicken nuggets. Of course, treats as well. Boxes of candies and popcorn. All the good stuff kids loved.

His phone buzzed in his pocket. He retrieved it and checked the message.

FROM JULIE:

Where are you? We're here and I need to get to the airport.

Charlie let out a big sigh. He curled his lower lip, biting down on it, but not too hard. He typed a response.

FROM CHARLIE:

> I'm getting the kids food at the store. Be there in 10.

FROM JULIE:

> ...

The text bubble disappeared for a moment and then continued with a brief message.

FROM JULIE:

> Hurry.

Charlie flung the phone back into his pants pocket. With a huff, he pushed the cart as quickly as he could through the aisle to the checkout lanes.

Luckily, the evening rush hadn't hit yet, and he was first in line at the checkout. He dumped his newly acquired goods on the conveyor belt almost as soon as he entered the lane. After a brief conversation of pleasantries, paying his bill, and gathering the newly bagged groceries, Charlie rushed out the automatic doors.

He stopped. Something caught his eye, causing him to turn back. A woman adorned with purple hair, dressed in all black, and wearing a black, wide-brimmed hat. The top in a curved point. A man in a black leather jacket held her hand. She reached to secure her hat as it almost blew off in the gush of air from the automatic doors.

He stopped for a moment. The ominous warning from Melissa moments ago coursed through his mind. He gave it a moment of brief thought.

A witch.

He shook his head to clear his mind.

"Nah," Charlie said under his breath. "It was a marketing gimmick to sell their wine."

He pushed his cart toward his car, deep into the parking lot. Delving into his pocket for his keys, he popped the trunk of his modest black sedan. Nothing special and quite common. A simple, used vehicle to get Charlie from point A to point B.

He shoved aside a few assorted items, including a black gym bag, to make room for his newly acquired goodies. After placing the final bag, he slammed the trunk and returned the cart to the cart corral.

Charlie jogged back to the car and flung open the door. He plopped onto the black cloth seat and shoved the keys into the ignition. The car roared to life, coughing and stuttering a little. The engine wasn't quite as finely tuned as it should have been. It almost squealed in protest. But it worked, and that was all that mattered to Charlie. He put the car into drive and headed off to meet his sister.

Charlie turned down the street, away from the center of Newbury Grove, passing streets of houses, Newbury Grove High School, and eventually the street he grew up on. He didn't live too far from his childhood home. His townhome complex was only a few streets away. Small, but a place to call his own.

He pulled into the parking lot. The rows of townhomes formed a horseshoe pattern. Though modern, they gave the appearance of an old English Tudor home. Brick on the first floor. Exposed wood beams formed inside stucco for the second. Intricate designs of metal and glass for windows. Pointed roof facades separated the individual units from the adjoining neighbors. Chimneys jutted up to the sky. Eight buildings in total with twenty-four individual units. Their appearance was something that could easily fit inside of a fairy tale.

To Charlie, it was a modest, simple home. It was only him and no one else. He preferred it that way. Only him. And his stuff. Most importantly, the one special item in the basement.

Charlie pulled into his assigned parking spot. His heart sank. Gritting his teeth, he slumped in his seat, trying to hide behind the dashboard. There, standing on the covered porch, her arms crossed and face in a scowl, was his older sister Julie.

Flanked by two young children sitting on the porch, his six-year-old niece and nephew—Ginny and Tyler. They beamed with glee the moment their eyes caught Charlie's face. They stood and waved, so they could be seen above the colorful luggage bags lining the cement walkway as a breadcrumb trail to his house.

Charlie waved back before turning off the engine and giving the car a much-needed rest. The clanking and moaning of the engine fell silent. Charlie exited the vehicle, tossing the keys into the pocket of his faded blue jeans.

"I thought I told you we'd be here at four o'clock," Julie said.

Charlie licked his lips, glancing at the grass retreating for its fall slumber. His eyes settled on the orange pumpkin on his front porch, ready for the upcoming Halloween season. He mustered the courage to face his sister, five years his elder, once again.

In a low, methodical voice, Charlie asked, "Did you want the kids to starve?"

Julie rolled her eyes. "Open the door," she said. "I'm in a hurry to catch the plane."

"Uncle Charlie!" Ginny and Tyler shouted in unison as they rushed to give him a hug. The double impact forced him back a step.

He wrapped his arms around both children. "Hey, you two monsters, how are you? Getting excited for this week?"

"Yeah," Ginny said.

"Mom said we have to be on our best behavior, so we can't have too much fun," Tyler said.

Charlie kneeled to meet his niece and nephew at eye level. "Being on our worst behavior is actually our best behavior, so we can be as bad as we want to."

The kids cheered. They darted off, running in circles in the common lawn space.

Julie furled her eyebrows, any proverbial daggers now completely unloaded onto Charlie.

Charlie shook his head. "We'll be good. I promise you."

"Open the door! I have to get going."

Charlie rose and delved his hand into his pocket once more to retrieve his keys. "Nice to see you too," Charlie said as he moved past his sister. He inserted the keys into the deadbolt lock and opened the door.

"Kids, get your luggage," Julie said. "Hurry."

Charlie headed back to the car to retrieve his bags of groceries from the trunk—four paper bags in total. He hoisted them up, cradling them in his arms, to carry them in one trip. With a flick from his elbow, the trunk slammed shut. He proceeded past the kids gathering their luggage and into his humble abode.

The inside of the rectangular townhome was quite cozy for an individual—small, but spacious enough for one. A stairwell off to the right side of the entrance led upstairs to the two bedrooms and a bathroom.

"Take your stuff upstairs, and then come back down," Julie said.

"Second door on the right," Charlie said. "You can fight over who sleeps on what side of the bed."

"No fighting," Julie said. She shut the front door behind her.

The kids tromped up the steps, dragging the luggage behind them. *Thump. Thump. Thump.* Each step bore the brunt of the wheeled luggage as they went.

"Don't drag your bags," Julie said.

"It's fine," Charlie replied. "It's only a problem if the neighbors knock on the wall."

Charlie proceeded into the sparsely decorated main living room. A worn and run-down couch sat under the front windows, the cushions indented with past occupants and well past their prime. A flatscreen TV mounted above the brick fireplace. Cords and cables jutted out the side and traced down the wall toward gaming consoles and media players stacked on cubed shelving.

"Your place smells," Julie said.

"It does not," Charlie replied. "I have some of those smelly wall things plugged in."

A black, leather recliner—formed and shaped with the outline of one man—sat in front of the TV. A square, white end table decorated with a few crushed beer cans from the night before sat next to the recliner. It was not of quality wood, but laminated particle board with screwed in legs.

"I thought I said no alcohol," Julie said.

Charlie stopped and turned around. He readjusted his arms to prevent the brown bags from slipping through.

"Those are from last night," he said. "There isn't a drop of alcohol in this place. I know I need to be on my best behavior while babysitting the kids. What do you take me for?"

Charlie turned and proceeded past the door under the stairwell that led to the basement. He entered the kitchen and placed the bags onto a speckled gray countertop. Charlie unpacked his newly acquired goods, placing them into their proper place in the cozy kitchen. A few cabinet drawers, a refrigerator, microwave, electric stove, and dishwasher. Enough for him.

"You could at least clean up after yourself," Julie said as she placed the empty cans into the trashcan.

"You sound like Mom," Charlie replied.

"What is this? An empty pizza box behind the trash?" Julie asked.

Charlie placed a half-gallon jug of chocolate milk into the fridge. "I'll take it out."

"How long has it been sitting here?"

He slammed the fridge door. "What does it matter? It's with the trash. I'll take it out when I take the trash out."

Charlie grabbed more items from the bags, slamming them down onto the counter.

"What did you buy them? Candy? Sugary cereal?" Julie asked, her tone pitched and condescending.

"I thought maybe they could have a little fun for the next week, considering everything going on in their lives at the moment."

"Fun. That's your excuse. *Fun.*" Julie crossed her arms and shifted her stance. Her brown hair drooped down her shoulder as she shifted her head to the side. Her eyebrows squinched closer together. "You live like a bachelor," Julie said.

Charlie flared out his arms, holding a handful of boxed candies, and gave a curtsy. "I take that as a compliment," he said. He placed the boxes onto the shelves of the cabinets.

"You know, you have a lot of growing up to do," Julie said. "You should be moving up. You should be moving on. You should be doing better."

"I'm doing good," Charlie said.

"You need more with your life."

"I have a life. I go to work. I work out. Hang with the bros. I'm good. I don't need anything else."

Julie paused for a moment. "You should be doing better."

"Better like how? Like *you*?"

"Yes!" Julie said. "A better job. A better house. A better . . . a better life. You should be with somebody. It's not good to isolate yourself."

Charlie waved his arms into the air. "I said I hang with my bros . . . every once in a while." He paused. His arms drifted down to his sides. "They're married now, so it's a little . . . harder, but we get together every once in a while."

"Charlie, you spend most of your life in here. In this place of squalor," Julie said. "Heaven only knows what was strewn about before we came."

Charlie flung a box of popcorn into the cabinet and slammed it shut. "Are you going to hound me the entire time you're here?"

"Yes," Julie said. "Maybe it will start to sink in."

"I get it enough from Mom and Dad. I don't need it from you too," Charlie said. "I have my reasons for staying in here. I like it this way. I like my life. I'm good."

"You need to grow up," Julie said in a raised voice.

"Is that all you're going to do? Hound me for how I live after I said I'd babysit your kids because no one else could?" Charlie said. His fingers flared out and tapped against his chest.

He took a deep breath. The next words slipped to the forefront of his mind. He guarded against saying them, but Julie pushed his buttons. The non-stop barrage from his family questioning his lifestyle had worn on his soul one too many times. The cracks in the dam burst through, and there was no stopping the deluge of years of emotions this time. No filter. The words flowed freely, and Julie was the one who broke the dam.

"Or . . . or . . . hear me out," he said. "Maybe your constant berating of other people, because they're not perfect like you . . ."

He leaned forward, eyes flared in anger. For emphasis, he raised his right hand. Touching his index finger to his thumb as if holding a proverbial dart, he waved it back and forth. Testing to find the right movement and speed needed to hit its target.

His voice elevated to a near shout. ". . . is the reason you're getting a divorce and your soon-to-be ex-husband is on the beach with someone else, instead of taking care of your kids while you go on a business trip."

Julie's face turned pale. Her mouth dropped. Tears glistened in her eyes. She stood with her arms crossed, frozen like a statue.

"Are you and Uncle Charlie getting a divorce too?" Ginny's voice said from around the corner.

Charlie slumped his shoulders and dropped his head. His dark brown hair fell forward, covering his eyes, shielding him from his indiscretion, if only briefly. He ran his hand through his hair and combed it back before raising up.

"We're not . . . we're not getting divorced," Charlie said.

He stepped out from behind the kitchen to view the children. They had sad, puppy dog eyes, and their lips quivered. Tyler hugged Ginny.

"Isn't that what people do when they don't love each other anymore?" Ginny asked.

Julie turned and rushed to her daughter. She kneeled and hugged her. "No, it doesn't work like that, sweetie."

"But you and Uncle Charlie were yelling like you and Dad," Tyler said.

Charlie joined his sister, kneeling to meet the kids at their level. "I'm . . . I'm sorry, little buddies. Your mom and I have been fighting since well before you were born. It's sort of what we do. But you know what, in the end we make up, apologize, and we take care of each other. Because we're brother and sister, and that's what we do."

He turned to face his sister. Julie's eyes met Charlie's.

"I'm sorry," Charlie said. "I shouldn't have said that. You have a lot going on. You're going on your business trip for the week. I shouldn't have said what I said. I should have been here sooner so you wouldn't run late."

Julie wiped a tear from her eye. "Apology accepted. I shouldn't have berated your home. I'm grateful I can count on you to babysit the kids for me. You're a good brother."

They leaned in to give each other a hug.

Charlie turned to his niece and nephew. "See, your mother and I made up," he said.

"Now come here and give Mommy a hug before I go," Julie said, stretching out her arms.

The kids rushed in, one on each of her sides, as she squeezed them tightly.

"I'm going to miss you," she said as she kissed them each on the head.

"We'll miss you too," they said in unison. Although they were fraternal twins, they still held a tendency to act and speak as one.

"You be good for Uncle Charlie," Julie said.

"We will," they said in unison.

"No rough housing, do what he says, and try not to stay up too late," she said.

"Staying up late is half the fun. They're on vacation from school while staying with Uncle Charlie," he said. "After all, this is the house of a bachelor, and in this house, we have some fuuuunnnn."

Julie released the children from her arms and stood. Charlie rose to his feet.

"Thank you for taking care of them," Julie said. "I mean it. I don't know what I'd do if it weren't for you."

Charlie shrugged his shoulders and grinned. "Don't worry about it," he said. "It's what younger brothers are for. Go have fun at your conference learning to sell more real estate or whatever you do."

Julie gave a slight laugh. "Thanks. It's all boring stuff, anyway. If I wasn't forced to be there, I wouldn't be going."

"Have fun. Let loose. You deserve it. Swim in the pool or something," Charlie said. "As a matter of fact, don't worry about a thing. You don't have to call to check in. If you don't hear from me, then everything is going great. Go. Have some fun. You could use a little fun."

"Thanks." Julie checked her wristwatch. "I have to get going."

Charlie escorted her to the front door.

"If you need anything . . ." Julie started.

"I have Mom and Dad on speed dial. They can answer questions all the way from Florida. We'll be fine." Charlie turned to face the children. His voice changed to a deep, playful voice. His hands raised and his fingers curled. "That is, unless we're attacked by the giant Goredellum, then all bets are off."

The kids laughed.

"A creature of immense size with elongated horns that can impale a person clean through." Charlie mimicked the size of the horns jutting out from his head with his index finger.

Charlie turned in time to catch his sister crack a smile. "Is that a smile I see?"

"You and your stories," Julie said with a small laugh.

"Always kept me entertained," Charlie said. He paused, slightly biting his lower lip. "It's all I needed."

Julie opened the door. "See you in a week." She exited.

Charlie waved. "Have a safe flight."

The kids ran to the door and waved as their mother entered her car and took off.

After a moment, Charlie closed the door and turned to the kids with a sly smile on his face. "Who's ready to have some fun?"

CHAPTER 2
CHILD'S PLAY

Charlie popped his head up from behind the couch. A metal mixing bowl adorned his head. But it wasn't a mixing bowl—nay—it was a helmet. A helm to protect him in the upcoming combat. His eyes peered over the rounded, plush top of the couch. His eyes surveyed back and forth over the battlefield.

They took refuge here. He, the leader of his army, and his two faithful lieutenants. They popped up after Charlie to get a view of the battle that was yet to come. A pasta strainer atop Lieutenant Ginny the Wise—the brains of the operation. A plastic popcorn bowl for Tyler the Brave—the muscles.

The field before them was beset with many traps and perils. The pizza box—an indication of quick sand. The overturned end table—a spike pit. A gathering of stuffed animals, generously donated by Ginny—minions of the beast they were tasked to hunt down. They'd have to fight through them if they wanted to quell their foe.

Perched atop its mighty castle, the black leather recliner moved to the far side of the living room, was the beast itself. Of immense size with horns four feet long, it stood on hoofed legs with the arms of a person. A bull like snout. Rage in its eyes. The Goredellum. The terror of the realm. A giant stuffed teddy bear, once again generously provided by Ginny the Wise.

They were tasked by the king and queen to vanquish the mighty beast. The prize . . . the many thanks of the people of the realm, and of course, a small monetary reward—chocolate candy. Though they did not fight for the candy itself, it was still nice to have when finished.

Charlie dropped below the top of the couch. He placed a hand atop both of his lieutenant's helms and slowly lowered them to join him in the safety of their hidden position. His mind scanned years of inspiring speeches he had learned from books, TV shows, and movies. A mishmash of ideas formed in his head like a shape out of molding clay.

The children intently focused on him.

"Troops," Charlie began. "I'm not going to lie. It's dire. A spike trap. Quicksand. An army of minions. I don't know how we're going to get through them. Then there's the beast itself. It's not good."

"What do we do, Uncle Charlie?" Tyler asked. He readjusted his plastic helm.

Charlie broke eye contact with his troops, focusing on a spot on the hardwood flooring. A discolored spot he'd have to use extra polish to buff out the next time he cleaned his floors. He conjured the right words to inspire his young troops. He puffed out his chest and held his head high to the ceiling.

"I'm not going to lie. Times appear dark and bleak. But in these moments, that's when legends are born and heroes are made," Charlie said. He turned to point to Ginny. "Heroes like you."

He turned to point to Tyler. "Or you. Heroes of great renown who faced the danger head-on."

Charlie shifted back and forth between the two children. "They never wavered or surrendered. They continued to move forward, never giving the enemy any ground. Regardless of the odds, they continued to fight. And fight they shall."

He picked up a wooden mixing spoon. His weapon of choice. His sword.

Charlie continued, "With our weapons by our side and resolve in our hearts, we shall never perish. Never falter. Never quit. For we fight not for us—nay—our fight is a good fight. A mighty fight. A fight for those who can't fight for themselves. For everyone back there in the kingdom who is counting on us. We fight for them. And most importantly . . ."

Charlie paused and breathed deeply to allow his words to linger. His eyes surveyed his captive audience, with grins on their faces and hope in their eyes. He hunched down closer. Tilting his head, his eyes met his eyebrows. A sly grin on his face.

"Most importantly," he said in a softer tone. "We fight for each other. For we are more than an army. We are companions. Compatriots. Family. We stick together and fight for each other. And with this in our minds and hearts, we'll never be defeated. No castle will keep us away. No foe is too great to be vanquished." He threw his right arm into the sky, the wooden spoon held aloft.

Ginny and Tyler did the same, holding up their plastic spatula and ladle, respectively.

"For we shall be victorious this day," Charlie shouted. "And we shall dine on the chocolate candies!"

The kids shouted with glee and excitement, "Chocolate candies!"

"Charge!" Charlie shouted.

Ginny took off around the right side of the couch. Tyler went around the left. Charlie leaped over the top, rolling down and bouncing off the couch cushions before springing to his feet. The trio easily dodged the two traps set out by the Goredellum, dancing and swerving their way around.

Easy enough. Child's play. But then, the minions. The real battle began.

Charlie mocked sword fighting, slashing enemies and parrying imaginary, retaliatory blows. Quick on his feet, he shuffled back and forth as if engaged in a battle to the death with a colorful, smiling, stuffed rabbit. The kids were quick to follow his lead.

"Keep pressing the attack," Charlie said. "We're almost through."

A dizzying display of wooden and plastic kitchen utensils swung through the air in figure eight shapes. Their blows struck their imaginary foes. Parry. Thrust. Strike. Charlie kicked over one of the stuffed animals. A felled minion. The children were quick to take note and followed suit until all the stuffed animals were strewn about the living room.

"Only the castle is left!" Charlie shouted. He thrust his wooden makeshift sword at the leather recliner. "Charge!"

The kids let out a great yell, leaping toward the black leather recliner. Ginny and Tyler climbed the sides of the chair, placing themselves on the cushioned arms. They all wobbled back and forth.

Charlie snatched a video game controller charging cable from next to the leathery seat. "Oh, no," he exclaimed. He wrapped the cord around his shoulders. "A hidden vine trap." He fell to the floor.

"Don't worry about me," he said. "Keep going."

"We leave no one behind," Tyler said. He leaped off the chair and rushed to his uncle's aid. He mimicked slashing away at the imaginary vines.

Charlie unwrapped himself, and with a quick push off from the floor, jumped to his feet.

The stuffed teddy bear Goredellum, draped over the top of the chair, slipped and slowly descended the back.

"Ginny!" Charlie called out.

The young girl turned her attention to her uncle.

Charlie continued, "It's getting away. Strike now."

Ginny wobbled back and forth on the chair. Her brown ponytail swung back and forth. She slipped and plopped onto the main seat, but only momentarily. As quick as she fell, she sprung to her feet. Ginny reared back with her plastic spatula.

The bear slipped further, now only the cute button face and arms holding onto the top.

"Ginny, swing now!" Charlie yelled. "Do it before it gets away."

She swung the black spatula, bopping the teddy bear on its head as it descended behind the chair. It landed with a thud onto the hardwood floor.

"I did it," Ginny shouted. She reared back, her arms held aloft, as the pasta strainer fell to the floor with a metallic thud.

"We did it," Charlie said, throwing his arms into the air. "The Goredellum is defeated."

Tyler ran around the living room, pausing to dance some latest internet craze. Ginny jumped up and down. The chair swung widely back and forth.

"You're the best, Uncle Charlie," Ginny said.

Charlie tousled her hair. "No, you're the best," he said. "You landed the final blow. Now, let's get down before you fall off and break an arm. I'll never hear the end of it from your mother." He picked her up beneath her arms and set her on the floor.

Bam. Bam. Bam.

The noise emanated from the stairwell wall.

"Oops," Charlie said. "We might have been a little too loud." He changed to a whisper. "We've got to use our inside voices now. But that's okay because it's candy time!"

The children shouted for joy. "Candy time!"

Bam. Bam. Bam.

Three more taps against the wall.

"Okay, seriously, now we have to keep it down," Charlie whispered.

THE NIGHT WORE ON, and the festivities for the day were done. Items strewn about the living room had been picked up and put away. The furniture was returned to its rightful place. The hour grew late, and another day awaited. A day Charlie hoped would be filled with more fun, excitement, and a bit of escapism for the children.

One by one, the children took their turn in the bathroom, brushing their teeth, removing the last remnants from their chocolate spoils of war. When finished, they entered their new bedroom for their nightly slumber.

Charlie turned down the bed for the children. His townhome wasn't big enough to provide space for a second bed, so they'd have to share. The room wasn't exactly spacious to begin with. A small desk in the corner with a computer. A closet that Charlie used for storage of odds and ends. A dresser with a lamp along a wall below a window that gave a less than elegant view to the backside of another building.

The children's suitcases laid open with clothes thrown about the floor.

"You can put your clothes in the dresser tomorrow," Charlie said. "That way you have more room for fun."

"Okay, Uncle Charlie," Ginny said. She removed a hair tie holding her ponytail together and placed it on the dresser.

"Brush your teeth?" Charlie asked.

"Yep," Tyler said as he placed his toothbrush bag back into his suitcase.

Charlie tapped the white bedsheets. "Hop into bed, and I'll get you tucked in."

The kids climbed the mattress and took their places. Charlie pulled back on the covers and whisked them over the kids. The white bedsheets fell like a parachute. He pulled them back, so the kids weren't completely buried beneath them.

"All set?" Charlie asked.

"Uncle Charlie, can you tell us one of your bedtime stories?" Ginny asked.

"A bedtime story?" Charlie said.

The kids wiggled under the covers.

"Yeah, tell us one of your bedtime stories," Tyler said.

Charlie let out a sigh. "I don't know. It's getting kind of late."

"Please?" Ginny begged. Her brown, puppy dog eyes pleaded for a story.

"Please, Uncle Charlie," Tyler said. He cleared his moppy, brown hair from his eyes. "You'll be the bestest uncle ever."

Charlie rolled his eyes. "Oh, alright," he said. "I can't say no to being the bestest uncle ever."

He plopped down at the foot of the bed. His hand on his chin, he stared at the ceiling, cycling through the stories in his mind. Flashes of images of characters, settings, and stories he practically knew by heart.

Charlie needed a story that was short, and not too long. Not too scary. He decided to test the waters with something simple. He shifted on the bed, raising one leg onto the mattress to get a better vantage point for his captivated audience.

"Okay. Game four. Bottom of the eighth. Two outs. Season on the line. Their longtime rivals, their nemesis, had them on the ropes. It was a cold October night."

"No sports stories," Ginny said.

"Yeah, we want to hear something else," Tyler added.

"No sports stories, huh?" Charlie asked. "But it was a good one."

"We want something fun," Tyler said.

"Alright. Alright. Alright," Charlie said. "Let me think. Another tale of the *Salty Sea Dogs?* . . . No. Let's do something different." His hand returned to his chin, once more cycling through stories. Images flashed through his mind, but only one returned.

The mirror.

He had only hinted at the mirror to his niece and nephew in the past. Charlie never told them the full story. Everything the mirror could do. What waited on the other side. The adventures he used to go on. It would do. After all, they defeated the Goredellum today. They deserved to know.

Charlie hunched low, leaning toward the children on the other side of the bed. "Okay, like all good stories, this began a long time ago," Charlie said.

He flared out his fingers, dancing them around like a puppeteer maneuvering imaginary marionettes.

"Once upon a time, there was a young boy and a young girl. Similar to you, but they weren't brother and sister. They were friends. Best friends. Inseparable," Charlie said. "And the little boy had a special mirror."

He paused for a moment to let the words linger in their young imaginations.

"This mirror could transport you to another world. A world where fairy tales are real. Rumpelstiltskin. Hansel and Gretel. Red Riding Hood. They all happened. It's a place where magic is alive. Filled with creatures and kingdoms and castles."

Charlie's eyes shifted back and forth between the two children. They were silent and unmoving, hanging on his every word.

"And that young boy and that young girl used to travel there all the time," Charlie added. "They met a wizard and a wonderful, kind king and queen. They were treated like royalty, for the king and queen could not have children of their own. They'd go on grand adventures, meeting all sorts of wonderful people. All was good and right. That was, until one night..."

His words trailed off. Charlie lost focus of the children, instead fading into a blank abyss only he could see. He inhaled deep into his soul.

"One night, the mirror stopped working." Charlie paused. "The boy was supposed to meet the girl on the other side. But when he tried passing through it..."

Charlie gulped. He wanted to stop, but the abyss was pulling him in.

"When he tried it, the mirror didn't work. The young girl was gone. The young boy tried to explain what happened, but no one would believe him."

His soul shouted for him to stop, but his mind was too far gone. He relived the night over and over. Flashes of the parents' faces. The officer. The years of therapy. The years of isolation. Loneliness.

"What happened, Uncle Charlie?" Tyler asked. His eyebrows arched with an expression of concern.

Charlie snapped out of his haze. He blinked a few times to clear water welling inside his eyes. Charlie rubbed his forehead. "Umm," he muttered. The words failed him.

"Was she trapped forever?" Ginny asked.

A rush swelled to his head. The room spun. His stomach turned in knots.

"Umm," he said again, failing to form words. "Uh, yeah. Um, no. She a . . . uh . . ."

He couldn't finish his words. Charlie wanted to tell the truth, but the innocence of the children's eyes pleaded for a happy ending. He inhaled sharply.

"She was able to get out, and they were reunited," Charlie lied.

"Good," Ginny said.

"A happy ending," Tyler said with a smile.

Charlie paused, biting his lip. "Yeah," he said. "A happy ending."

He rose with his arms placed on his hips. "I think it's bedtime now," he said.

"Good night, Uncle Charlie," Ginny said.

"Good night," Tyler said as he rolled over to face away from his sister.

"Good night, you two," Charlie replied as he moved toward the door. "We've got a big day tomorrow." He flicked the switch, reached for the doorknob, and shut them in for the night.

Charlie stood in the hallway. His mind raced, continually focusing on the mental image of the mirror. It had been a few days. Or it could have been a few weeks. Definitely not months. He had lost track. Tonight was as good as any to try again.

Charlie placed his hand on the rail to help guide him down. He traversed the steps slowly, to not wake the kids or disturb the neighbors for another time that night. The living room was quiet and dark, only the hum of the fridge and a light from the kitchen.

"What . . . what harm could it do?" Charlie said in a hushed voice.

His eyes drifted to the basement door. His index finger tapped against his leg. The soft nylon material of the black gym shorts he wore as pajamas itched his finger.

Charlie strode toward the door, flinging it open—the entryway to a darkened basement. He flicked the switch, and the light fought back against the darkness. Freshly painted white steps with strips of carpet led his way down. Carpeted flooring awaited him below. The musty smell rose to greet him, tempting him down like a siren's call. The steps creaked as he proceeded down.

The basement was rectangular and sparsely populated. A few boxes of odds and ends scattered the floor. A boxing training dummy in the corner stood opposite the stairs. Painted cinderblock walls. Decent lighting. A drywalled section that housed the utilities, washer, and dryer. Nothing impressive, but better than Charlie expected when he first moved in.

Charlie focused on the tannish orange boxing training dummy. Charlie wasn't a boxer, but he used it for other purposes. Beneath the stairs, a dark brown wooden sword rested in a cylindrical, metal trashcan.

He withdrew the sword, pulling it up to his face. He struck a fighter's pose. Sword out and pointed at his foe. Feet shoulder-length apart. His right foot pointed at the dummy, the left perpendicular for balance. His off hand raised to his shoulders.

"So, we meet again," Charlie said to the training dummy. "Tell me what you've done with the princess, and I shall let you live."

The training dummy remained silent.

"To the death, it shall be then," Charlie said.

He thrust forward, poking at the dummy. It wobbled back and forth. Charlie shuffled his feet, practicing his footwork. He swung the sword in a triangle pattern, a technique he learned from taking a few fencing classes. After a few more pokes, he gave up.

"You're a valiant foe, and we shall meet again," he said as he placed the sword back in its rightful place.

Charlie went deep into the basement, around the walls of his utility space. Standing in the corner, nestled securely on the floor, was the object he sought. The mirror.

He stood in front of the mirror, breathing deeply. He examined himself, head to feet. His pulled back his brown hair, long enough to cover his ears and kiss his neck. His brown eyes betrayed his sadness, heavy and a bit baggy. A youthful, boyish face. Clean shaven and little to no physical scars. Broad shouldered. His grayish T-shirt was tight against his chest.

Twenty years might have passed, but he was still the scared thirteen-year-old boy who stood in a room full of disbelieving adults.

He breathed deeply. His heart raced. Every attempt to activate the mirror held both optimism and despair, usually only finding despair. Charlie rubbed his hands together, caressing his fingertips with each pass. His brown eyes focused on the dial. The image of the other realm was clear in his mind. Of castle walls and medieval furniture. He stepped forward, and his fingers lightly touched the radiant dial.

A few times clockwise. A few turns counterclockwise. All an instinctive motion. One final turn of the wooden sun, and he released his grip.

"Please work," he whispered.

His fingers dropped to the reflective glass, hovering inches from them. His mirror reflection shone back. Filled with hope, but ready for disappointment. He touched the glass. His fingers bent with resistance.

The mirror was still closed.

Charlie lowered his head and let out a sigh. His hair fell in front of his face to hide his shame and disappointment. He tapped the mirror twice more.

"I'm sorry," he whispered. "I'm sorry I wasn't there for you."

Charlie faced his reflection once again. Tears welled in his red eyes. Charlie ran his fingers through his hair, returning it back to its proper place. He let out a drawn-out sigh, turned, and went upstairs. He had enough play for one day.

CHAPTER 3
ONCE UPON A NIGHTMARE

"Uncle Charlie," Ginny said as she pushed on his shoulders. "There's a monster in my room." She continued to push against his body over the comforter.

Charlie's eyes flicked open at the constant barrage from the young girl. Half his face buried into the pillow. Drool ran down his chin. Torn away from a dream mid-scene, its images fading into an abyss and forgotten. He inhaled sharply as if he was struggling to breathe.

"Wha-what?" he mumbled. "What's happening?"

"Uncle Charlie, there's a monster in my room," Ginny said.

He rubbed his face and eyes. The room came into view. In the orange glow of his bedside clock, the time materialized into focus. 3:30 a.m. Far too early to get up.

"There's no monster. It's your brother," Charlie said. "Get back to bed."

He buried his face back into the soft, cool embrace of his pillow. His eyes drifted off to sleep when the barrage started again.

"Uncle Charlie, there's a monster in my room. I need you to take care of it," Ginny said as she pounded on Charlie's shoulder.

"The monster is your brother. Go back to sleep."

Ginny moved to the other side of the bed. A spare pillow crashed down onto the exposed half of Charlie's face, jolting him awake.

"Uncle Charlie, there's a monster in my room, and I need you to take care of it. Now!"

Charlie rolled over onto his back. "Alright. Alright. I'll take care of the monster."

He flung the covers off. He swung his legs over the side and sat up. His feet planted into the plush beige carpet of the bedroom. Charlie rolled his neck and shoulders.

"Hurry, Uncle Charlie," Ginny said, now standing in the doorway.

"I'm coming. I'm coming," he said as he stood. Charlie followed the young girl to the adjoining room.

She stood in the doorway and pointed into the room. "The monster is in there," she whispered.

Charlie stuck his head in. Tyler slept on one side of the bed. The dresser was in its proper place. Same with the computer desk. Their luggage was still on the floor. Nothing out of the ordinary.

"The only monster in there is your brother," Charlie said as he placed a hand on her back. With a small push, he guided her into the bedroom. "Now, go back to sleep."

Ginny flicked on the light switch. Charlie shielded his eyes from the blinding light with the back of his hand.

The young girl pointed to the window. "Uncle Charlie, the monster was right there," she said. "It was wearing a hat."

"A hat?" Charlie asked. "What hat?"

Tyler stirred in the bed from the noise.

"It was a funny hat. Kind of tall," she said.

"Is it morning already?" Tyler asked.

"No," Ginny replied. "I saw a monster."

Tyler popped up in bed. "A monster?"

"Your sister didn't see a monster," Charlie said. "Go back to bed."

"I did too, and it was right here." She pointed to the ground in front of the window. "The bedroom door was open, and the monster was in the room."

A noise came from the kitchen—the sound of a cabinet opening and closing. Charlie spun around; his eyes focused down the staircase.

"It's the monster!" Tyler said.

"Shh," Charlie said to quiet the children and not alert the intruder they were awake.

The kids fell silent, following Charlie's lead.

Another cabinet opened downstairs and slammed shut.

"It's the monster," Ginny whispered.

Charlie strode over to the closet door, and without thinking, flung it open. He rifled through a few items to find a baseball bat hidden in the back corner. He withdrew his wooden weapon, eyes now focused on the bedroom door.

"You two, get back in bed and stay there," he said. "Do you understand me?"

Tyler climbed out of bed. "We want to help you fight the monster," he said. "Like earlier."

This wasn't playtime. It was a home invasion. In the years of living here, Charlie had never encountered any issues. It was rather quiet. However, there was a first time for everything.

His lungs rose and fell as adrenaline surged through his body. Short breaths, in and out. His mind raced. His arms and shoulders tightened and tensed up. His feet planted securely on the ground, not moving with his command. Charlie was frozen.

"I want you two to say here. Do you understand me?" Charlie asked.

"But we want to help you," Ginny said as she moved to join her brother.

"Stay here," Charlie said in a raised voice.

He wasn't frozen out of fear for himself. Quite the opposite. He'd taken a few self-defense courses and fencing classes—only a few. He was a novice who knew a few moves. He had tried to hone the rudimentary sword skills he learned as a kid in the mirror.

Charlie was frozen because of his duty of care to babysit his young niece and nephew. Fear of failing them if they got hurt or worse. He couldn't let his mind sink into such despair. He needed to act. Defend *his* kingdom. His fencing sword was in the basement. The bat would have to do.

He left the bedroom, baseball bat pulled back over his shoulder, ready to strike. His foot met the first step. A small creak. It would give away his position. He gingerly lowered his foot to the next step, not wanting to alert the intruder to his presence.

More cabinets opened. The sound of bowls, pots, and pans being thrown around.

Charlie descended to the bottom of the stairs. His stealthy moves had evaded the intruder so far. He turned the corner. The kitchen light spilled into the living room. The intruder was hidden behind the wall, deep in his kitchen. The basement door was slightly ajar.

Using his fencing footwork, Charlie maneuvered through the living room. He advanced without making a sound. His toes met the cold hardwood before lowering his heels. His left foot forward. His right for balance. His wooden bat held aloft, ready to strike.

The stairs creaked as the children began their descent. Charlie's eyebrows furled at the thought of them disobeying his order. He couldn't see them, but he wanted to yell for them to stop. He held in the anger, not wanting to alert whomever or whatever was in his kitchen.

Charlie gripped the handle tightly. His fingers wrapped around the tan wood. The knuckles of his hands aligned, ready to strike at a moment's notice. With the kids descending and the intruder in the kitchen, the element of surprise wouldn't last. There was no way around it. Charlie needed to strike and strike now.

Charlie maneuvered past the basement door. He inhaled deeply and held his breath. *One. Two. THREE.*

Charlie sprung forth. He bellowed a barbaric yell as he charged into the kitchen. He held the bat high above his shoulders.

"Who are you?" Charlie yelled.

"It's okay," an impish voice said. "Don't hurt me. I'm searching for someone."

Charlie stopped. He let go of the bat with one hand, and the bat dropped to his side. His face turned white and pale as if he'd seen a ghost. Standing in his kitchen, was a person he hadn't seen in twenty years.

A pale, impish figure roughly the size of his niece and nephew. Skinny with a pointed nose and pointed ears. He wore a black top hat with a tuft of black hair coming out from beneath. A tattered black suit jacket with tuxedo tails and a gray vest. Fingerless gloves held aloft to shield himself from the oncoming attack. Gray and white striped pants with black, leather buckled shoes. The creature's appearance was something out of an old vaudevillian play.

"Half-pint?" Charlie asked as his voice cracked. He gulped, but something caught in his throat.

"I'm trying to find Charlie Grimm," Half-pint said.

"Half-pint, it's me," Charlie replied. "It's Charlie."

The impish figure lowered his hand. "You're too big to be Charlie. The Charlie I knew was this big." He held a hand to his eye line.

"It's been twenty years since I last saw you. I'm taller now," Charlie said. "I was that size when I first met you."

"Oh, right," Half-pint said. "I forgot. Time passed."

Ginny and Tyler rushed into the kitchen, not brandishing weapons, but hiding behind their uncle's legs. They each hugged a leg, nearly knocking Charlie to the ground as he lost his balance from the rushing children. They poked their heads out from behind.

"That's who I thought was you," Half-pint said as he pointed to the children.

"These are my niece and nephew," Charlie said.

Half-pint raised his hands to the sky. "Oh, you're a father now." He waved to the kids. "Hello, niece and nephew."

Charlie shook his head. "I'm not a father, you numbskull. I'm their uncle."

"Oh, that makes much more sense," Half-pint said. "I was wondering why you would name them niece and nephew."

"Uncle Charlie, what is that thing?" Ginny asked.

"Is it a minion of the Goredellum?" Tyler asked in a hushed tone.

"I know a couple Goredellums," Half-pint said. "Fantastic people. They make some of the sweetest pies. Very even-tempered."

Charlie freed himself from the scared children and dropped to a knee. He placed an arm around each of the children's shoulders. He locked eyes with each of them before moving to the other.

"This isn't the minion of the Goredellum," Charlie said. "This is an old friend. He shouldn't be here."

"And yet, here I am," Half-pint said. His arms flared out. His fingertips wiggled.

Half-pint took a step closer to the group. "Allow me to introduce myself," he said. He dove his right hand into his jacket pocket. "My name is Cornelius Cromwald Harrington Bartholomew Alexander Aloysius Alexander Bartholomew Harrington Cromwell Cornelius the third. But my friends call me Half-pint."

He removed his top hat with his left hand and took a bow. He flung his right hand into the air and scattered glitter all over the kitchen floor and countertops. The tiny metallic particles glistened as they fell like a shower of colors.

"Did you glitterbomb my kitchen?" Charlie asked.

The children laughed.

Half-pint raised ever so slightly. A smirk formed on his face. He winked. "Be amazed as my magical particles are whisked away with the snap of my fingers," the impish figure said. He snapped his fingers, and, as if by magic, the shiny dust cloud of glitter flew off the kitchen surfaces and into his awaiting top hat.

The children clapped and shouted with joy.

Charlie rolled his eyes. "Don't encourage him."

Half-pint tipped over the hat, but nothing fell out. He tapped the top of the hat twice, but still, nothing spilled out. The impish creature proceeded to place the hat on his head and was doused with a gush of water.

Half-pint raised his hands to shoulder height, palms reaching the sky. "Ta-da!"

The children laughed louder. Their laughter boomed and echoed throughout the townhome.

"And now my floors are wet," Charlie said with a sigh.

Half-pint scowled at Charlie, an eyebrow raised. The smile turned into a discerning smirk. "You used to laugh at this. When did you become such a grumpy bum?" He snapped his fingers. The water evaporated from the floor. His clothes appeared dry.

"Uncle Charlie is a grumpy bum," Tyler said.

Ginny laughed. "A grumpy bum."

"That was twenty years ago," Charlie said.

Half-pint moved closer to the children. He removed his hat and presented it to the children upside down. He bounced it a few times, no doubt wanting tips for his little performance.

"They're kids," Charlie said. "They don't have gold."

Half-pint pouted as he placed the hat back on his head.

Charlie stood and paced back and forth. "This is a dream, right?" Charlie asked. "Some induced psychosis. I overdid it today. I overdid it today, and now I'm living some dream."

Charlie stopped and paused. His chest rose and fell as his breath quickened.

"This isn't real," he continued. "You're not here. You can't be here. You're not here."

"But I am here," Half-pint said. "And the princess needs your help."

"Uncle Charlie, the princess needs us," Tyler said with a hint of glee. "Like in your stories."

Charlie resumed his pacing, his arms crossed and tight against his chest. A hand on his clean-shaven chin. "This isn't real. My therapist said this could happen. Some sort of psychosis. I didn't need it to happen while I'm babysitting the kids. It'll be okay."

Half-pint retrieved a plastic coffee container strewn about the floor. He chucked it at Charlie. The red, plastic container smacked Charlie in the arms. Instinctively, Charlie grabbed the impact point.

"Ow!" Charlie yelled. "What was that for?"

"Real enough for you?" Half-pint said. He picked up a bag of chips and tore it open. He reached in for a handful and shoved them into his mouth. Talking with a mouthful, he said, "We need to get going."

He withdrew another handful of kettle cooked chips and engulfed them. His words became jumbled as he spoke. "We need to get going if we're going to help the princess. She needs you."

"What princess?" Charlie said. "The king and queen didn't have any children."

"That's not true," Half-pint said. He gulped the last of his chips. "Well, kinda true. But the princess is the ruler of the kingdom now. And she needs your help."

"What are you talking about? What princess? What help?" Charlie asked. "How could a princess need my help?"

"Oh, right. Time. You don't know," Half-pint said. He removed his top hat, holding it close to his chest. "The king and queen are dead."

Charlie stepped back and hunched slightly over. "The king and queen are dead?"

"Yeah. Everybody was sad. And the princess was crying." He paused for a moment, his eyes wandering off into the distance. "She carries on, and she'll be the new queen. Everyone loves her, so that's good. At least, I think they love her. There was the one incident, and they kind of don't like her now. The kingdom is in trouble, and she's trying to get help, but no one will help her."

Charlie focused on the imp. "Help her with what?"

"The attacks from Castle Verafell. There's a lot going on. And you have to come with me," Half-pint said. "To help her."

Charlie shook his head. "I'm not going anywhere."

"Can we go, Uncle Charlie?" Ginny asked.

"I want to go," Tyler added.

"We aren't going anywhere," Charlie said. "I've already lost . . ." His words trailed off.

He continued, "I've already lost enough to that place. I'm not losing any more. I have to babysit these kids. I can't leave. I can't take them with me."

"I was worried you were going to say something like that," Half-pint said. He placed the bag of chips onto the ground. "But the princess needs you."

"I don't know what princess you're talking about," Charlie said. "There was no princess."

"But there is now," Half-pint said. He paused for a moment, eyes wandering from Charlie to the kids, and then back to Charlie.

"I'm sorry, but there's no other way," Half-pint said. "I hope you forgive me."

"Forgive you for what?" Charlie asked.

Half-pint snapped his fingers and disappeared into a cloud of smoke. He reappeared next to Tyler, grabbing the child's arm. With a snap, he disappeared again with the young boy. The two reappeared at the basement steps. As soon as they appeared, they were gone. Another puff of smoke led into the basement.

Everything happened in an instant. Charlie reeled back on his heels, caught off guard.

"Tyler!" Ginny said.

Charlie rushed to the basement door.

"Uncle Charlie!" Tyler yelled from downstairs. "Help me."

Charlie flew down the steps, his feet almost slipping on the half carpeted open stairs. He rumbled down, reaching a full sprint to appear around the corner.

Half-pint stood in front of the mirror, holding the arms of the young boy. His face contorted in fear. He wiggled and struggled to break free, but the imp held both arms tightly.

"I'm sorry it had to be this way, Charlie," Half-pint said. "But I need you to come with me." Half-pint pulled the child close to him and fell backward into the mirror.

"Uncle Charlie," the boy yelled.

They disappeared inside the mirror, as if traveling through a wall of water. The silver, reflective mirror was replaced with a swirl of purple, blue, and silver.

"Tyler!" Charlie shouted.

Ginny rushed around the corner. "Uncle Charlie, it took Tyler. We have to go get him."

The room swirled. Blood rushed to his head. It pounded and throbbed. His heart raced. Charlie sharply inhaled and exhaled. Every rush of emotion surged through his body. He focused on the little girl.

Her eyebrows arched and mouth agape. Arms tucked in close to her body. Fingers interlinked. "We have to help him," Ginny said in a whimper.

Charlie focused on the swirling mirror. The moment he waited twenty years for had arrived. He had hoped for better circumstances, but this was it. He already lost one person to that realm. He wasn't going to lose another.

Charlie glanced back at his niece. He stuck out his hand, his palm awaiting hers. She placed her hand into his. "It's like walking through water," he said. "Except you don't get wet. Stick close to me."

Ginny nodded.

They stepped toward the mirror and disappeared into the swirling vortex.

CHAPTER 4
WELCOME TO GLIMMERFELL

"Tyler!" Charlie shouted into the void. Total darkness enveloped them as they emerged from the other end of the mirror. Charlie held firmly onto Ginny's diminutive hand. "Ginny, don't let go of me."

"Okay, Uncle Charlie," she replied behind him.

"Tyler? Are you here?" Charlie shouted. His bare feet met chiseled stone, cold and damp to the touch, as if stepping onto a cement basement. "Tyler?"

"I'm here, Uncle Charlie," Tyler shouted back. "I can't see anything."

"Neither can I," Ginny said.

"Stay where you are," Charlie cried out. "I'm coming to you." He took a step forward, only to be met with sharp pain ripping across his exposed shin.

"OW!" Charlie shouted. The pain ripped up his leg. He bent over, dragging Ginny closer. He rubbed his shin with his free hand while gritting his teeth.

"Are you okay?" Tyler asked.

Charlie only returned an audible grunt.

"Hold on a moment," Half-pint said. "I'll open the curtain."

"Half-pint, you better run as fast as you can," Charlie said through his closed teeth. He opened his mouth. "As soon as I can see, we're going to have at it."

"I already apologized," Half-pint's voice echoed through the room. "It was the only way to get you here."

"Tyler, call out where you're at, and I'll come to you," Charlie said.

"I'm over here," the boy said.

Charlie shuffled toward the sound of Tyler's voice. His feet scraping across the stone floor, Charlie reached out with his toes for any other obstacles before continuing. At first, he only found stone before his toes hit the soft cotton of pajama pants.

"Something touched me," Tyler said.

"That's me," Charlie said.

His hand jutted out and tapped the moppy hair of the young child. He traced down his arm and took the young child's hand.

"Don't let go," Charlie said.

A cacophony of sounds erupted as objects crashed to the stone floor on the other side of the room. "I'm okay," Half-pint said.

"Not for long," Charlie was quick to reply. "Get us some light, so we can get out of here. Where are we, anyway?"

"My private study where I've been working," Half-pint said. "I've been working for years to get that mirror going again. And it worked. I honestly can't believe it worked."

More objects, metallic in sound, crashed to the ground. The pitter-patter of the edges from an iron lid bounced off the stone before coming to a rest.

"I don't think I'm okay now," Half-pint said. "That one . . . that one stung."

Pitch black. Not a sliver of light spilled in through the cracks and crevices of a doorway. The darkness enveloped them. Charlie stood frozen, not wanting to move in case he ran into another object.

Worse, the kids could run into something. He waited for the imp to finish his task.

Charlie breathed in and out to soothe his nerves. "Half-pint, you have about thirty seconds until I start grabbing things and tossing them toward you," Charlie yelled.

"It's the defenses. I keep the room in darkness, so no one will find the mirror," Half-pint said. "They must have gone off when I went through. We'll be fine after I open the curtains."

Gong. Gong. Gong.

The sound of a clock tower echoed through the room.

"What's that, Uncle Charlie?" Ginny asked. Her voice was raised with a hint of terror.

"That's a . . . That's a clock tower," Charlie said. The realization of where exactly the mirror led them crept into his mind. *Glimmerfell.*

Gong. Gong. Gong.

"Not any clock tower," Half-pint said. "The royal clock tower."

Gong. Gong.

"Eight o'clock," Half-pint said. "Perfect."

Curtains flung open, spilling light into the room. Everything turned a shimmering bright white. Charlie closed his eyes and turned his head, temporarily blinded by the light. He blinked a few times, adjusting to his new reality. He turned back toward the source —a window with a long-forgotten view.

The shining, glimmering city came into focus. A city he hadn't seen in twenty years. He could only draw on the specifics from memory. A fading memory that had deteriorated over time. Small holes were renewed with fresh eyes.

He gulped and let go of the children's hands.

Half-pint stood in front of the large window, twice the size of Charlie. Intricate metal bands crisscrossed the glass. A metal band ran down the middle. Half-pint opened the window inward. A dazzling display of deep blues, golds, and reds showed on the rooftops outside—the colors of the kingdom.

"Welcome back to Glimmerfell," Half-pint said.

Charlie approached the window with short steps. His mind still grappled with the fact that after twenty years, he had finally returned. His hands clasped the stone windowsill. Charlie leaned out of the window to get a better view.

With walls made of glimmering stone marble, the city below shined like a beacon. The sky was a deep blue, rich in color. Full trees lined the streets. People dressed in a tapestry of deep, rich colors went about their day. Some with booths on the street peddled fresh wares, fruits, baked goods, or flowers. Shop owners invited people inside their stores. The city was alive with activity.

Towers and other spires rose to greet the sky. Buildings with stone bases and exposed wood formed in a stucco like material. Pointed, wood tiled roofs were painted with deep, rich colors. A clock tower in the center of the town loomed almost as high as the castle keep. A clock faced in all four directions. A mighty, glistening golden bell hung below the pointed blue roof.

Charlie scanned the city, unable to find the royal keep. He peered over the edge to the ground below, a good four, five stories down. He couldn't find the castle keep because they were in it.

Charlie had waited twenty years for this moment. Twenty years of dreaming to return. He breathed deeply. Fresh air filled his lungs, rejuvenating his body. He held his breath for a moment before exhaling. He backed away from the edge and turned toward Half-pint.

Half-pint backed away; his hands raised. His palms faced Charlie. "Now, I know . . . I know I shouldn't have done what I did, but you weren't listening."

All the anger directed at Half-pint ceased. Charlie ran a hand through his hair. He blinked, holding back tears that welled in his eyes.

"Do you know how long I've waited for this view?" Charlie said in a low voice. "I never thought I'd see it again."

"So, you're not mad at me?" Half-pint asked.

"Oh, I'm furious," Charlie said. His voice picked up. "You're lucky I got this view."

"Can we see?" Tyler asked.

Charlie motioned to the window with his head. "Come here. Don't fall out the window. Your mother will be mad at me."

The kids rushed to the windowsill, peering outside. "Whoa," they said in unison. "It's a real kingdom."

Charlie held the windowpanes and stood behind the children, taking in the view.

"This place is the from the stories I told you," he said. "This is where I came as a kid. All the adventures I told you about. They all happened here."

"Wow," the kids said in a drawn-out exclamation.

"Uncle Charlie, take us on one of your adventures," Ginny said.

"Yes," Tyler said. "Please take us on an adventure."

"You're already here, so why not?" Half-pint added.

"We'll stay for a bit," Charlie said. "I'll show you around or walk around or something."

"Yeah!" the kids shouted as they ran around the room.

The room was circular, with high walls. Various odds and ends were strewn about. A wooden end table, no doubt what Charlie's shin greeted upon arrival, sat in front of a high-back chair. A drafting table of sorts with a well-worn grimoire opened atop it. Bottles, vials, and jars decorated shelves. A black cauldron tipped over onto the stone floor, its lid off in the distance. Behind them stood an exact duplicate of the mirror they had traveled through in Charlie's basement.

A lightheadedness befell Charlie. He wobbled on his feet. The room spun. An uneasiness formed in his stomach as if he were about to throw up. He moved toward the high-back chair. His feet became unsecured on the stone floor. He caught himself on the end table before tumbling toward the leather chair. He slumped into the plush leather, clutching his head with one hand.

Ginny rushed to his side. "Are you okay, Uncle Charlie?"

He closed his eyes. "I'm . . . I'm fine," Charlie said. His head swirled. "I'm . . . It's a lot. It's a . . . It's a lot to take in at the moment."

Charlie's heart raced. He breathed in and out. It had been a few months or maybe years, but Charlie recognized what was happening. He had worked through them multiple times with his therapist. A panic attack had set in.

He inhaled slowly, letting each breath linger over his tongue. He held it for a moment, then exhaled twice as long as the inhales. His fingers tapped against the supple, worn leather of the chair's arm.

A small hand cupped his. Not a child's hand, but a gloved, bony one. Charlie opened his eyes, greeted by the smiling imp.

"Charlie," Half-pint said. "Welcome home."

Charlie spoke not a word. They both smiled at each other for a moment.

"Now," Half-pint said, letting go of Charlie's hand. He moved toward a brown, wooden door. "The princess needs our help."

"You keep saying a princess. What princess?" Charlie asked.

"Oh, that's right. You don't know," Half-pint said. He touched his cheeks with his open palms and held them there for only a moment. "I keep forgetting these things. Princess Nessa."

"Nessa?" Charlie leaped out of the chair. His shoulders pulled back and head held high. "My Nessa?"

"Mm-hmm," Half-pint said. "The princess needs your help."

Charlie stumbled, nearly falling back into the chair. A smile arched from ear to ear.

"She's . . . she's okay?" Charlie asked. "Vanessa is okay?"

"Oh, yeah," Half-pint said. "She's great, except she's Princess Nessa now."

He paused for a moment. His face contorted, lips held tight, and eyebrows narrowed as if he were deep in thought.

"Well, she's not great at the moment," Half-pint said. He scratched the back of his head. "She's also kind of sad because of the king and queen and all. Plus, the other thing that people are kind of mad at her for, but that's for later. I guess . . . I guess maybe she's not doing okay."

"She's the princess?" Charlie asked. "Vanessa is the princess?"

"That's what I said," Half-pint answered.

Charlie plopped back into the seat. He slouched in the chair, covering his face with his hands. "Oh, I need a moment."

"We don't have a moment. The meeting will be taking place at half-past the hour. You have to be in that meeting," Half-pint said.

"What meeting?" Charlie mumbled through his hands. He splayed out his fingers to catch a glimpse of the imp.

"The meeting of the kingdoms," Half-pint said, waving his arms in animated gestures for emphasis. "To deal with Castle Verafell. She needs your support in the meeting."

His fingers lingered across his face as Charlie dropped his hands. Half-pint maneuvered to the front of the chair, grabbing onto one of Charlie's arms. The imp pulled back, arms flailing back and forth in an attempt to drag Charlie out of the chair. The imp was no match for his size and weight. Charlie didn't budge.

"You have to go now!" Half-pint said. "You two, come help."

The kids rushed over and grabbed Charlie's other arm. They tugged, but still, Charlie didn't budge.

"Alright, alright," Charlie said as he waved his arms, freeing himself from their grasp.

The three let him go.

"I'll go. I'll go," Charlie said. "But I'm barefoot, wearing a T-shirt and gym shorts. Do you have something I can wear? At least shoes? These stone floors aren't good for my feet."

"Got it," Half-pint said. He jogged over to a wooden chest and flung it open. He withdrew pants and shirts, holding them aloft. "Right here."

The clothes were small enough for his niece and nephew.

"Half-pint," Charlie said. "Those are half my size. Combined."

"Oh, right," Half-pint said. He examined the red-and-yellow-striped shirts and brown linen pants. "Growth over time."

He paused, lowering his head. He popped his lips and clicked his tongue. "I have another idea," Half-pint said. "But you have to kind of go with me on this one."

Charlie closed his eyes and shook his head. "What is it?"

"I have a buddy in the guard," Half-pint said. "We'll get you a nice suit of armor. That way it will be easier to get you in."

Charlie's eyes sprang open. "Easier to get me in?" He sat forward in the chair. "Hold up. I thought she was expecting me."

Half-pint licked his lips. "Well . . ." he started.

Charlie leaned forward, nearly falling off the seat. "Half-pint, what's going on?" he asked. "She's expecting me? Right?"

Half-pint shrugged his shoulders. "Well . . . not exactly."

Charlie raised his voice. "Not exactly?!"

"You see, umm . . . well . . . umm . . ." Half-pint said. "She doesn't know you're coming."

"She doesn't know I'm coming?" Charlie asked. "I thought you said she needed my help."

"Well, I thought it would be better if it was kind of a surprise for you to be there to support her because the other kingdoms aren't," Half-pint said.

Charlie's mouth dropped open. He sat in silence for a few seconds. The room swirled again, but his anger rushed to fill the void. He closed his eyes. Gritting his teeth, he soothed his temples with his index and middle fingers.

After a count of ten, Charlie's eyes shot open and locked onto Half-pint with a searing intensity. Charlie licked his lips before speaking. He inhaled and exhaled a few times to quell the anger.

"Half-pint," Charlie said. "I need you to start back at the beginning. Tell me everything."

"Uh, how far back?" Half-pint asked. "And which beginning?"

Charlie clutched his fists. "Start with the mirror not working," he said.

"Ah, yes, the mirror," Half-pint said. "You see, the mirror was broken. Like shattered in pieces. We didn't know how to put it back together—"

"Who's we?" Charlie asked.

"Wynden the Wise," Half-pint answered.

"Where is he now?" Charlie asked.

"He's with the princess getting ready for their meeting," Half-pint said. "He's greeting the special guests."

"Who's Wynden?" Ginny asked.

"He's a smart wizard," Half-pint said. "He's a good friend of mine. And Charlie's. And Princess Nessa. Come to think of it, he's friends with a lot of people."

The children gasped.

"It's like in your story, Uncle Charlie," Ginny said as she pushed his leg back and forth.

Half-pint flailed his arms about as if he were drawing a picture on a tapestry. "Well, the mirror was in pieces, and we couldn't put it back together. Also, Nessa was here. And she couldn't go back home because the mirror was in pieces. But the king and queen took her in and raised her to be the princess."

Charlie leaned back in the chair. His heart raced, beating against his chest. "The mirror broke when she was here?"

"Yeah," Half-pint said.

"That's why it didn't work." Charlie tapped the arms of the chair. "The mirror was broken on this side. I knew it. All those years. I knew it had to be something on this side."

"After the king and queen died, Princess Nessa took over. But now, the kingdom is in trouble . . . or could be in trouble. I'm not certain," Half-pint said. "The other kingdoms are coming today, and they're going to talk about it and maybe help, but maybe not help. Except this one guy. I don't think he's going to show up."

"Why?" Charlie asked. "Why won't he show up?"

Half-pint exhaled. His eyebrows arched high, and he smacked his hands together. "Whoa. We don't have enough time for that story. That's a lot to unpack there. Also, that's kind of why people are mad at her."

"How am I supposed to help with this?" Charlie asked.

Half-pint paused. His eyes narrowed, focusing on Charlie. "Because you're Charlie," Half-pint said. "You and Nessa were a team. *Are* a team? She needs you. I've spent years trying to get that mirror to work again. But when she said she needed help, there was only one person who I thought could help her. I did what was necessary to get the mirror working again."

Half-pint approached him and pointed at Charlie's heart. His bony finger dug into Charlie's chest.

"That person is you," he said. "I read every book and scoured every tome I could find. For twenty years, I kept faith that it would work again. And on this day, when I needed it to work the most, the portal opened once more."

Charlie blinked his eyes and sniffled to hold back a tear. He placed both hands on his hips. "Alright," Charlie said. "Alright. Get me that suit of armor. I'll go into the meeting, and I'll do what I can."

"Yeah!" the children cheered. They ran around the room.

"We get to stay," Ginny said.

"We get to go on adventures," Tyler shouted, following behind his sister.

Charlie raised a hand. "Calm down," he said. "Pick out some clothes, whatever can fit. I don't need you running around in your PJs."

Charlie turned to Half-pint. "They're going to need shoes. Do you have any shoes?"

"Shoes?" Half-pint said. "Shoes run in my family. My cousin twice removed on my mother's side is a shoemaker. I'll find some shoes."

"I don't think we have enough time for you to make shoes," Charlie said.

"Oh, I'm not going to make them," Half-pint said. He tapped his fingers together. "I'll ... acquire them. Through means."

Charlie gripped the arms of the chair and bolted out of the seat. "Alright," he said. "Take me to the princess."

CHAPTER 5
ROYAL RECEPTION

Princess Nessa paced around the circular chamber of the council room. Her blue eyes focused on the round wooden table in the center of the room. She examined every element awaiting her honored guests.

Two wooden chairs, exquisitely built with elaborate wood carved designs, were placed at evenly spaced intervals around the table. Plush, leather cushions were on the seats and backs. They were draped with colorful heraldic banners of the various kingdoms represented at the table. High backs to honor the royalty. Nessa's eyes barely gleamed over their carved, wood tops.

Red, black, and white for the mountainous kingdom of Ironfell. Silver and gold for the pastoral kingdom of Emberfell. Green and purple for the forest kingdom of Mystfell. For the northern snow kingdom of Frostfell, a light blue and purple banner with a third chair—a kingdom ruled not by a king and queen, but a council. A sea green banner trimmed in gold for the pirate kingdom of Brightfell. Finally, while not the head of the circular table, but positioned to face the entrance, were the chairs of her kingdom.

Glimmerfell.

Draped down the back was a deep blue heraldic standard trimmed in gold. The plush leather seats were well-worn from the previous occupants—King Aric and Queen Valeria. Honored and cherished members of the council for the realm of Everfell, they were known for their kindness, fairness, and generosity. Their absence from this meeting, the first since their deaths, would be a large void for Nessa to fill.

She paused. Her eyes focused on the empty chairs. She breathed in and out to soothe her nerves. Nessa fiddled with the end of her braided ponytail draped over her shoulder. She flipped the ends of her once golden blonde hair, now darkened. Streaks of natural gold and red gave it a glimmering shine. After a moment, she flicked the end back over her shoulder. It swung back and forth until it settled at her waist.

This was her first council meeting. She had called it at the behest of her advisors. What was natural for the former king and queen was daunting and overwhelming to the princess. If she failed, then her kingdom could face ruin.

A threat loomed large over the land, and it was up to her to rally the forces. The king and queen would have had no issues. Their reputation alone would have gathered the support from the other kingdoms in the realm. Their arms would be ready to charge into battle and face the new threat head-on. For Nessa, this would be her first test as the new leader of the realm.

She exhaled, letting the breath linger over her tongue.

The table was adorned with a leather map featuring the realm of Everfell, each kingdom represented with their colors. To the southwest, a land was marked in boundaries of black ink—the land of shadows and nightmares. A wooden statue of the castle was placed in the center of the land, nestled along a winding river. The threat that loomed large over everyone—Castle Verafell.

Nessa focused on the wooden statue representing the castle. The decrepit tower had been left to crumble and age in the land of Shadowfell. A once shining kingdom and the most robust in all the realm.

It was besieged by an evil wizard. He sought nothing but power. He mastered the arts of dark forces. The kingdom was blighted, and the tower fell to ruin.

The wizard was defeated before he could accomplish his goals. The land was left to rot and house the monstrous creatures he let loose on the world. The kingdom had been contained for hundreds of years. But now a threat loomed deep in the heart of Castle Verafell.

Nessa continued her inspection ahead of the arrival of her guests. She tugged at the banners, straightening them as much as possible. She adjusted their positions ever so slightly. Around and around the table she went. The leather of her shoes clacked against the stone flooring, echoing off the walls.

Her eyes caught a green vine sprouting through the cracks in the stone floor. Her deep blue dress ruffled as she kneeled. She plucked the green sprout from its cracked crevice. She examined the leafy vine, rotating it in her hand before popping back up.

Nessa snapped her attention to her personal bodyguard, holding the vine aloft for her to see. Her eyebrows furled. "There's another vine," Nessa said. "I thought we had these under control?"

The heels of Lyra Thornvale, Nessa's personal bodyguard, clicked as she snapped to attention. The gold epaulet swayed back and forth on the shoulders of her blue leather coat. The image of a gold rising sun was embroidered on the front. A brown leather belt tied around her waist. The golden filigree handle of her dueling sword was at her side. Her white pants were tucked neatly into her boots.

Lyra stood poised, ready to defend the princess, head held high with her blonde hair pulled back into a ponytail. Her white-gloved hands curled into fists at her side. Lyra's eyes found Nessa's. "I shall personally ask the gardeners to search the castle grounds once more, Your Highness," Lyra said.

Nessa straightened her stance. "See to it these vines are found, plucked, and eliminated. I don't want the castle to be overrun with these things."

The hem of Nessa's blue dress glided over the stone floor as she moved toward Lyra. She presented the green vine.

Lyra unfurled one hand and accepted the discarded weed. "It will be done, Your Highness," Lyra said.

"Very well," Nessa said. She paused for a moment. Her lips curled into a half smile. "Thank you."

Bang. Bang. Bang.

Three knocks at the wooden door signaled the arrival of their honored guests.

Nessa inhaled, pulling her shoulders back. She strode over to her chair—the chair once belonging to Queen Valeria. Her rightful place. Nessa hadn't yet had her coronation as the official queen of Glimmerfell. It wasn't yet her right to wear the crown of the queen.

She adjusted her gold-plated tiara, which matched the highlights in her hair. She ran her fingers through her light brown hair, securing the gold band before waving to the guards to open the doors.

The wooden double doors, twice the size of a person, opened inward. A cadre of six trumpeters entered single file in columns of two. They stood in front of the doors and turned inward to face each other. They raised their elongated, buisine trumpets. A banner of Glimmerfell dangled from brass horns, waving back and forth. The trumpeters' lips were pursed and ready to blow. They played a melodic tone to announce the arrival of the various dignitaries.

The first to enter was Nessa's advisor, Wynden the Wise, a wizard and wielder of powers beyond her comprehension. He had hair as white as snow and scraggly like a bush with a neatly trimmed white beard stretched to his waist. He was old. Nessa wasn't exactly sure how old. Some said he was as old as the castle itself. He wore a dark purple robe, trimmed in gold, with crescent moons embroidered on a stripe of black along the edges. His staff, made of the wood of a juniper tree, clanged against the stone floor as he circled the table. He used it as less of a tool to walk and more of a pronouncement for his arrival.

Wynden took his place to the left of Nessa. He had served as advisor to the king and queen. Now, he served as advisor to the princess. His wise, sage advice helped guide Glimmerfell for many, many years. Nessa hoped it would continue.

She glanced at Wynden, her eyebrows arched high. He gave a quick smile and winked. Nessa smiled in return.

The lead trumpeter lowered his instrument. His shoulders pulled back and his head held high. His voice boomed and echoed off the stone walls. "Your Majesty," the lead trumpeter yelled. "We are proud and honored to welcome our guests from the land of Ember-fell. Her majesty, Queen Gabriella of the Cinder Ash, and his majesty, King Christopher."

The royal couple emerged from the columns of trumpeters. Glass clanged against stone. They should break, yet, the queen's magical glass slippers held firm. She wore an elegant, silver dress trimmed in gold. The reflective silver hugged her upper body before billowing out toward her ankles.

"I could use a fairy godmother right now," Nessa muttered under her breath. "I wonder how you contact one."

Silver and gold velvet draped King Christopher, as well as a white fur trimmed cape. A black leather belt hung around his waist with boots to match.

Two bodyguards, tall and lanky, with slim facial features followed the king and queen to their seats. The couple bowed to Princess Nessa. She returned the gesture in kind before the couple took their seats.

The trumpeters bellowed again.

"Your Majesty, Princess Nessa," he said. "We are proud and honored to welcome our guests from the land of Ironfell. Her majesty, Queen Eirwen of the Winter Snow, and his majesty, King William."

Entering through the column of trumpeters, arms locked together at the elbows, were the King and Queen of Ironfell. The king was dressed in the regal colors of his kingdom. A thick, red pleated cloth mantle down his front with the symbol of a hammer striking an anvil embroidered in white. Black pants and fur draped over his shoulders.

The queen was dressed in her namesake colors. A white dress with streaks of red matched her cheeks. Black trimming matched the color of her hair. A golden apple brooch, encased in a band of iron, was pinned to the center of her lapel below her throat.

Following behind were two dwarfs, armed with hammers and dressed in gold-plated armor. Their helmets had no face guard, as to proudly display their bushy beards that reached to their waists. They followed the king and queen to their seats.

"Your Majesty, it's an honor you would invite us to your kingdom," Queen Eirwen said.

The king and queen bowed their heads.

Nessa returned the gesture. "Thank you to the King and Queen of Ironfell for accepting my call."

The king and queen took their seats. The wood scraped along the stone floor as the dwarfs pushed them closer to the table—an easy task for the muscular bodyguards.

Queen Eirwen leaned over the side of the chair and thanked them for their assistance.

The trumpeters bellowed out once more.

"Your Majesty, we have the distinct honor to present her majesty, Queen Rosemond of the Briar, and his majesty, King Anders of Mystfell."

The couple took their turn through the rows of trumpeters, hand in hand. Her hair was pulled up into a bun, wrapped around a piece of broken spindle from a spinning wheel. Her purple dress, trimmed in green, swished back and forth as she approached the table.

The king wore a regal green velvet cloak trimmed in purple over a white jacket. A white star embroidered in the center. A black cape draped over his shoulders, flowing down to his waist.

The couple marched toward their seats, accompanied by two bodyguards armed with long pikes. They followed behind the couple in lockstep formation. The king and queen bowed before

taking their positions at the table. Nessa bowed in acknowl-
edgement.

The trumpeters lowered their instruments. They filed out one by
one in their single file columns.

Nessa turned to her side and whispered to her advisor. "What
about the other two?"

Wynden leaned in, speaking in a hushed voice. "The council of
three from Frostfell declined the invitation."

"What about Cyrus?" Nessa asked.

Wynden paused, biting on his lower lip as if he didn't want to
answer.

"What about the Prince of Brightfell?" she asked again.

Wynden glanced at the floor, licking his lips. He shuffled uneasily
in place. "He said . . ." Wynden started in a low voice so only Nessa
could hear. "He said you can go to hell."

Nessa closed her eyes and breathed in deeply, holding it for a
moment. She kept her composure, not wanting to project any sign of
weakness. Her body stayed straight, her fit frame poised and unmoving. She thought of her counting exercises to soothe her nerves.

One. Two. Three.

She exhaled and opened her eyes.

"Thank you," she whispered. "Let's begin."

Nessa motioned to the two guards in full plate armor standing
near the door. Lockstep, they turned and exited through the entryway. They each pushed a wooden door closed.

A hand emerged through the crack of the doors. Armored in full
plate, the silver hand stopped the doors from closing. The wood
crunched against the steel gauntlet. The guards opened the door and
allowed their fellow guardsman to enter. The noise drew the attention of the crowd.

He saluted, but awkwardly, as if he struggled to raise his arm. His
face shield was down, covering his face. The guard pivoted and
turned to his left, shambling along the walls. His metal plates
clanged together. The boots stomped along the stone floor.

Nessa followed his every step. Her glare grew more intense as her eyebrows narrowed, and her eyelids nearly closed. The guard found an open spot along the walls, pivoted, and faced the table.

"I apologize for the slight disturbance," Nessa said, drawing everyone's attention back to her.

"It's quite alright," Queen Eirwen said with a smile.

A slight, almost imperceptible half-smile shaped Nessa's lips as she returned the pleasantry.

Nessa bowed her head and gathered her thoughts. She stood at the ceremonial head of the table, leaning over. Her arms spread out, she placed her fingertips on the polished wood. She pulled back her shoulders, trying to project an image of authority and confidence.

She had witnessed her adoptive parents hold court, yet never had the opportunity to do so herself until now. They projected a coolness. A calm. Jovial in their attitude. The king and queen were well-liked and respected. They could sway and convince anyone of anything, as if they agreed all along. She needed that strength. Especially now.

Nessa faced the council of the realm on her own. The kings and queens seated at the table were at least fifteen years her seniors. Though youthful in appearance, they had far more years of experience under their leadership. Far more reasons to tell her she was wrong and that her plans were foolish. Though thirty-three-years-old, Nessa's youthful face betrayed any attempt at gravitas.

She was a child seated at the adults' table.

"Thank you all for coming," Nessa said. Her voice boomed through the chamber. "I know the journey was long, but we thank you in this dire time. I wish we were gathered under happier circumstances, especially considering the passing of King Aric and Queen Valeria."

"We're sorry for your loss," King Anders said.

"Yes," Queen Rosemond added. "If there's anything the kingdom of Mystfell can do to help with the transition, please don't hesitate to ask."

Nessa smiled from ear to ear, but her drooping eyebrows

betrayed her sadness. "I appreciate that. I hope you'll all attend the coronation in two moon cycles."

"Of course," Queen Gabriella said. "We wouldn't miss it."

"It would be an honor," King Christopher added.

"But that isn't why I've called you here today." Nessa glanced at the map laid out before everyone as she motioned toward the man to her left. "Thanks to the consult of my advisor, Wynden the Wise, we strongly believe there's a dark force gathering within Castle Verafell."

The kings and queens glanced at their partners before glancing at the rest of the seated members.

"What do you mean dark force?" King William asked.

Nessa drew in her hands, interlocking her fingers. She placed them on her stomach. "We believe a spirit of a wizard is actively building an army and preparing for an invasion of Everfell."

"You're certain of this?" Queen Rosemond asked.

Nessa inhaled deeply, puffing out her chest, and drawing her shoulders back. "We've seen an increase of attacks on the border towns. Most recently, an entire town was wiped out from an incursion of monsters from Shadowfell."

"We share a border with Shadowfell as well," Queen Rosemond said. "We've had our share of encounters with the creatures that wander out of the shadow kingdom. This is nothing new."

Nessa gulped. She had expected resistance, but she hoped someone would speak up for her side. "The incursions are becoming more frequent. Tactical, as if they were planned. We've stationed troops to those towns. However . . ."

She paused as something caught in her throat.

"However, they were unsuccessful in saving the town," she finished.

The royal dignitaries shifted their focus from one to another.

"We're sorry for your losses," King William said. "Do you need assistance defending the towns?"

Princess Nessa inhaled sharply. "Defending the towns isn't why we called you here today. We have a proposal to deal with the threat once and for all."

"Do you have proof of this threat?" Queen Gabriella asked. "I thought containment has been the policy of all kingdoms for years."

"It has," Wynden said. "But containment allowed the dark forces to gather strength."

All eyes turned their attention to the wizened wizard.

Wynden circled the table, gaining a better vantage of the map laid out before everyone. He used his staff to point to the wooden replica of Castle Verafell. "I first discovered it around twenty years ago on one of my many scouting missions into Shadowfell."

The guard who entered last shuffled his feet, clanging against the wall and drawing Nessa's ire.

Wynden continued, undisturbed by the noise. "Something form-less and shapeless stirred within the halls. I consulted with the Council of Mystics. We've kept an eye on it."

He tapped the wooden replica of Castle Glimmerfell with his staff. "It was the policy of King Aric and Queen Valeria to contain the threat within the borders of Shadowfell for the time being," he said. "With the passing of time, the darkness grew. Now, its forces are ready to march on the realm."

Wynden slammed the gnarled and twisted head of his staff onto the map. The wooden castle replicas bounced around. The replica of Castle Glimmerfell tumbled over. "They will no doubt invade. One by one, the kingdoms will fall. First, with Glimmerfell."

He swiped the piece off the map.

"Then Mystfell," he said as he knocked over the castle. "Followed by Emberfell, Ironfell, and Frostfell. Brightfell would be the last to fall, but their ships would find nowhere to port."

The captive audience shifted in their seats. They gave knowing glances to each other.

"How certain are you?" King Christopher asked. "Shadowfell has been off limits. Now, you're asking us to do what . . . marshal our troops deep in the forests?" King Christopher shifted in his seat, leaning away from the table. "They're filled with creatures and abominations that have thus far been contained. If there's anything in there, it would be contained as well."

"I agree," King Anders said. "It would be useless to march into Shadowfell. Why not follow the process of containment that we have now? If you need additional assistance guarding your border towns, we could provide a company of knights . . . should they be required."

Nessa's fingers twitched and trembled. She dug them deep into her interlocked hands, hoping to not show any signs of weakness. The heel of her foot was raised, rocking back and forth, itching to run.

Taking a deep breath, she locked eyes with everyone one by one around the table. She exhaled, soothing her nerves and finding the clarity she needed.

"If what Wynden says is correct—" Nessa said.

"*If?*" King William asked. "So, you're unsure of the threat of invasion?"

Nessa closed her eyes. Her foot trembled once more. Her breath quickened. Her stomach fluttered and twisted in knots. She was losing them. She needed to be more careful with her words.

"We're very sure," Wynden said. He placed his staff upright at his side.

"Have you seen it with your own eyes?" Queen Gabriella asked.

Nessa snapped to Wynden, her eyebrows shooting upward. She never considered the fact that he hadn't visited Castle Verafell. At least, not in recent years. He had only used his mystical ways of obtaining knowledge.

Wynden shifted in his stance. His fingers repositioned around the brown staff. "I scried the location using the power of farsight," he replied.

"Scried?" Queen Eirwen asked. "You ask us to risk our armies. Our knights. Our citizens. All because you've scried?"

"How do you know what you saw was real?" Queen Rosemond

asked. "If this was a spirit of a powerful wizard, how do you know he didn't show you what you wanted to see?"

"I ... umm ..." He struggled to find the words.

Nessa's heart raced, beating against her chest. She was losing them. Her chest rose and fell as she inhaled deep breaths. Panic invaded her mind, leaving it a blank slate of nothingness. She couldn't find the words to justify a valid reason for them to pledge their army to stop whatever stirred deep within the ruined castle's halls.

"If you haven't seen it and offer no other proof, then we can't justify the armies of Mystfell marching into the land of shadows," King Anders said.

The King and Queen of Emberfell glanced at each other. A silent exchange told through the subtle shifts in their eyes.

"We agree," Queen Gabriella said. "Border town incursions by a select few aren't enough to justify us sending our citizens into the dark forest."

Nessa glanced at Queen Eirwen. Her eyes begged for Eirwen's help. Nessa's eyebrows raised, holding back tears. Nessa only found a half-smile and sorrowful eyes hidden behind narrowed eyebrows.

Eirwen shook her head, her black hair waving back and forth. "Without proof, we can't justify sending anyone ourselves," Queen Eirwen said. "I wouldn't ask the citizens or dwarfs to go if I wasn't willing to do so myself."

Nessa fell back into her chair. She closed her eyes and bowed her head. She had failed her kingdom.

"If you have something real, something to offer as proof, perhaps we can send our soldiers into battle," Queen Gabriella said.

"Until then, we're sorry," Queen Rosemond added. "The policy of containment remains in place."

Nessa gathered her composure. She was still the princess and ruler of Glimmerfell. She might be devastated with the answer, but she needed to project poise and confidence as a leader. She inhaled to soothe her nerves, raising her eyes to meet the other royal dignitaries.

"Understood," Nessa said. "I want to thank you for making the trip to Glimmerfell. I hope to see—"

"Wait!" a voice shouted. "Don't give up yet."

Everyone drew their attention to the guard against the wall.

Lyra drew her sword and charged at the disrupting guard. The bodyguards of the kings and queens did the same. They moved in and surrounded the man who had entered last.

"What is the meaning of this?" King Christopher said as he bolted up out of his seat.

King William and King Anders followed suit.

The man cowered as an assortment of dueling swords, pikes, and hammers, all surrounded and pointed at him.

"I can explain," the man said. He held his arms out at shoulder height.

"Guard, remove your helmet and identify yourself," Nessa shouted. "Immediately."

The guard removed his helm, revealing his boyish young face and slicked back brown hair. A face that was somewhat familiar to Nessa, but she couldn't quite place it.

The man's eyes glanced from weapon to weapon, mere inches from his face. "My name is Charlie," he said. "Charlie Grimm. I'm here to help."

CHAPTER 6
THE ROYAL TREATMENT

"Charlie?" Nessa whispered as she slumped back into her chair, her mouth agape. She couldn't believe her eyes. She hadn't heard that name uttered aloud in many years. So many. Now, a man stood before her claiming to be Charlie.

This isn't real, she thought. *This must be a trap.*

She glanced at Wynden, who was already focused on her. He shook his head as if to disavow any knowledge of his sudden appearance.

"What is the meaning of this?" King Anders asked. "Is this some sort of joke?"

"I'm . . . I'm as surprised as you are," Nessa said.

"So, he's a spy?" King Anders asked. "I shall have my pikemen run him through."

"Whoa, whoa, whoa," Charlie said. "No . . . no need for that. I'm a friend of Nessa's. I was summoned, but I was a little late."

"Was he supposed to join us?" Queen Gabriella asked.

Nessa couldn't answer. If Charlie was here, then that meant the way was open. That the mirror was working again. That she could go home.

"I agree," King Christopher said. "If he's a spy, then he should be dealt with."

"Nessa, tell them I'm not a spy. We're old friends from when she was a child," Charlie said. A hint of panic appeared in his voice as his words tripped over themselves to get out. "Nessa, tell them."

Nessa stood and locked eyes with her friend—a reunion twenty years in the making. But what if it wasn't Charlie? Some sort of trick sent from Castle Verafell to sabotage the meeting itself. The mirror was broken and shattered. It hadn't worked for twenty years.

The life of Vanessa Davis ended on that day. She had lost all connection to home. Her family. Her previous life. Her previous relationships. Her mother. Her father. Charlie. All were gone on the day the mirror shattered. Instead, she was born anew as Princess Nessa of Glimmerfell. King Aric and Queen Valeria had raised her as their daughter.

Still, she had to know. Was this the real Charlie? She scoured her memory for a question she could ask him. A question to verify it was him. A question only he would know. Twenty years of a new life clouded her memories. Only images remained. The emotions of her memory had long since faded. Only the pictures of a life once lived remained. But as her former life flickered by, her mind settled on a single image. A small white brick with a dangling cord.

Nessa pulled back her shoulders, puffing out her chest. A discerning glance crossed her face as her eyebrows narrowed. She scrutinized the man standing before her. Her heart wanted to believe it was Charlie, but her brain refused to accept it. No, the mirror was inoperable. There was no way for Charlie to come back or for her to leave.

Nessa shifted in her stance. "If you're Charlie—"

"I am," he said. "I'm most certainly Charlie Grimm."

"Then tell me. What was our favorite song to listen to, and how did we listen to it?"

"Our favorite song was "All the Small Things"," Charlie

answered. "And we used to bounce around your bedroom listening together on your iPod. I called you a pop-punk princess."

Nessa's heart nearly skipped a beat. Her stomach fluttered. She did her best to fight back the tears, but she couldn't as they forged a streak down her cheek. Her best friend and once close confidant had returned.

She rushed around the table. The hem of her blue and gold dress swayed back and forth. She dipped a shoulder and squeezed between the guards. Her arms wrapped around Charlie, the force nearly knocking him back. He returned the favor. The metal gauntlets lightly tapped against her back.

She held him for what felt like twenty years—twenty years of missed conversations and play and experiences. Nessa buried her head into his shoulder, the plate armor cold to her cheek. He placed his head on hers.

"I missed you," she whispered, fighting back the tears.

"I missed you too," Charlie whispered.

The two swayed back and forth—life-long friends reunited once again.

A tear streamed down her face. "I never gave up hope," Nessa said.

"Neither did I," Charlie said. "I kept the mirror safe. I kept it safe, and I waited for so long."

"Would you two like some private time?" Queen Gabriella asked.

As joyous as the reunion was, Nessa was still a princess and needed to conduct court. She released her grip on Charlie. Her hand raised to her face and wiped away the tear. She gave two taps on Charlie's shoulders and turned to face the crowd.

The guards had lowered their weapons and backed away from the couple.

"I—I apologize for the disruption again," she said. "This is Charlie, a close personal friend I haven't seen in many years."

"I'm happy about your reunion," Queen Rosemond said. "I know the pain of waiting for a long time."

Queen Eirwen stood. "Perhaps we can table this conversation for another time," she said. "It seems the princess has other matters to attend to."

The joy fluttering in Nessa's heart sank, leaving her with an emptiness. "No, please wait," she said. "Let's discuss this more."

"I'm sorry," Queen Gabriella said. "Without proof, and with your little reunion going on, perhaps it's best to wait."

"If you can give us something . . ." King Christopher said. "Anything . . . then we would consider taking action."

"Until then, you're chasing ghost stories," King William said.

Nessa dipped her shoulders and lowered her head. Her first official court as Princess of Glimmerfell was a failure.

The kings took their queen's hands as they rose from their seats. Hand in hand, they all proceeded toward the double doors, followed by their respective guards.

Nessa had failed. She failed her kingdom, her duty, and most importantly, her adoptive parents. Another tear fell from Nessa's eyes; this one filled with sadness instead of joy.

Queen Gabriella stopped and let go of her king's hand. She wrapped her arms around Nessa, giving her an extra squeeze. "Felt like you needed it," she said.

Nessa smiled back. "Thanks."

Gabriella winked at her and released her hug. She clasped Christopher's awaiting hand, and the pair exited.

Lyra sheathed her sword. The golden filigree hilt smacked against the leather of her scabbard. She stood at attention, her arms at her sides and shoulders pulled back. She glared at Charlie.

Nessa closed her eyes and licked her lips. She mentally counted to three before turning in place. She smiled at Charlie, but she squinted, projecting her inner sadness.

"Why . . . how are you here?" she asked. "What are you dressed in?"

"Half-pint dressed me. He said it was how I could get in," he said, wobbling back and forth on his feet. "How does anyone move in this thing? It's so restrictive."

"Only the finest warriors are fit to wear the armor," Lyra said.

Charlie held out his armored hand. "Hi, I'm Charlie. Nice to meet you."

Lyra kept her guarded pose.

"Charlie, this is Lyra. She's my personal bodyguard," Nessa said.

"Whoa, personal bodyguard. Nice," he said. "I guess it comes with being a princess."

He flailed out his arms and crouched in his stance to bow. "Speaking of which, congratulations . . . Princess. I was worried you were going to be on the streets or something. *Princess*. Well, I used to call you a pop-punk princess. Now, you're a real-life princess."

"Pop-punk princess? I haven't heard that in a long time." Nessa chuckled. "I'm not so much a pop-punk princess these days."

"At least you're doing well," Charlie said. "Even if it's a little less punk rock."

Nessa glanced around the council chambers. "The king and queen took very good care of me."

Wynden joined the reunion. His staff echoed through the room each time it struck the stone floor. His eyes shifted from flared excitement to squinched discernment as he examined Charlie. "How are you here?"

"I don't know," Charlie said. "Nice to see you again too."

"Yeah, yeah, yeah. That's all fine and dandy," Wynden said, waving his free hand in the air. "But how are you here?"

Charlie pushed up his grin into his cheekbones as he shook his head back and forth. His eyebrows pushed up high as he shrugged his shoulders. "I don't know. You tell me," Charlie said. "The mirror hasn't worked for twenty years, and then all of a sudden, Half-pint was standing in my kitchen."

Wynden's face dropped, solemn and expressionless. His eyebrows furled. "The imp!" He said. "I should have known. Where is he?"

"In a room in the keep," Charlie said, pointing to the door with his thumb. "He's keeping an eye on my niece and nephew."

Wynden exited the room, slamming his staff into the ground to announce his presence.

"Niece and nephew?" Nessa asked.

"You've missed a lot in twenty years," Charlie said.

"So have you, Charlie," Nessa said. "Let's go take a walk."

THE BIRDS' song filled the air with beautiful melodic tones. The stones of the castle keep shone brightly in the sunny, blue sky. The citizens of Glimmerfell went about their day, shopping, playing, and conversing. Jovial in their attitudes.

Nessa had rarely strolled through the city in the past two years. She kept to herself in the keep ever since the incident with the kingdom of Brightfell—the embarrassment of her kingdom. She couldn't linger on those thoughts. It had happened a few years ago. Time passed, yet not all wounds had healed. He didn't show up today.

"Your Highness, do you think it's wise to be out and about?" Lyra asked in a hushed whisper.

"We're fine," Princess Nessa said. "These are my people. We'll be fine. Besides, I want Charlie to stroll through the town again."

The keep of Castle Glimmerfell was reserved for the royals. The town, held within the walls, was for its citizens. A collection of two-story buildings. A few towers. A place of commerce and fun, where the citizens could live their lives in peace. Pastoral farms covered the landscape outside the castle walls. A patchwork of tilled lands, where farmers could grow crops and tend to livestock. It was a thriving, bustling kingdom with happy people.

Nessa adjusted her hennin—a long, pointy gold hat with a string of blue ribbon sewn into the tip. Tiaras were reserved for official royal business. The hennin headwear was worn despite protests. Not for function or purpose, but at the behest of the royal guards and her official bodyguard. It was designed so that Nessa stood out in a crowd. It made her easier to spot and locate in times of trouble.

Nessa scratched her light brown hair. She despised wearing the hennin. It never sat right on her head. It itched and constantly slid off. Nessa fiddled with the end, trying to find the right spot, only for it to shift with her every step. She preferred to remove the hat.

It drew the ire of the citizens, who could easily spot her. Throngs of people going about their day increased. The cobblestone streets were filled with their joyous activities. Some carried carts of vegetables, freshly picked from the fields. Others pushed their carts of food and other items for sale. Her throat tightened as the crowds poured into the streets.

A few noticed her presence. They glanced and smiled. Before they could turn away, their faces soured. Nessa's heart sank. She was the leader of Glimmerfell, yet she couldn't inspire anyone. Not in the way King Aric or Queen Valeria inspired the citizens.

Nessa's thoughts raced—thoughts of running or getting away. She had spent so much time isolated in the keep following the incident with the prince of Brightfell. The increased attacks on the border towns hadn't helped her reputation or her legitimacy as the rightful princess. Luckily, word hadn't spread of her failed meeting with the council of the realms.

Facing the citizens wasn't the reason she ventured outside. No, it was the man on her right. The man in plate armor, taking his first stroll through these streets in twenty years.

"Does that bakery still make the best scones?" Charlie asked.

"Oh, yeah," she said. "I have bakers at my disposal, but I request them to get fresh bread from there every day."

"That place smelled so good," Charlie said. "I loved the free samples when we were younger."

Nessa stopped. "Do you want to get some?"

Charlie smiled. "You don't have to ask me twice."

Nessa and Charlie rushed over to the bakery, weaving in and out of the crowd. His armor clanged together. Her braid flopped behind her, the blue ribbon waving in the breeze. One hand held the hem of her skirt, and the other held her hennin hat.

Lyra rushed through the crowd to keep up. "Your Highness, please wait," Lyra said.

Charlie rushed through the door first. His shoulders drooped, and his knees buckled. He inhaled, closing his eyes and smiling. "It's exactly as I remembered," he said. "The smells are heavenly."

The scent greeted Nessa as she entered. The rich aroma of freshly baked goods tantalized her senses, drawing her deeper inside. Freshly baked breads, cupcakes, pastries, and pies were scattered across the bakery in wicker baskets or metal pastry stands. All were enticing. She wanted them all.

"How may I help you today—" The words of the baker trailed off. A middle-aged woman with a slight hint of gray in her black hair bowed her head. "Your Highness, it's an honor. To what do I owe the pleasure?"

Nessa politely chuckled, raising a hand. "It's quite alright," she said. "My friend would like a sample of your goods."

"Do you have any of those delicious scones?" Charlie asked.

The baker smiled. "Blueberry or raspberry?"

"Oh, blueberry," Charlie said.

The baker retrieved a paper bag and placed a scone inside. She turned toward the princess. "For you, Your Highness?"

"I'll take the raspberry," Nessa replied.

The baker placed another in the bag.

"And you?" the baker asked Lyra.

Nessa's bodyguard shook her head. "Nothing for me."

The baker handed the bag to Nessa. "On the house," she said.

Nessa shook her head in protest. "That's not necessary. Please let—"

"I won't hear of it," the baker said. "I remember when you came here as a child. When the king and queen brought you here. I consider it a favor to them."

Nessa smiled. "Thank you."

The trio gathered their newly acquired goods and left the store.

Charlie retrieved his blueberry scone, passing the bag to Nessa. He took a bite. "As good as I remembered," he said with a mouthful.

Nessa retrieved hers and bit down. The raspberry filling teased and delighted her taste buds with its sweet flavor. She was transported back to when she was the young girl who sampled the scones for the first time many, many years ago.

It was heavenly.

The trio continued their journey toward the fountain square, a large basin filled with crystal clear water. A marble statue stood at the center, carved with the images and likenesses of the first four kings and queens of Glimmerfell. Their arms and hands were outstretched. Water poured forth and spilled into the basin below.

Nessa sat on the stone ledge. Charlie sat by her side. Lyra stood at attention, scanning the streets.

The citizens came and went through the town square. They glanced at the princess. They bowed, but were quick to move on.

"So, what's the big deal?" Charlie asked as he finished off his scone.

"Big deal with what?" Nessa asked as she took another bite.

"Why do you need my help?" Charlie asked. "Half-pint said you needed my help."

Nessa sighed. "I need a lot of help."

"Well, I'm here," Charlie said. "What do you need?"

"Things are bad, Charlie," Nessa said. "Our border towns are under attack. Wynden wants to storm on Castle Verafell. I can't get anyone to support me. The citizens aren't exactly thrilled with me right now. I'm worried they'll protest me being their queen. They know I'm not of royal blood. I need to show them that I'm their leader."

She lowered her head. Her voice dropped to a whisper, nearly drowned out by the bustle of the daily activities. "I don't know if I can do it alone."

A street performer had set up across from the fountain—a cart that converted into a mobile puppet stage. He raised a red curtain backdrop. He ducked inside the cart. Kids and curious spectators gathered around.

Lyra focused on the gathering performance.

"Oh, it's a puppet show," Charlie said. "We loved these as kids."

Nessa focused on the curtain. She leaned back, her hands holding onto the ledge of the basin. A smile formed on her face.

Two puppets, a king and a queen, popped up from beneath the makeshift stage. The puppets had crowns on their heads and smiles on their faces. They danced back and forth across the stage.

"Once upon a time," the puppeteer said. His voice boomed. "There was a king and a queen, and they were loved by all in the land."

The puppets disappeared below the stage. Another puppet, a princess wearing a hennin hat similar to Nessa's, appeared. The puppet's arms were crossed, and a sour expression was on its face.

"They had a daughter. A princess," the puppeteer said. "She wasn't a happy princess."

He jolted the puppet forward, mimicking the tantrum of a child. The kids in the audience laughed.

"Hmm. I'm the sour princess," he said. "Nothing pleases me. All I do is stay in the castle."

Another puppet appeared. A man on a horse.

"Your Highness," the puppeteer said in a deep voice. "I'm a prince from a faraway land. I'd like your hand in marriage."

The man on the horse bounced toward the princess.

"But the princess was far too sour," the puppeteer said. He turned the princess puppet away from the man on the horse. "I shall not marry you, for I'm the sour princess. I'd much rather be turned into a frog."

The princess puppet disappeared, replaced by a frog puppet. "Ribbit. Ribbit," the puppeteer said.

The children laughed.

Nessa leaned forward. She flopped her braid over her shoulder. Holding the braid with one hand, she flicked the ends of her hair back and forth with the other. Her eyes remained on the puppet show. Her story played out before her—the story of how the citizens of Glimmerfell viewed her.

Charlie leaned in and whispered, "Maybe we should get back to the keep."

Nessa never said a word. She focused on the puppet show. She drew in her lower lip. Her eyes watered. She wanted to cry. Bawl her eyes out. She needed a hug. She needed the king and queen.

"Ribbit. Ribbit," the puppeteer said. "I'm much happier being a frog." The frog puppet bounced around the stage.

The children in the audience laughed.

Charlie stood. The metal of his armor clanged together. He tugged on Nessa's dress. "Hey, let's . . . let's get away from here."

She glanced at Charlie. A tear traced a familiar line down her soft cheek.

"I want you to meet my niece and nephew," Charlie said. "They'll love you."

Nessa brushed the tear away. "I'd love that," she said.

"Come on." Charlie held out his hand.

Nessa grabbed his hand and rose to her feet.

The trio slunk away back toward the castle keep, not wanting to draw the attention of the crowd.

CHAPTER 7
GLASS REUNION

"Are you a real princess?" Ginny asked.

Nessa bent down, tucking in the billowing hem of her dress, to meet the young girl at eye level. "I am," she said. "I'm Princess Nessa of Glimmerfell. Welcome to my kingdom. And who are you?"

"My name's Ginny. It's short for Virginia, but people call me Ginny," the young girl answered.

"Well, it's a pleasure to meet you." Nessa held out her hand, and Ginny shook it.

"Is there a prince of Glimmerfell?" Tyler asked. "Does that make you queen if the other king and queen are dead?"

Nessa pivoted in her squared stance to meet the young boy eye to eye. Both children were dressed in far too baggy clothes. Leather belts kept their pants from falling down.

"No. No. No prince," Nessa said, shaking her head. "I will be queen, but not yet."

"When?" Tyler asked.

"Umm . . ." Nessa said. "Soon. There will be a huge party, but first we're mourning the loss of the king and queen."

"Oh," Tyler said. He squinted one eye in a confused expression. "Sort of like when we lost our hamster. Mom and Dad said we couldn't have a hamster for a while."

Nessa offered a tight-lipped smile with a hint of amusement. She had never considered the line of succession for the leader of Glimmerfell to be similar to replacing a family pet. Yet, out of the mouths of babes came the truth. "Kinda."

"Do you have any food?" Tyler asked. "I'm hungry. Uncle Charlie didn't feed us."

Nessa glanced back at Charlie with a sly grin. "Your uncle doesn't feed you? Shame on you, Uncle Charlie."

"Yeah," Tyler said. "Shame on you."

"Hey," Charlie said as Half-pint tugged on the rear-brace armor wrapped around Charlie's bicep. "I gave you food."

"Not today," Tyler said. "I'm hungry."

Nessa leaned in and whispered to Tyler, "I have a full kitchen that can make whatever you want, including pies and desserts."

"Cake?" Tyler asked.

"Yeah, I want cake too," Ginny said in an excited voice.

Nessa perked up. "Sure. Anything you want."

"Yeah," the twins said in unison. "We want cake."

"Ow," Charlie yelled. "You're pinching my arm."

Half-pint tugged harder on the metal plate. "Well, it's not coming off."

"Did you unbuckle it?" Charlie asked.

"No," Half-pint said. "It should slide right off."

Charlie buried his head in the palm of his hand. "Unbuckle it," he said as the imp tugged him back and forth. "You're supposed to unbuckle it."

"Fine," Half-pint replied. He removed the buckles, and the plates fell right off, crashing onto the ground. "See, it slides right off."

"That's because you have to unbuckle it first." Charlie rubbed his bicep over the white shirt. "That's going to bruise."

Nessa rose and turned to Lyra. "Please take these two to the kitchen and have the staff prepare anything they request. Especially if it's cake."

Lyra stood at attention. Her shoulders pulled back, chest pulled back, and arms tight to her sides. A display of authority. "Your Highness, given the events of today, I shouldn't leave your side. They were able to sneak into the castle, so others could as well."

"We didn't sneak in," Charlie said. "We sort of walked through that." He pointed to the mirror.

Lyra glared at him.

"It will be okay," Nessa said. "Wynden and Half-pint are here if anything happens. I'm asking you to guard the children as if they were my own."

"Yes, Your Highness," Lyra said with a slight bow.

Nessa bent down to meet the kids at eye level. "I want you two to follow Lyra and do as she says, okay?"

The kids agreed.

"When you're done, can we explore the castle?" Ginny said.

Nessa winked at her. "I'll give you the royal tour."

"Yeah!" the kids screamed as they ran through the door.

"Kids, wait," Lyra said as she jogged to follow the rambunctious youths.

Nessa turned to the man standing in front of the mirror. The wise sage stroked his beard, examining every inch of the glass. He poked the mirror, his finger sinking into the spiral void. Wynden swirled it around before finally retracting his index finger.

"You reassembled the mirror?" Wynden asked.

"Yep," Half-pint said as he joined Wynden in front of the glass. "I read through your books for how to get it working again. I scoured the realm to get the necessary components. That's why my room is so messy."

The wizened wizard glared at the imp. "You took my books?"

"Only the important ones I needed," he said. "I couldn't find what I was searching for, so I scoured the realm. I did find this transportive spell. Also, I may have made a bad choice to acquire it, but that's for later. When I used the spell, *poof*, it started working again. But not really."

"What do you mean, not really?" Charlie asked. "It clearly worked."

"No, it worked," Half-pint said. "Sometimes I could see through it. Sometimes there was nothing. But then something happened, and it started the swirl again."

"I turned the dial," Charlie said. "I hadn't turned the dial in years. But we were playing, and I told the kids a bedtime story about the mirror. I thought, why not? Why not give it one more try? I touched the mirror, but nothing happened."

"Maybe it was on a delay," Half-pint said. "But it started to swirl, and that's when I found you."

"What happened anyway?" Charlie asked. "Why did it break?"

Nessa and Wynden glanced at each other, tilting their heads back and forth in an unspoken conversation. Nessa had considered telling Charlie the truth earlier—the reason she spent the past twenty years stuck in Glimmerfell. The words failed her. The truth was far too devastating. A simple mistake altered the course of her life.

"What?" Charlie asked. "What is it?"

"Charlie, I need you to sit down," Nessa said. "We'll tell you what happened."

Charlie plopped down on one of the crates strewn about the room.

Nessa took a deep breath. "Charlie, the day I went through the mirror was the day it was destroyed on purpose."

"On purpose?" Charlie said, squinting and shaking his head. "Why? Why was it broken on purpose?"

"I broke it," Wynden said.

Charlie shook his head. "*You?* Why did you break it and trap her here?"

Wynden lowered his head. He glanced at Charlie through the bottom of his eyebrows. "I didn't know she was here."

"But why?" Charlie asked in a hushed voice, as if he couldn't speak. "Twenty years. Twenty years gone. Why?"

"The same reason we had the meeting today," Nessa said.

Wynden raised his head, meeting Charlie's gaze. "Whatever shadow roams the halls of Castle Verafell knew of the portal in the mirror," Wynden said. "It rambled about how the path was opened. How it sought to find a way home. I heard the words during my scrying on the tower the first time a presence was felt. Whatever roams the halls of Castle Verafell is not of this realm. As long as the mirror worked, it was a threat to this kingdom."

Wynden stroked his beard, focusing on the swirling vortex in the mirror. "I consulted with King Aric and Queen Valeria. They were devastated. They knew what must be done in order to protect the kingdom. They so much enjoyed the company of you two. However, wearing the crown forces you to make decisions you don't want to make.

"I feared that whatever shadow stirred, once it left, it would be unstoppable on the other side. I had contemplated the dangers of such a portal and was considering shutting it off, anyway. I was giving you two some time. However, the threat was too much to ignore." He turned toward Charlie. "They asked me to destroy the mirror."

"But you destroyed it with Nessa here," Charlie said.

"Charlie, it wasn't done on purpose," Nessa said. "It was a circumstance of bad timing."

"Bad timing?" Charlie asked. "I'd say that was bad timing."

"Following their approval, I immediately rushed toward the mirror," Wynden said. "I used my staff over there to smash the mirror and seal it off."

"I was hiding in the room, waiting for you to join me that day," Nessa said. "I was tucked behind a corner, listening to my music when it happened. I was only here for ten minutes."

"I wish I could fully express my regret for what happened that night," Wynden said.

"I was fortunate the king and queen took me in," Nessa said.

Charlie shook his head. He hunched forward, his elbows on his knees and fingers in his hair. "Twenty years because of ten minutes," Charlie said. "Twenty years of torment because of ten minutes. Did you not try to find another way home?"

"We did," Wynden said. "But finding a portal to another realm at the right time wasn't easy. Sure, there have been other visitors to this realm. But they used other means. There were the brothers; they used books. Others came through dreams. Some traveled through a magical pool of water. These portals are random. I tried to get the mirror working again, but nothing worked."

Tears welled in Nessa's eyes. She fluttered her eyes to contain them, but she couldn't. The emotions of that day came back. The fear. The anger. The desperation. All emotions long buried, but now stirred up like the bottom of a murky lake.

"Charlie, it hasn't been easy on me, either," she said. "My life ended the moment the mirror broke. Everything was gone. Family. Friends. My life. All gone. I'm lucky the king and queen took me in and accepted me as their own. If not for them, I don't know what I would've done."

"If I could take it all back, I would have spoken to you two first," Wynden said. "I was too hasty. That's my burden to bear."

Charlie bolted up from his seat. "Well, it is what it is," Charlie said. "If you'll excuse me, I need to go find my niece and nephew before I lose them to this place as well. Don't destroy the mirror while I'm gone. We actually would like to get home." Charlie stormed out of the room, almost breaking into a sprint.

"Charlie," Nessa said. A tear traced a path down her soft cheek. "Charlie, wait."

He didn't respond, continuing out the door. Nessa buried her face into the palm of her hands and cried. A cry she had held in for twenty years. A bellowing, weeping agony built up over time.

Nessa's old life, newly restored, was gone once again.

CHAPTER 8
THE WEEPING TREE

Night fell over the kingdom. The bright, sunny day gave way to the coolness of the night. A sea of stars blanketed the sky. They twinkled as they danced across the vast landscape—a familiar sight to Princess Nessa.

She rocked back and forth as she settled into her usual comfy spot of grass to gaze at the stars. Her hands folded behind her head as a pillow. Nessa gazed at the night sky, allowing her mind to wander, recalling the events of the day—a disastrous day. She wasn't sure how much worse it could get.

Her first diplomatic conference fell apart in shambles. She had asked the dignitaries from the various kingdoms to come for a highly urgent conference, only for two of them not to show and the remaining three to walk out on her without offering any support. Her father and mother would have at least had an offer of aid, be it scouts or soldiers to travel deep into Shadowfell and confirm Wynden's suspicions.

Then there was the surprise of the day—the surprise of two decades—Charlie Grimm.

It had been so long since they were together. So very long. Nessa had given up any hope of seeing her old life again years ago. When she was a small child, she would come to this spot and cry. Cry for the loss of everyone she knew—her mother, her father, and Charlie. All lost to her.

This secluded plaza was meant as a peaceful retreat for the royals, a well-maintained area for privacy. Wooden benches, positioned by stone railings, offered an exclusive view of the kingdom below. A single apple tree, encircled by a ring of grass, stood in the center of the round plaza. She called it her weeping tree.

Nessa allowed herself to have a good cry whenever she was scared or alone or mourned her former life. Queen Valeria encouraged it. She told her it was okay to be sad for the past because that meant Nessa cared deeply. That it was special. Although it was over, the memories lived on.

The weeping tree hadn't always been a place of mourning—quite the opposite. It was a place of joy. A place where Charlie and Nessa played and ate apples. When they ventured through the mirror, they ran and explored the halls of the great castle. They were given access to places closed off from the normal citizens. The king and queen treated them as their own—two rambunctious children they allowed to play in the halls.

Charlie and Nessa would pick apples, sometimes with the help of Half-pint using his abilities to pluck the higher, better apples for them. The juiciest, sweetest, most delectable apples she ever ate.

Nessa smiled at the memories of times long past. She inhaled, holding her breath for a moment, letting the memory linger before the slow, controlled release.

Charlie—her former best friend—the best friend she thought was lost forever. His anger over those fateful ten minutes was understandable. Nessa had cried so much over those ten minutes. She replayed the events of that day many times in her head. If she had waited for Charlie, then the mirror wouldn't have worked, and she would have gone on with her life as normal.

If she had stopped at home for a drink first. Or dropped off her backpack first. If she had grabbed a snack. Maybe she could have . . .

The thought trailed off. She had been down that road before. It was never a good path to follow. It always led to despair. The past had happened. There was nothing she could do to fix it. If she dwelled on the what ifs, then she couldn't focus on the right now. At least, that's what she had told herself over these many years.

Nessa focused on the stars above and their shimmering, glimmering twinkles.

"I thought I'd find you here," Charlie said.

Nessa turned her head. Charlie emerged from the archway door and stepped into the plaza. He appeared to have found some suitable clothing after removing his armor. Now he wore loose, black cloth pants and leather boots. A billowing, white, long-sleeved shirt with a slight V-neck. A black leather belt wrapped around his waist.

"I've been searching all over for you, and then I remembered the tree," Charlie continued.

"It's my favorite spot," Nessa said. "*Our* favorite spot."

Charlie shifted in his stance; his sad, droopy eyes focused on Nessa. He twiddled his thumbs above his interlocked fingers, as if he was trying to determine what to say. They hadn't spoken since he stormed out of the room earlier in the day. Nessa gave him the space to process everything.

"I—I want to apologize for my behavior earlier," Charlie said.

"It's okay, Charlie," Nessa said.

Charlie shook his head. "No. No, it's not okay," he said. "I shouldn't have acted that way. I've been avoiding you all day. I waited twenty years for this, and it didn't go the way I dreamed it in my mind."

"Same, Charlie. Same." Nessa patted a spot on the grass next to her. "Come. Join me."

Charlie glanced toward the other occupant in the plaza—Nessa's personal bodyguard, Lyra Thornvale. She stood at attention along the wall of the castle with a direct line of sight to the princess. Her eyes scanned back and forth for any potential threat to the princess.

"I can come back if you two were having a conversation or something," Charlie said.

Nessa laughed. "Lyra is always with me. She's my watchful guardian. It'll be alright. Come. Join me." Nessa patted the grass once more.

Charlie joined Nessa on the grass. He laid down, gazing up at the stars with his hands behind his head, the same as Nessa. Their heads were inches from each other, reunited once again.

Nessa smiled.

"So, what's it like being a princess?" Charlie asked.

"Everything you hoped it would be and the worst at the same time," Nessa said. "It's rigid in what I can and can't do. Advisors order me around all the time."

"Shadows following you around," Charlie said.

"Lyra!" Nessa shouted. "Come join us."

"If it's quite alright with you, Your Highness, I'll maintain my position here," Lyra responded. "It's the best tactical position."

Nessa turned her head to Charlie. "See. Rigid."

"Sold out to the man, huh?" Charlie said with a hint of teasing in his voice. "What happened to the rebellious, pop-punk princess I used to know?"

Nessa licked her lips. An image of her rebellious youth flashed in her mind. The short hair. Leather bracelets. Baggy pants. Band shirts. A smile crept across her face.

"She became a real princess," Nessa said.

"But you've gotten to explore a lot of the realm, right?" Charlie asked.

"Oh, yeah," Nessa said. "I've been on trips with my mother and father."

"You mean the king and queen?" Charlie asked.

"Well, yeah," Nessa said. "Since they took me in, I called them mother and father. They were my mother and father. I miss them."

Nessa's eyes welled with tears. The thought of losing them hadn't hit her yet. She had been so preoccupied with trying to run a kingdom that she hadn't allowed herself the proper time to grieve.

"What happened to them?" Charlie asked.

"They were old, Charlie," Nessa said. "They were old when I was young. Time finally caught up. They went together, holding hands in their bed."

"That's the way to go," Charlie said. "Holding hands with the person you love."

"Yeah," Nessa said.

A silence fell over the pair. The twinkle of the stars blurred as Nessa's eyes watered. She wiped her eyes to clear the tears threatening to spill forth.

She sniffled. "So, you're an uncle?" Nessa asked.

"Yeah. Those kids are the best," Charlie said. "They got a belly full of food, and now Half-pint is keeping them entertained. They're begging me to stay for the entire week."

"Well, you're welcome to stay as long as you want," Nessa said. "My castle is your castle."

"Thank you," Charlie said. "We play all the time. I'm babysitting them for the week. My sister went out of town for a work conference."

"How nice of you," Nessa said.

"Yeah, but they're going through stuff right now. Their parents are getting a divorce. A nasty one. The scumbag cheated on my sister. Their fights are shouting matches. All played out in front of the children. I gladly took the kids for a week. I wanted my sister to go on the trip to get away for a while. I wanted to give the little ones a fun week to remember before life . . ." His words trailed off into silence. He paused for a moment.

"Before they were forced to grow up," Charlie said.

Nessa allowed the silence to linger.

"Yeah," she said. "Yeah. We both know what that's like."

Nessa turned on her side to face Charlie. He did the same. Their gazes locked together. Both had watery eyes as if they wanted to let the deluge of tears flow.

"What . . . ah . . . what happened with my mom and dad?" Nessa asked.

Charlie exhaled, pushing out his lips. "They're good. It took them a while, but they're good. It was a rough couple of years. You have a sister."

"I have a sister?" Nessa asked.

"Yeah. She was born a few years after you went missing."

"They replaced me?" Nessa asked.

"No. No. No," Charlie said. "They cared about you. They mourned you. A picture of you hung in their living room until they moved. Your parents never gave up hope."

Nessa scooted closer. "What about you?"

"I waited for you. I waited every day," Charlie said. "No one believed me. I tried to tell everyone, but they told me I was imagining it to cope. I saw therapist after therapist. They tried to tell me this place was imaginary. That it wasn't real."

"What did you tell them?" Nessa asked.

"I told them to shove it."

Charlie and Nessa laughed.

"I tried that mirror every day for ten years straight," Charlie said. "Then it was every other day. Every other week. Every other month. My mom wanted to throw it away. I begged her not to. My therapist said it was good to hold on to the mirror to help me process it. I cared for it, made sure nothing happened to it. I never gave up hope. I couldn't move on."

"I moved on, Charlie," Nessa said. "I had to."

Charlie blinked a few times. His face was solemn, and his lips parted. "Well, I didn't. I couldn't. I couldn't abandon you. I held out hope that one day you would return."

"And do what?" Nessa asked. "I can't abandon this place now. I'm going to be the queen. Others depend on me for leadership and guidance. This is my home now."

Charlie's chest rose and fell as he breathed deeply. "I was afraid you were going to say that."

Nessa smiled. "The way is open again, Charlie," she said. "It doesn't mean it can't be like the old days."

"Yeah, like the old days." Charlie rolled onto his back.

Nessa did the same, greeted once again by the blanket of shimmering stars.

"Maybe I'll bring some weed killer next time. Do you know you have vines all over the castle?"

"I know. I know," Nessa said in rapid succession. "The groundskeepers are trying to combat them. They spring up out of nowhere."

Charlie raised an elbow, pointing to the tree. "We better pull those vines before it constricts the base of the tree."

Nessa squinted. There were no vines at the base of the tree. There was nothing growing around it when she laid down. She rolled over to verify Charlie's claim.

Green, twisting vines climbed up the trunk of the apple tree, like a serpent's tail constricting its prey. Large, heart-shaped leaves followed the path, vibrant green in the glow of the bluish-white moon.

"Those vines weren't there earlier," Nessa said. "It's as if they sprang up out of nowhere."

Charlie rolled over on his stomach. "Vines don't grow that fast."

They turned toward each other, meeting each other's gaze.

A bell echoed throughout the kingdom.

Gong. Gong. Gong.

Not a bell to tell the time. The strikes were far too quick. It was a warning. Nessa snapped her focus to Lyra.

Lyra placed her hand on the golden hilt of her dueling sword. She took two steps toward the entrance of the plaza. Horns and trumpets called out.

Nessa's eyebrows slowly raised, and her jaw dropped at the realization of what was happening at this late hour. They were under attack.

The vines around the tree grew, reaching higher up the trunk. A small, round sphere appeared on the vine, followed by another. A few more appeared. They grew in appearance, taking the full shape of a pumpkin. They enlarged and fell to the ground, rolling down the slightly elevated hill.

Lyra rushed toward Nessa, grabbing an arm and lifting her. Charlie pushed himself up and sprang to his feet.

Nessa froze. Unable to move, she focused on the pumpkins as they formed and shaped into monstrosities. A torso, arms, and then legs made of dirt and earth appeared. Twisted vines weaved in and out as if it were the structure holding the monstrosity together. Soon, eyes formed. Angry, terrifying eyes and mouths with jagged teeth formed in the orange rind of the pumpkin.

The creatures turned to the trio.

"We have to get you to safety, Your Highness," Lyra said as she drew her sword.

"The kids," Charlie said. "We have to get to the kids."

The pumpkin monsters, three in total, shambled toward the trio. Claw-like fingers were ready to strike.

"Run!" Lyra shouted.

The trio turned and dashed toward the entrance to the castle.

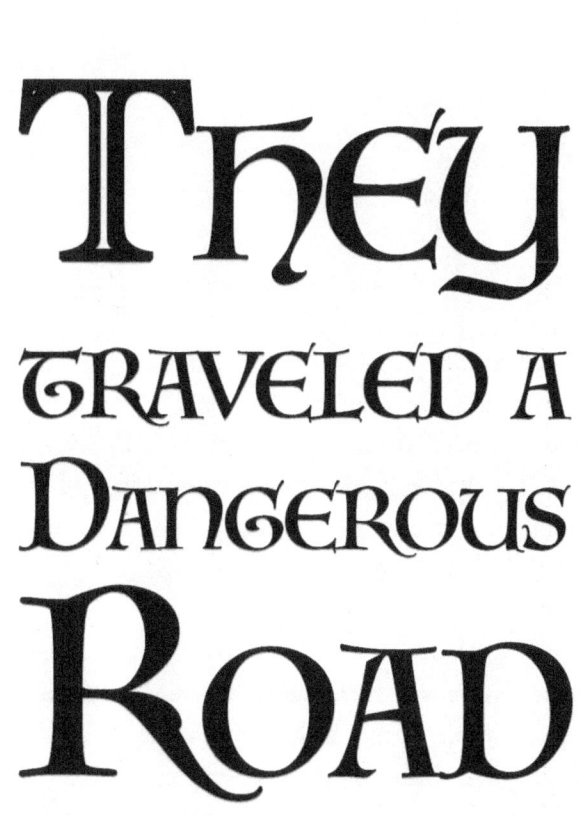

They
Traveled a
Dangerous
Road

CHAPTER 9
INVASIVE PLANTS

The kids, Charlie thought. *I have to get to the kids.*

Screams echoed through the halls of the castle. Twisted vines erupted from every crevice in the stone. They worked their way up the walls, following the outline of the stone bricks. The bells and trumpets created a cacophony of maddening sounds that mimicked the sentiments of the screams.

Chaos. Total chaos.

The various stewards and housemaids of the castle ran through the dimly lit hallways as candlelight flickered from wall sconces and candelabras to illuminate their paths. A guttural noise from the pumpkin monstrosities echoed throughout the halls.

The trio rushed as fast as they could. Nessa lagged behind. The dress of a princess wasn't the most suitable attire to run into combat. She lifted the skirt of her dress as to not trip over the excessive material. Lyra slowed to run beside her, sword out and ready to strike.

Charlie couldn't wait. A few steps ahead of them, he sprinted down the hall. His lungs burned as they pumped in and out. His heart raced. Adrenaline surged through his body. Lifting his knees, he forced himself to go faster. The race through the castle was a sprint, not a marathon. He couldn't lose time.

He turned a corner. One of the pumpkin monstrosities greeted Charlie with open claws. It towered over him. The monster swiped its hefty arm at Charlie.

Without thinking, he collapsed to the ground. The sharp, bark-like claws narrowly missed. The monster lifted its foot, flat and jagged at the edges, no different from an uprooted tree stump. The monster stomped down onto Charlie.

He rolled out of the way. The force of the stomp reverberated against Charlie's torso. Without time to think, Charlie crawled forward. He needed space and distance from the monstrosity. The monster lifted his foot again. Charlie sprang to his feet.

"Stay back, Your Highness," Lyra said. She thrust her dueling sword forward.

The blade pierced the monster's earthen body. Yet, the monster seemed unfazed. It marched forward, drawing the sword further inward.

Lyra retracted her blade, but the monster wrapped its hand around it. Lyra kicked against the vine-wrapped torso. It stumbled backward.

Lyra freed the blade. She shuffled back from the monster. Her lead foot moved forward, and her back foot was angled. The sword pointed at the beast, primed in a defensive position. She slashed across the creature, chopping off dirt and green vines.

The monster persisted with its pursuit.

Charlie lifted a tall, free-standing candelabra. The five lit golden candles flickered. He swung it around and wielded it as a spear. He let out a guttural scream. Charlie charged forth and struck the beast. The candles stuck in its torso. The earthen dirt doused the flames.

He lurched at the monster. Over and over, he struck, driving the candelabra into its torso. The dirt was torn asunder.

Still, the monster continued its pursuit. It swung widely, attempting to strike Charlie.

He drove the candelabra into the torso one final time. Thrusting, it drove deeper into the earthen dirt. The beast grabbed onto the candelabra. It pushed out, attempting to remove it. Charlie slid on the stone floor. Its overpowering strength was too much.

Charlie's fingers tightened around the steel. He drove one foot forward, and the other braced behind him. Charlie bent his knees, squatting down for leverage. Thrusting forward with all his might, Charlie's arms strained to hold the beast back.

"Go for the head," Charlie shouted. "I'll hold him back. Strike the head."

Lyra swung back and then struck. She forced the blade deep into the orange rind.

The monster let out a screeching howl. Its unearthly scream echoed off the stone walls.

"Do it again," Charlie said. "Destroy the pumpkin."

With quick strikes, Lyra hacked away at the head. Small pieces fell away. The beast screamed in agony.

It let go of the candelabra. Charlie drove it deeper into its chest.

Lyra withdrew the sword and bent down. She sprang up. Swinging her sword down with enough force, it cracked the pumpkin in half.

Mumbled gurgles emanated from its mouth. The monster collapsed into a pile of dirt and vines.

"Good call," Lyra said.

"Teamwork makes the dream work," Charlie said.

More monstrous screeches echoed throughout the halls of the castle.

"Come on," Nessa said as she ran past the mound.

Lyra and Charlie followed.

An armored flank of guards and knights rushed past, armed with shields and swords.

"Your Highness," the lead guard said. "We need to get you to safety."

"As head of the royal guard, I'll keep her safe," Lyra said. "You can deal with the threats."

"Yes, ma'am," he said. The guard saluted.

Lyra returned the gesture.

"Go for the heads!" Charlie yelled back.

The three continued with their mission.

Charlie sprinted into the stairwell at the end of the hall. A dark, winding staircase led to the upper levels of the keep. The bluish-white moonbeams spilled in through slits in the stone walls to guide the way.

Nessa and Lyra were right behind him. He held the candelabra to his side, pumping it back and forth with his arm as he climbed. It was his only weapon against another attack.

Around and around the staircase they climbed. The bedrooms were a few stories up. That's where the kids were secluded—the guest bedrooms. Normally reserved for dignitaries and other invited guests of the king and queen, his niece and nephew had picked out one of the few rooms with two beds. It offered a wonderful view of the city below. They should be safe.

Charlie's mind filled with worry and dread. They had to be safe.

Besides, Half-pint was with them. No doubt he had lightened the mood. Yes. Half-pint would have lightened the mood as chaos enveloped the kingdom. They were safe. They were safe with Half-pint. They had to be.

Charlie huffed and puffed as he climbed. His legs burned in protest with every step. His leg muscles were on fire. He couldn't give up. Couldn't relent. Charlie needed to reach the children.

Light spilled into the stairwell. *The exit.*

Charlie bolted down the hall toward the bedrooms. His foot slipped, tumbling forward. The end of the candelabra jabbed into the floor. Charlie picked himself up.

Leafy, green vines covered the stone floor and the wooden doors. They stretched up to the ceiling and reached back down like gnarled fingers.

Charlie held his breath, frozen in sheer terror. His eyebrows raised. His heart thumped and beat against his chest. His mouth drooped open.

The kids. They came for the kids.

"My word," Nessa said. Her words broke Charlie free from his frightened state.

"We have to get to the kids," Charlie said.

He took off. The vines and leaves grabbed at his leather boots. He stumbled and tripped, but he held firm, not able to reach full speed without tripping. Charlie couldn't sprint, but he moved as fast as he could.

Each door was constricted by the vines and flung open. Charlie reached the end of the hall. His heart sank, and his throat tightened. The door to the kids' room was ajar. The leafy vines had crept inside. No sound came from the room.

"Ginny!" Charlie shouted. "Tyler! Are you in there?"

Only silence answered.

The candelabra bounced off the vines as it tumbled from Charlie's hand. The ground was covered so much that it never echoed off the stone. He pushed the door open.

The vines fought back, restricting the door's movement. Charlie slammed his shoulders into the wood, pushing it open only a few inches. He grunted and gritted his teeth as he slammed his shoulders more and more. Pain seared through his body with each slam.

"Let us help," Nessa said.

Nessa and Lyra pressed against the door. The three of them shoved in unison, breaking the door free from the constrictive vines.

Charlie rushed in, frantically searching the room. He overturned the bedspreads and mattresses, searching for any signs of the kids. Both beds were empty. Charlie flung open the wardrobe doors. They were nowhere to be found.

Charlie's heart skipped a beat. His neck tightened. Some unseen forced grabbed the back of his head and shook it. His hands clenched. Charlie hunched over in agonizing pain. His body erupted in a flood of emotions.

Charlie had failed. He failed to protect the kids. Now they were gone. He let out a scream, a guttural, deep scream that echoed through the room. His fists clenched. The whites of his knuckles showed. He collapsed to his knees with his forehead on the floor.

His world ended. Charlie only saw darkness. He tried to wake from this nightmare. He couldn't have lost them. They couldn't be gone. Not again.

Charlie gave a quick thought to their location. *They must be hiding somewhere. That's it. They're hiding somewhere. Somewhere safe.*

He needed to get up and continue searching. They were scared, probably hiding in the castle. *Yes. That's what they did. They're hiding somewhere in the castle.*

A hand rested on his back, breaking him free from his darkness. "Charlie, you need to get up," Nessa said. "We have to keep searching."

His chest rose and fell. He breathed in and out in short bursts. She was right. He needed to get up. He needed to keep going. Keep moving forward.

Charlie stood. The blood rushed from his head.

The dizzying sights of the room returned. Nessa stood next to him. Her eyes locked onto his. She put a hand on his shoulder. An eyebrow narrowed. An expression of concern passed over her face.

Charlie wiped his nose. "Yeah," he said. "They have to be hiding somewhere."

"I haven't found anyone in the adjoining rooms," Lyra said. "No signs of the monsters either."

"Half-pint is with them," Nessa said. "Maybe he got them out."

Charlie bowed his head. The thought of Half-pint poofing them away toward safety played out in his mind. "Yeah. Yeah. Of course. Half-pint."

"I found something," Lyra said. She swung the door closed. "There's something behind the door."

Hanging on the back, bound and squirming in twisted vines, was the imp—Half-pint. His arms were tied at his sides. Vines twisted around his legs and torso, interlaced around each finger. His expressive eyes portrayed a sense of panic and terror. He mumbled something, but it was inaudible. The vines wrapped around his mouth.

"Cut him down," Nessa said.

Lyra hacked away at the vines keeping him tied to the door with her sword. Charlie ripped the vines from his mouth. One by one, they peeled back, slowly freeing the imp from his prison.

"They took the kids," Half-pint said. "I couldn't use my hands to poof away. I couldn't poof the kids away."

Charlie stumbled. His legs grew weak. The room spun. He did lose the kids. His niece and nephew were gone. He failed to protect them.

"I tried to stop them," Half-pint said. "But the monsters were too much. They grabbed the kids and took them. It was a horrible shade. He wore a pumpkin as a crown. He stopped me from poofing away. He grabbed the kids and poofed away."

"Where?" Nessa asked. "Where did he take them?"

Half-pint shook his head. "I don't know. They left that." He pointed to a note tied to his jacket.

Nessa removed it. Her eyes followed every word written on the piece of yellowed parchment paper.

"What does it say?" Lyra asked.

Nessa handed the note to Charlie.

The way portal has been opened.
We have those who do not belong.
Bring the way portal to Castle Verafell.
You have three nights if you wish to see them again.
—The King of Verafell

Charlie and Nessa locked eyes. An unspoken conversation was held between their shared glance. Charlie handed the note to Lyra and exited the room. He retrieved the candelabra from the hallway floor.

"Where are you going?" Half-pint asked.

"To your room," Charlie replied. "To the mirror."

He sprinted toward the stairwell. The green, leafy vines tugged at his feet. He thrust the candelabra into the vines to brace himself. He twisted the shaft in hopes of breaking them up.

Charlie rumbled down the steps. The soft leather soles of his boots nearly slipped on the smooth stone. He braced himself against the wall with his free arm. Charlie gathered his composure and continued down.

He bolted through the castle hall. Guards tended to the wounded. Mounds of dirt and vines were scattered with shattered pieces of pumpkin strewn about. Charlie didn't stop. He sprinted as fast as he could.

His legs burned in protest. His lungs sucked in as much air as they could. It didn't matter. The only thing that mattered at that moment was the safety of the mirror. He had to secure the mirror.

Charlie's mind wandered to his niece and nephew, but he stopped himself. All that mattered was the mirror right now. It needed to be safe so all three of them could go home.

He ran past the royal dining hall—an elongated table in the center of the room with multiple chairs running down the sides. He sprinted past the door to the council room chambers—the room where Nessa had held court with the other dignitaries earlier in the day. The doors to the council room remained closed, ensnared by the twisted vines.

Charlie pushed forward. He rushed toward another stairwell, toward the tower containing Half-pint's room. He began the climb. One foot per stair. He skipped steps. The strain on his legs was too much. He stumbled and fell to the ground. His hand slammed into the edge of the step, bracing himself. A sharp pain reverberated up his arm.

It didn't matter. He had to brush it off. Charlie picked himself up. Rising to his feet, he continued the ascent.

His muscles burned and ached for him to stop. He powered through. One step at a time. One stair at a time. The mirror was his primary focus. He wasn't going to trap himself or the kids here.

The kids. They must be so scared.

No. Not now. Charlie couldn't let his thoughts linger on them. Not now. He had to focus.

Charlie reached the top. He bent over, hands on his knees. The wind rushed into his lungs. He gasped for breath, his legs weak. His eyes were on the door at the end of the hall. There were no vines here. No signs of marauding pumpkin monsters.

Charlie flung the door open. He rushed inside. Shadows bathed the room in darkness. Dim light flickered from a few candles. Charlie could see the faint outline of the wood frame and a man holding a staff.

"Stay back," Wynden shouted. "Do not tempt the powers of a wizard." Wynden wielded his gnarled staff and guarded the swirling vortex.

Charlie dropped the candelabra and hunched over with his hands on his knees. A pain shot across his stomach. His gut pumped to fill his lungs with air. He raised a finger, waving it back and forth.

"It's me," Charlie said through gasps. "It's Charlie."

"Oh, thank the stars," Wynden said with a smile. "I thought you were one of those monsters."

"They have the kids," Charlie said in a low voice.

Wynden's face sank as the smile disappeared. He lowered his staff. "Who has the children?"

"The pumpkin monsters took them," Charlie said, forcing the words from his mouth.

"Oh no," Wynden said. He cupped a hand over his mouth.

Charlie stood up straight. With his hands on his waist, he tried to catch his breath. "They took them," he said. "They took the kids. We have to get them back."

CHAPTER 10
KNIGHTLY PLANS

"What are we doing?" Charlie asked. "Let's get the troops and knights together and march on the castle."

"We will, Charlie," Nessa said. "We'll get them back. I promise."

Charlie shook his head. "Promises aren't good enough. I made a promise to protect them, and now they're gone." He ran his fingers through his hair, pulling it back behind his ears.

"We'll get them back. You have my word," Nessa said.

Charlie placed both hands on his hips. "I've already lost one person to this place. I'm not losing anyone else."

Nessa closed her eyes, narrowing her eyebrows. The hurt was clearly visible on her face. Charlie had overstepped.

He placed a hand on his forehead. "I'm sorry. I didn't mean it like that. It . . ." He paused to carefully choose his next words. "It's happened again," Charlie said. "That's all I meant. That once again someone I truly care about was put in danger because of this place. That's all."

Nessa opened her eyes, raising a hand. "It's okay."

"What do we do now?" Half-pint said, sitting in his high-back leather chair.

"We march to the castle and get them," Charlie said.

"There are a few injuries the guards are dealing with," Lyra said. "We wouldn't be at full strength."

"So?" Charlie said. "The kids are in trouble. We need to save them. I need to save them."

"We will. We have to think about this logically." She turned to face the wizard standing in front of the mirror. "What do you say, Wynden?" Nessa asked.

He was silent, stroking his beard with one hand and holding the yellowish parchment with the other. Wynden was no doubt lost in thought. "Fascinating," he said.

Charlie slapped the sides of his legs. "I'm glad you're fascinated by all of this."

"No, I find it fascinating that this King of Verafell knew the mirror activated," Wynden said. "That he could tell the children weren't from here. Fascinating."

"So?" Charlie said. "How does that help us?"

"How long have the vines been invading the castle?" Wynden asked.

Nessa shook her head. "I don't know. A week or two."

Lyra stepped forward and stood at attention, as if addressing a superior. She held her arms straight at her sides and her shoulders pulled back. "A week and a half to be precise. We instructed the castle groundskeepers to pluck and remove any sprouts that appeared."

Wynden turned to the imp sitting cross-legged in his chair. He pointed the paper at Half-pint. "When did you piece the mirror together?"

Half-pint rose in his seat. His lips pressed together as if he were a student called upon for a pop quiz. "Umm . . . about a week and a half ago. Don't ask me how I got it to work."

"That's twice you've mentioned not asking you," Charlie said.

"Well, don't," Half-pint said. "It's . . . personal."

Wynden turned back to the mirror, continuing to stroke his beard.

"But it didn't work until today," Half-pint said.

"What does this have to do with getting the kids back?" Charlie asked.

"Everything," Wynden said. "It has everything to do with it." Wynden turned to face the group. He raised his arms high, smiling. "I was correct."

Charlie crossed his arms. "I'm glad you're excited about being right," Charlie said in a sarcastic tone. "But what are we going to do?"

"Give me a moment," Wynden said. "I'll get there."

Wynden moved to a drafting table off to the side. A large piece of parchment lay across the wooden table. He flung it off to reveal a clean sheet below.

"Hey!" Half-pint said. "That's my work."

Wynden didn't stop. He picked up a charcoal pencil and started drawing. On one side, he drew a pumpkin and a castle. On the left, a few stick figures, an oval, and a small circle.

The group gathered around the table. Half-pint disappeared and reappeared on a bookshelf—a better vantage point for him to see.

"This was me, twenty years ago," Wynden said, pointing to a stick figure. "I used my scrying ball to check on the castle here."

He drew a line from the ball to the castle. "That's where I found the shade wandering the halls. It talked about returning home and said there was a way."

Wynden pointed to the mirror. "I broke the mirror," Wynden said as he crossed out the oval. "And severed the connection to your realm, stopping whatever was in the castle."

"But what about me?" Nessa asked. "Wouldn't it have keyed off of me?"

"Correct," Wynden said. "But without the mirror, maybe it no longer saw you as not belonging. Or you were here long enough that by the time it was ready to march, it saw you as belonging."

Wynden drew another oval. "Then the mirror was restored, and it felt the connection once again. It sent the vines as scouts."

Wynden sketched serpentine shapes with small leaves. "When you had your meeting today, it listened in. It knew we were onto its plan and had to act. It waited until dark and took the castle by surprise."

"But why the children?" Charlie asked. "Why did it take them and not come for the mirror? There wasn't a single vine coming up the stairs or in the hall."

The charcoal pencil sketched out two small stick figures. "That's what I'm not certain about," Wynden said, turning with a finger raised for emphasis. "But I find it fascinating."

Wynden turned back to the paper and circled the two small stick figures. "These two must have put out more of a signal than the mirror for the King of Verafell to find them first."

Wynden poked the paper with the pencil a few times. "They probably drowned out the mirror. He must have been frustrated. That's probably why he took them. That, and leverage for us to hand it over."

"Wonderful," Charlie said. "My niece and nephew were beacons for a monster."

"This could be to our advantage," Wynden said.

"How so?" Nessa asked.

Wynden smiled. "If we marched in with troops, he would no doubt see it as a threat, and the children would be endangered."

Charlie pressed his lips tighter and let out a high-pitched hum. "They're pretty endangered right now."

Wynden pointed back to the paper. "This is our advantage. As long as he has the kids, it's his only bargaining chip. He wouldn't risk the mirror being turned off again. And if he sees outsiders the same as the mirror, then he won't know it's not coming."

"What do you mean?" Nessa asked.

Wynden drew three more stick figures on the paper with a fourth one half the size of the others. "What I'm proposing is that the four of you march to Castle Verafell alone, and you take the children back. He will see no difference between Charlie and the mirror."

"Absolutely not," Lyra said. "I won't put the princess in harm's way."

"I'm in," Nessa said.

"Your Highness, I can't let you endanger yourself," Lyra protested.

"Let's suit up. Let's go," Charlie said. "Hell yeah, I'm in."

"Me too," Half-pint added from above.

"Your Highness, you have to think of your safety and your kingdom," Lyra said.

Nessa turned to face her bodyguard. "I *am* thinking about their safety. On how we called for aid from every other kingdom, and no one stepped up. What sort of leader would I be if I'm not willing to do what I ask of my own people?" Nessa faced the rest of the group. "I'm in."

"I guess I have no choice," Lyra said. "I'll follow you."

"What about you, Wynden?" Charlie asked.

He placed the pencil down and dropped his shoulders. He hung his head, unable to meet anyone's gaze. "Unfortunately, I need to remain here," Wynden said. "If anything happens to you or they come back for the mirror, someone needs to do what's necessary."

"Necessary?" Charlie asked.

Wynden glanced toward Charlie. His eyes met his eyebrows. "The mirror will have to be destroyed."

Charlie's heart sank. "Destroyed?"

"Unfortunately, yes," Wynden replied. "We can't risk this King of Verafell getting out into your world. Could there be anyone in your realm to stop him?"

Charlie pondered the thought. There were no witches and wizards, at least to his knowledge. No magic or anyone that could stop the King of Verafell from taking over Newbury Grove, or worse. The weight of what was being asked caught up to him—his life or the mirror. He had to take the risk. Not for him, but for Ginny and Tyler.

"Alright," Charlie said. "Alright. Do what you must. The four of us will go."

Nessa placed her hand on her chin. A solitary finger traced over her lips.

"What?" Charlie asked. "What are you thinking?"

"What if there was a fifth member of our party?" Nessa asked.

"I'd prefer a full army of knights, but I'll take a fifth member," Charlie replied.

"There is someone, but I don't know if he'll agree," Nessa said.

"Great!" Charlie said with a hint of glee. "Let's go ask him."

"He's . . . He's in Hollowreach," Nessa said. She played with the end of her braid, flicking the loose strands of hair back and forth in her fingers. "We'd have to stop there first."

"I love Hollowreach," Half-pint said. "A great town. That's where I got the spell to fix the mirror." He paused for a moment. "Don't ask me how."

Charlie glanced up at the imp. "I feel like you're dying to tell us."

"No. No," Half-pint answered. "It's . . . umm . . . personal. Don't worry about it."

"Your Highness, would he be willing?" Lyra asked. "Especially since the incident. He didn't show up today."

Charlie's heart sank. As excited as he was for a fifth member, he'd prefer someone more reliable. "You want to ask this guy for help? What did you do?"

"We'll have to convince him. Appeal to his good nature," Nessa said.

Charlie clapped his hands together. "Wonderful, but we'll take the help if we can. What can he do anyway?"

"He's the greatest swordsman in all of the realms," she said.

"Fantastic!" Charlie said. "But what's the problem?"

Nessa paused, tilting her head to the side. "Well . . ." she said. "I might have . . . I might have embarrassed his whole kingdom and mine by breaking off a wedding engagement with him."

Charlie's mouth dropped open. His heart shattered into a million pieces. He had never considered Nessa marrying someone on this side of the mirror. He never fell in love on his side. Sure, there were the occasional dates, but nothing serious. Charlie always called them off before the relationship went anywhere. He was always hopeful that one day . . . one day the mirror would work again, and he would fulfill a promise he made when he was twelve.

"You were going to marry him?" Charlie asked.

"I couldn't go through with it. Ruling one kingdom is hard enough. I couldn't be responsible for another, especially the maritime kingdom of Brightfell." Nessa shied away, hiding her eyes from Charlie. "I asked him to join us today. He told me no."

"I believe the full answer was, 'Go to hell'," Wynden said.

They all turned to the wizard, glowering at him.

"What?" Wynden asked. "It's the truth."

"So, our best hope is appealing to the kind heart of a man left at the altar," Charlie said.

"It wasn't at the altar," Nessa said. "It was the night before the wedding. The King and Queen of Brightfell were upset. He was upset. The citizens of Glimmerfell were upset. The only ones not upset were King Aric and Queen Valeria."

She paused. Her voice cracked, betraying a hint of sadness. "They were the only ones who comforted me. So, I mainly stayed in the keep. I wasn't able to face the citizens."

"I wasn't upset with you," Half-pint said.

Nessa chuckled, wiping away a tear. "No," she said. "I could always count on you to be there for me."

Wynden retrieved his staff from its spot against the wall. "I believe this is enough conversation for the night. You'll need your rest for the journey ahead. It's about a day's ride to Hollowreach, and we don't have any time to waste. You'll need to leave at dawn break."

"Ride what?" Charlie said. "I haven't ridden in years."

Nessa smiled. "You'll love what we have for you to ride," she said. "But first, let's go get some sleep."

"If we can," Charlie said.

CHAPTER 11
THEY KNOW HIS NAME

The sun peeked over the horizon. Its orange and gold rays bathed the early morning sky and fought back against the darkness. A slight chill was in the air. Charlie's breath left a ghostly, vaporous trail as he headed toward the royal stables. Nessa and Half-pint were by his sides. Lyra led the way.

"How did you sleep?" Nessa asked.

"Didn't," Charlie said. His eyes were heavy and tingled with sleep. "You?"

"Same," Nessa replied.

"You cut your hair," Charlie said.

The long, braided hair of the princess was gone. The flipped out ends of her hair kissed her shoulders as it bounced back and forth with each step.

"It's more my style anyway," she said. "More of a . . . pop-punk princess." She winked at Charlie.

He smiled back.

"Besides, it was too long anyway," Nessa said. "It would be terrible in battle. Plus, it's better to blend into a crowd."

"I brought special berries for everyone," Half-pint said. "Crunch on these, and they'll wake you right up."

They each took one and bit down on the reddish-purple berry. A surge of energy rushed through Charlie, jolting him awake.

"Where did you get these?" Charlie asked.

"Hollowreach," Half-pint said. "You can find anything there."

They were all dressed and ready for travel. Charlie wore black linen pants and leather boots with a white, billowing long-sleeved shirt. A blue leather vest and a black leather belt were around his waist. A dueling sword hung at his side.

Nessa and Lyra appeared as traveling mercenaries, wearing black leather boots, black linen pants, dark blue shirts, and a black leather vest. Nessa wore a blue cloak around her neck and a bandana to hide her image from the unsuspecting public.

Half-pint . . . Well, Half-pint was Half-pint. He wore the same raggedy clothes that gave him the appearance of a pauper performing in a traveling show.

The group entered the royal stable. The dirt floor was immaculate, clean and well-kept. Elegant designs and symbols of the kingdom were carved into the wood of the paddocks. Blue and gold streaks were painted along the posts.

The stable master stood ready and at attention. He was an older gentleman dressed in a blue military uniform with gold trimmings.

He bowed to the princess. "Your Highness," he said. "They are saddled and prepped as instructed."

Nessa bowed in return. "Thank you, Sir Reginald."

"The unicorns are extra frisky this morning," Reginald said, leading them deep into the stable.

"Unicorns?" Charlie said. "I'm not riding a unicorn."

Nessa turned to face him with a sly smirk on her face. "I'll have you know, the unicorn is the fiercest and most deadliest of all horses."

"Deadly?" Charlie asked.

"Oh, yes," Reginald said. "A wild, untamed spirit. Stubborn and fierce. They use their horns to attack. On command, that is."

"Attack horses. I like the sound of that," Charlie said. "Do we each get an attack horse?"

"I'll be riding my pony, thank you very much," Half-pint said. "It's more, uh, my size."

"I have my personal stallion," Lyra said. "Besides, it wouldn't be prudent for me to ride the royal unicorns."

Nessa smacked Charlie's shoulder. "It's you and me."

Charlie smiled.

"This way," Reginald said.

Grunts came from the back of the stable—not the typical neigh of a horse, but something deeper. Something more guttural. Something with attitude.

Their twisted black horns appeared first over the edge of the stable wall—not like the horn Charlie had envisioned. This was a growth emerging from the forehead of the white horse. A twisted, gnarled growth. With another grunt, the unicorn slashed the horn downward.

"Pet them and give them respect, and you'll be alright," Reginald said.

"Be alright?" Charlie asked.

"Don't worry," Nessa said. "I ride them all the time."

The white unicorns poked their heads over the stable gate.

Nessa petted and rubbed each of their heads. "How are my unicorns doing this morning?"

They grunted as if to respond.

"That's good," she said.

She scratched around their horns. The unicorns kicked up stray hay with their front legs, excited by the attention.

Reginald opened the gate, and Nessa entered. She placed her boot in the stirrup and hopped up into the saddle.

Charlie approached his unicorn with methodical, easy steps. He extended his arm. "Hey," Charlie said. "Hey, boy." He petted the unicorn's head.

"Don't be afraid, son," Reginald said. "Hop on up."

Charlie placed a boot in the stirrup, and the unicorn moved. "Whoa. Wait for me."

He placed his hand on the saddle horn and hopped up onto the animal. He lifted the reins, ready to ride.

"Can you handle him?" Nessa asked.

"It's been a while since I've been on a horse, but I think I can manage it," Charlie said.

She winked at him before turning to Reginald. "Thank you."

He bowed before her. "My pleasure, Your Highness," he said. "Your secret is safe with me. If anyone asks, I'll tell them you took them out hunting, which is technically true."

"Ready?" Nessa asked.

"Lead the way," Charlie said.

Nessa clicked her tongue against her mouth and gave a slight tap to the unicorn with the heel of her boot. One by one, the group exited the royal stables. They picked up speed, heading onto a secluded path that would lead them out of the kingdom and toward rescuing the children.

On they rode. The lush fields gave way to forests. Hearty trees lined the road to Hollowreach, their leaves rich and green. Birds chirped and sang as the group galloped past. On and on they rode. Minutes turned to hours. They passed other travelers, all heading toward the safe confines of Glimmerfell.

"We should stop," Lyra shouted. "Give the horses some rest."

The group slowed their animals, coming to a full stop. Charlie's unicorn meandered off the road, bending down to eat a tuft of grass.

"Hey," Charlie said, pulling on the reins. "Get back over here."

The unicorn refused his call, heading deeper into a grassy area.

"Having trouble?" Nessa asked.

"I'm fine, thank you," Charlie said. "The stupid unicorn is the problem."

"Maybe it's the rider," Half-pint said.

Charlie glanced over his shoulder, scowling with furrowed eyebrows. He tugged a few more times on the reins. "Come on, you glorified rhinoceros."

The unicorn refused his call, continuing to munch on the blades of grass.

Nessa chuckled. "You have to take charge of the unicorn."

"What do you think I'm doing?" Charlie asked. "It has a mind of its own."

"Perhaps you'd like to switch," Lyra said.

"I'd like the animal to pay attention to what I'm doing," Charlie said.

"We should stop," Nessa said. "We've been traveling for a while. Perhaps the break would do the horses some good."

"While I agree with you, Your Highness, maybe we should continue up the road for a moment. There could be a safer spot," Lyra said.

"This place seems safe enough to me," Charlie said.

Slender trees surrounded the dirt road. Their lush, green foliage nearly blocked out the sun as it carved a path across the sky. The rays broke through openings in the canopy to provide a decent amount of light. Shadows crept in deeper in the woods.

The unicorn meandered closer to the tree line.

Charlie tugged on the reins. "Come on, you beast," he said.

"A couple of lost travelers," a high-pitched man's voice said.

Lyra drew her dueling blade. She scanned around, no doubt searching for the source of the voice.

Charlie scanned the tree lines as well, placing a hand on his sword's hilt. Nessa did the same. The two of them were ready to draw and defend themselves.

They were well outside the jurisdiction of the kingdom and its various outcroppings. They had already been on guard for the various creatures that roamed the forests of the realm. Wolves. Bears. Worse.

Of course, they always had to be vigilant for the dreaded high-waymen that plagued the land—rogues and knaves who sought the goods of unsuspecting travelers caught off guard. They would take everything they had, robbing them of their goods. Sometimes they took more.

"Who's there?" Nessa asked.

Charlie's head was on a swivel. He scanned the trees back and forth, yet found nothing.

"Who am I?" the voice said. "Well, that's the question of the day. I know who you are."

"We're merely a band of travelers," Nessa proclaimed. "We carry nothing of worth."

Lyra pointed her sword at various positions along the tree line. "You will only find the end of our blades and nothing more."

The voice laughed. "Oh, no. I could not best your blade, Lyra Thornvale."

Charlie's throat tightened. *How did he know her name?* He drew his sword, passing a knowing glance to Nessa.

Their eyes met without words. An unspoken agreement expressed with the furl of eyebrows.

"Be not a stranger, and show thyself," Nessa said. "We are but humble peasants. Come, we can break bread together."

The voice laughed maniacally. "Oh, but dear princess, you're so far away from your kingdom. I didn't have to know your name to know who you were. You're riding two unicorns. Did you think a mere peasant would be as fortunate as the wannabe queen?"

Charlie swung his legs over his mount and jumped down to the ground. Shoulders pulled back, he readied his stance. His feet were perpendicular to each other. The lead foot pointed ahead, the back foot bracing his stance. He led with his right arm, his dominant arm. The left arm hung in the air behind him to counterbalance himself.

It had been a few years since he had taken fencing classes—an elective he had taken in college. Most students took it because it was fun or to flirt with their classmates. Charlie took it to keep up the basic skills he learned as a young boy. He knew a few good strikes and defensive measures. Not enough for a skilled swordsman like the one they sought in Hollowreach, but enough to defend himself.

"If you seem to know us, then stand and deliver," Charlie said.

There was only silence.

"Come on," Charlie said. "Are you a coward? Present yourself."

"You're intriguing," the voice said. "I don't know you. You're a stranger in a strange land."

Charlie kept his sight on the trees. He took small steps, pivoting around. Every time he thought he knew where the voice was coming from, it changed on him.

"It's not that strange to me," Charlie replied. "Show yourself."

"One doesn't become who I am by merely charging into battle," the voice said.

Charlie pivoted toward the origin of the sound, but found nothing. "What do you want?"

"Three of you should consider yourselves lucky," the voice said. "I'm not here for you, although the unicorns would fetch a nice price."

"Show yourself, and I'll personally introduce them to you," Nessa said.

"Of course not," the voice replied. "I'm well aware of their temperament. I find my position a much more . . . advantageous position."

"Then who are you here for?" Lyra asked.

Charlie glanced over at the normally talkative imp. His head was buried in his shoulders, and his hat hung low over his eyes.

"Half-pint," Charlie said. "You said you made a deal to get the spell. What deal did you make?"

The imp raised his hand, lifting his index finger. He opened his mouth, only to close it again.

"Half-pint?" Nessa asked.

"Ah, yes," the voice said. "The small imp . . . That's who I'm here for. We struck a bargain. He sought a spell to cross worlds. I offered it gladly."

"What was the bargain?" Charlie asked.

"A thousand years of servitude," the voice said. "I'm here to collect."

"Half-pint, why would you do such a thing?" Nessa asked.

Half-pint pulled down his hat and held it with both hands. His fingers tapped along the black felt rim. Half-pint glanced at the ground. "You said you needed help. I did what I could to get you help."

He raised his head. Half-pint's lips quivered. "I thought I had more time. I would have figured something out."

"And yet, here I am," the voice said.

I know his name.

Of course. Of course, it had to be him. That's who Half-pint made his deal with—a scoundrel of ill repute. Others in the realm might fall for his trickery. Charlie, however, wasn't from this realm, and he had heard stories.

Charlie laughed.

"What's so funny?" Nessa asked.

He ran over to the princess, leaning in to whisper in her ear. "Don't say my name," he said, winking at her.

Nessa's jaw dropped, and her face formed a half-smile. She winked at him.

Charlie sheathed his sword with a flourish. The metal hilt bounced against the leather scabbard. He brought a finger to his lips, hoping Lyra and Half-pint would take the hint. Lyra returned the gesture. With a questioning glance, Half-pint squinted, furrowing his eyebrows in confusion.

"Clearly, you won't engage in a battle of strength," Charlie said. "Perhaps you'll engage in a battle of wits."

Charlie was met with silence.

"Are you afraid to battle me with nothing but your mind?" Charlie asked.

"What's in it for me?" the voice said.

"An offer," Charlie said, lifting both of his index fingers up to his shoulders. "If I win, your deal with my impish friend here is null and void. Should you win, I'll take his place."

"Why should I take you over him?" the voice asked. "He could be very useful to me."

"Because I'm an enigma," Charlie answered. "You don't know who I am. I don't know who you are. You said yourself I'm not from here. Clearly, that's more valuable to you than a regular old imp."

"Your offer does intrigue me," the voice said. "What are the terms of the battle?"

"Three guesses," Charlie said. "We have three guesses to name each other. If I get your name and you don't get mine, then I win. If you get my name and I don't get your name, you win. If neither of us guesses correctly or we're both right, then you can take the imp. You have a two-thirds chance of winning."

"Those terms are acceptable to me," the voice said. "To be a good sport, I'll let you go first."

Charlie grinned at Nessa, and she returned the gesture.

Half-pint rotated the hat in his hands. He opened his mouth, but Charlie was quick to shush him. He gave the imp a quick wink.

Charlie pivoted, turning around to scan the trees. There was no sign of anyone—no one hiding off in a bush. No scattered items or signs of civilization. Only untamed wilderness.

"Well, let's see," Charlie said. "What do I know of you? You're wise. Intelligent. Perhaps you're small or feeble. Meek. Well, you would have to be if you rely on your brain more than your physical prowess."

Charlie moved around. He was hoping to run into something unseen, to get a jump on the origin of the voice. He paused. Charlie needed to answer soon so as not to draw out suspicion.

"Henry. Your name is Henry," Charlie said.

The voice laughed. "You're incorrect."

Nessa's eyebrows popped up. Charlie smirked and shook his head, hoping to portray an air of confidence in his game.

"My turn," the voice said. "You're a stranger. Willing to fight. Willing to throw yourself into danger. It must be a strong name. A hero's name. A name like William."

"Oooh," Charlie exclaimed, pushing out his lips and drawing out the sound. "Good guess, but you're wrong."

"Round two," the voice said. "I go first."

"Fair enough," Charlie said.

"Perhaps your bravery is a mask," the voice said. "You hide behind fear. You refuse to show your true self. I've known people like you. They weren't heroes. No, they were something else. They were survivors, doing what was necessary for self-preservation. William isn't a fitting name for you. No, your name is Ch—"

Charlie's throat tightened at the syllables.

"Your name is Chance," the voice said.

Charlie gulped. He stilled his body, hoping not to give away any sign that he was close. He whistled, popping his lips at the end for emphasis. "Seems you're wrong yet again," Charlie said. He paced around once more, kicking out his feet, hoping to strike something.

"Well, it seems that you love a good bargain. A good offer. Perhaps you're a collector. Yes. A collector. Someone who hoards precious items. I know the perfect name. Frederick."

The voice laughed. "Wrong yet again. Round three."

"To show you that I'm a good sport, I'll let you go first again," Charlie said.

"I tire of this game," the voice said. "I don't believe you'll guess my name. The question you have to ask yourself is, would I prefer you or the imp?"

"A valid question," Charlie said.

"I already have a contract with the imp," the voice's sound changed. No longer high-pitched, it deepened, silky smooth, as if to charm Charlie into a lulled state. "I'd have to create a new one for you. I much prefer the imp. I name thee Half-pint."

Charlie whistled. He slapped his hands together. "I kind of figured you were going to do something like that."

"Name me," the voice said. "Name me, and I'll claim my prize."

Charlie turned to see his diminutive friend's face buried in his hat. Lyra focused on the princess, hand at the ready to draw her sword. Nessa concentrated on Charlie. Lips pursed and eyebrows arched high, widening her gaze. She didn't utter a word, but her eyes screamed for him to finish this up.

Charlie grunted as he rotated around, swinging his arms. "Ah, well, you see, that imp over there is my friend. We've known each other since I was a little kid. See, I've known all kinds of stories about this place. It sort of runs in my family. A legacy, you could say."

Charlie stomped around, feeling out for the man behind the voice. "I've heard all kinds of stories," Charlie said. "Stories of princesses and princes. Of wolves. Of bears. Of lost children. There was one story about a short man. He made these promises. Promises of gold spun from straw. Of course he wanted a price. Similar to you."

The voice said nothing in return.

"Well, in this story, he couldn't refuse a challenge and offered to break his contract if this young woman could say his name. She failed the first two times."

The voice was still silent.

"But she was smart. She figured out where he was and listened for him to give up his name. Which he did because he was far, far too confident. Foolish. Arrogant."

No words responded to Charlie's monologue.

Charlie halted his pursuit of the invisible man. He no longer needed to track him. His next words would draw him out.

"I know exactly who you are," Charlie said. "You're a gnome who makes deals with desperate people in exchange for lives. Be it their own or their firstborn. You're the thief in the night. You're a curse on this land, and you should be banished, especially for your deal with the miller's daughter. I name thee Rumpelstiltskin."

An ear-shattering screech echoed along the road. The horses neighed and bucked up. Lyra and Nessa struggled to control their animals before finally calming them down. Charlie continued his search for the gnome, yet he found nothing. The voice sounded as if it was coming from everywhere all at once.

On it screeched. The noise overwhelmed Charlie. He slammed his hands over his ears to shield them from the onslaught.

"You think you've won," Rumpelstiltskin said. "The imp may be free from his obligation, but you have yet to see the last of me. For every time someone is desperate, I am there. There will always be someone else."

The voice trailed off as it headed into the woods. "Until we meet next time."

"How did you know his name?" Lyra asked.

Charlie smiled. "Nessa and I knew the story of the miller's daughter. Where I'm from, a lot of people know his name."

Lyra glanced at Nessa and said, "Maybe he's worth keeping around."

Half-pint lowered his hat. "Does this mean I don't have to go with him?"

Charlie strode over to the imp, his chest puffed out and head held high. He snatched the hat from Half-pint's hands, giving it a few spins before placing it back on the imp's head. Charlie tapped the black velvet top twice.

"Nope," Charlie said. He winked at Half-pint. "Now you owe me a favor."

Charlie jogged over to his unicorn and bounced up into the saddle. He clicked his tongue on the roof of his mouth and gave a slight bump to the unicorn with his feet. Charlie winked at the princess as he rode past.

"Perhaps we should find someplace better to rest," Lyra said.

"I think that's a good idea," Nessa said. "Some place far, far down the road."

CHAPTER 12
SPILLING THE TEA

Nessa tied the reins of her unicorn to the branch of a tree off the side of the road. The group found a spot to rest the animals far away from their previous encounter. Far, far away. Perhaps they had overworked the animals. They could arrive in Hollowreach before sunset, but only if the animals were properly rested.

Flipping open her saddle bag, Nessa removed a small oatcake and fed it to the magical horse. She gladly accepted the offering, munching down on her treat.

"Good girl," Nessa said as she petted the unicorn's side. "You've done well."

"The tea will be ready soon, Your Highness," Lyra said.

The princess turned and gave a quick nod. She joined the group, resting by a small, crackling fire. Charlie and Half-pint sat in front of the broad side of downed logs, using them as back rests. The tree bark was dark brown as rot set in.

Lyra bent down on one knee to tend to the fire with a cast-iron kettle suspended above it. Smoke spilled out of the spout as the water inside boiled.

"Why do you call her Your Highness all the time?" Charlie asked.

Nessa gracefully sat down on the makeshift seat Charlie provided for her.

"It's proper etiquette," Lyra said. "It would be disrespectful for me to call her anything else."

Charlie leaned back, rolling his back over the curve of the log. "I mean, I get that in the castle and stuff," he said. "But out here? I mean, who are you trying to impress?"

Lyra straightened her posture. "I'm not trying to impress anyone. It's my duty to protect and give respect to the princess and future queen."

Charlie rolled his eyes. "If I were king—"

"If *you* were king?" Nessa asked. She raised an eyebrow.

"Yeah, if I were king . . . I would keep it more casual."

"Define casual," Nessa said.

Charlie rolled a hand in a flourish. "I wouldn't have someone call me 'Your Highness' all the time."

"I rescind my comments on his usefulness," Lyra said.

Charlie sat up. "If someone followed me around all day, tending to my every need, I wouldn't treat them with a condescending attitude. That's not very punk rock of you to be called *Your Highness*."

"What is *punk rock*?" Lyra asked.

"An energetic, rebellious attitude. Rocking out to music. Not caring what anyone else thinks. Doing things on your own terms," Charlie said. "That's punk rock."

Nessa straightened in her seat, tilting her head. She narrowed her eyes, pondering what prompted Charlie to object to how she was addressed. "What brought this on?"

"Did we ever call the king and queen *Your Highness*?" he asked.

Nessa replayed conversations through her mind. Though they had faded, the images and sounds played like a skipping CD. The images and sounds skipped, but the next would play, filling in the gaps. She couldn't recall any time they had addressed the king and queen so formally.

Nessa cleared her throat before answering. "No," she said. "I guess not."

"See," Charlie said, slapping his thigh, no doubt as a point of emphasis.

The kettle whistled, signaling it was ready. Lyra lifted the cast-iron pot from the suspension chain and poured the boiling water into four awaiting tin mugs. The tea leaves were already placed inside. The steam roiled and bubbled over the lips. She picked up a small spoon and stirred each one.

Lyra carefully cupped Nessa's mug, holding onto the handle and placing the mug into her leather gloved hand. She rose from her spot and slowly stepped toward the princess.

"Your tea, Your Highness," Lyra said.

"Thank you," Nessa said as she gripped the metal handle.

She held the mug up to her lips, allowing the steam to wash over them. She puckered her lips and blew. It wouldn't make that much of a difference to the temperature, but she enjoyed it. The hot liquid washed over her tongue—a sensation of citrus and spices imported from the kingdom of Brightfell.

"Apologies for the tin mug," Lyra said. "Given the situation, it was best to travel with field equipment."

Nessa smiled. "It's quite alright. Thank you for the tea."

Lyra returned to gather another cup. She carried it to Half-pint.

He outstretched his hands, ready for the hot refreshment. "Thank you, m'lady," the imp said.

Lyra bowed her head. "You're very welcome." She returned to her wilderness kitchen and picked up one more cup. Pivoting, she sat down on the makeshift wooden bench.

Charlie focused on his mug sitting on the ground and then glanced up at Lyra. She took a sip, never taking her eyes off Charlie. When she finished, she pointed to the mug with an open palm.

Nessa grinned. "I thought you wanted to keep it casual. That you weren't into the frivolity of royalty and high tea." She took another sip.

"Fair enough," Charlie said, tilting his head to the side and pursing his lips.

Charlie rose and dusted off his cotton pants. He strode over to the mug with the confidence of a drunken sailor—shoulders pulled back, head high, chest out. A display, no doubt, that his ego was a little hurt. At least, Nessa hoped his ego took a glancing blow.

He bent down and retrieved his mug before raising it in a toast. "Thank you."

Lyra slightly bowed. "You're welcome." She took another sip. "Your Highness."

Charlie smiled. "Funny." He took a sip and returned to his seat. "I'm merely saying . . . I mean, I get that you're the princess and all, but she's been with you every step of the way in everything you do."

"That's my duty," Lyra said. "It's my charge."

Charlie turned to Lyra. "Do you find it odd and tiresome?"

"No, it's a great honor. The highest honor and position one in the service of the king or queen could aspire to hold. Personal bodyguard of her majesty, the Princess of Glimmerfell," Lyra answered.

"I mean, do you get any breaks?" he asked.

"Breaks?" Lyra asked.

"Lyra is always with me," Nessa said. "I have my alone time, but she makes sure the room is secure before taking her leave."

"So, you're like sisters," Charlie said.

"I wouldn't say sisters," Nessa said.

"It's my duty," Lyra said.

Charlie pointed at Lyra with his mug. "How long have you been doing this?"

Lyra took a sip. "Doing what?"

"Taking care of her," Charlie said, pointing to Nessa.

"Lyra guards me. She doesn't take care of me," Nessa replied.

"How long?" Charlie asked.

"Well, when the king and queen took me in, I was assigned a handmaiden. Someone roughly my age. We grew up together. Bonded together. Played together—" Her words trailed off.

Nessa was deep in thought, reconsidering the past twenty years.

"Like a sister," Charlie said.

Sister?

Nessa had never considered Lyra a sister. She was there, charged with a duty of care, but not as a sister. They spent nearly every day together over the past twenty years. Lyra was by her side the entire time, guarding her and caring for her, protecting her from threats— the older sister she never had.

"I wouldn't consider our relationship to be like sisters," Lyra said.

"Sure," Charlie said. "You two are basically sisters."

"I wish I had a sister," Half-pint chimed in. "Or a brother. Actually . . . I might have both. Maybe. I haven't seen them in a long time. Hmm . . ."

"I fight with my sister all the time. Always have. She was the protective big sister, always taking care of me, but sometimes she could be so annoying," Charlie said. "We fought right before . . . right before she left for her trip. A rip-roaring fight in front of the kids. I said some things I shouldn't have."

Charlie paused as only the crackle of the fire could be heard. After a moment, he took a sip. "Question," Charlie said, drawing in his stretched-out legs and leaning forward. "Do you two ever fight?"

"It would be improper for me to fight with the princess," Lyra said.

"Okay, but do you wish you could fight?" Charlie asked.

Lyra glanced at the ground and became silent.

"Lyra Thornvale!" Nessa shouted in a playful tone. "Have you wanted to fight with me?"

She held her tongue, sealed in by her lips. Lyra shuffled the tin mug around in her hands, never raising her eyes to meet Nessa's.

"I give you permission to speak freely," Nessa said.

"There you go again," Charlie said.

Nessa scowled at Charlie. Her eyebrows narrowed.

"To be honest . . ." Lyra said. "I thought you treated Prince Cyrus unfairly."

Nessa sat up. "Unfairly?"

Lyra sat up, mirroring Nessa. "Yes, unfairly. I thought you two made a great couple, and you would have been happy. It was a mistake for you to call it off."

"The man we're going to see?" Charlie asked.

"Yes," Lyra said.

"Well, spill the tea, sister," Charlie said.

"Spill the tea?" Lyra asked. "Why would I spill my tea?"

"It's a saying," Charlie said. "My niece and nephew taught me about it. It's similar to spilling the beans or telling the details."

"Hopefully not actual beans," Lyra said.

"The last time beans were spilled, a beanstalk grew, and we had a giant problem on our hands," Nessa said. She motioned high into the air, imitating the height of the beanstalk.

"Well, I thought you treated Cyrus poorly," Lyra said. "You kept him close, but not too close. He offered grand adventures and trips for the two of you, but you always turned him down. You never seemed fully excited to see him. I thought it was very . . . rude. Especially since your marriage was supposed to unite the two kingdoms in a new partnership."

Unite? More like, offered as a prize.

Nessa took a drink of the now cooled liquid. She glanced over the rim of the mug. Her eyes met her eyebrows.

"It . . . it would have never worked out," Nessa said.

"Why?" Charlie asked.

Nessa couldn't reveal the true reason. She couldn't. It would complicate things. Besides, it was in the past. She couldn't be the queen of two realms. She could barely manage one. Overworked, overwhelmed, in over her head . . . All she needed was to be the head of a merchant kingdom, sailing across the seas.

Still, that wasn't the true reason she had rejected Cyrus' offer. And now she found herself on the way to ask him for assistance—a huge ask for the man she rejected.

"I have my reasons," Nessa said. "First . . . well, mostly . . . And this stays between us four."

Charlie motioned across his lips as if pulling on a zipper. "My lips are sealed."

"How can your lips be sealed if you're talking?" Half-pint asked.

"Figure of speech," Charlie said.

"Well, I'm not going to say anything," Half-pint said.

"Your secrets are always safe with me, Your Highness," Lyra said.

Nessa shifted in her seat. "I appreciate that," she said. "The truth is I'm overwhelmed. I wasn't prepared for this task. Not as much as I should have been. It seems easy to be the leader of a kingdom, but the crown is heavy, and I haven't put it on yet."

Nessa focused on the fire. The flames danced and kissed the air as their embers dwindled. Nessa pondered her words carefully, but something wanted her to divulge the truth. To open up to her childhood best friend seated across the fire, her longtime friend to the left of her, and her personal confidant seated to her right.

"Cyrus is a great guy. He's kind, caring, and very, very charismatic. He taught me a few of his sword moves, but it would have never worked. I can barely keep one kingdom together, let alone two," Nessa said. "I wished it ended differently. I was too nervous to end it before I did. I was nervous that everyone would be disappointed in me, and I let the whole kingdom down."

"Well, *Mister I'm the greatest swordsman in the world* sounds like a great guy. I can't wait to meet him," Charlie said as he stood. He threw the rest of his tea onto the fire. "Shall we get going?"

Lyra stood as well. "We should," she said. "Mr. Pint, if you wouldn't mind, take care of the fire for us."

"Sure thing," he said, snapping his fingers.

The flames were doused into black charcoal. A vaporous trail of smoke rose into the air.

Lyra broke down the metal tripod and gathered the other items for tea.

Charlie proceeded to his unicorn, untying the reins from the tree branch. He placed his boot into the stirrup and hopped up onto the animal.

Nessa wanted to tell the truth—why she never wanted to be with Cyrus. How her heart never belonged to Cyrus. But she couldn't. The ramifications would destroy their rescue party. So, she must remain silent.

"You coming, Princess?" Half-pint asked as he mounted his pony.

"Yeah," she replied. "Let me get my unicorn. I'll be right there."

A tear formed in Nessa's eye. She wiped it away, blinking a few times to prevent any tears from falling down her cheek. She rose and removed the reins from the tree branch.

"Next stop, Hollowreach," Half-pint said.

CHAPTER 13
COMFORT FOR
THE WEARY TRAVELER

"Welcome to Hollowreach!" Half-Pint exclaimed with a hint of pride in his voice.

The group paused, taking in the sights of the town nestled along the river below. The sun descended below the mountains, bathing the town in an orangish-red glow. Nessa loosened the unicorn's reins. The corners of her lips broke the solemn expression into a half-smile.

"A shining town nestled in the valley hollow of the bright cap hills. All roads in the realm lead to Hollowreach. Any destination, any item, any desire can be found in or through Hollowreach." Half-Pint sat upright in the saddle, his chest puffed out. He readjusted his top hat and pulled on the lapels of his jacket.

He cleared his throat before continuing, "You have to be cautious, though. There are some unsavory parts as well."

"Sounds fantastic," Charlie said. "I take it this is where we can find *Mister greatest sword guy in the realm, but might be mad at the princess?*"

"Unfortunately," Nessa said.

"Wonderful," Charlie replied.

Lyra maneuvered her horse to the front of the group. Her eyes scanned the town below. She pointed to an area on the outskirts of the city. "That's our best place to stow the animals," she said. "We'll be on the outside. That way no one will see us come and go."

Nessa pulled the hood of her green cloak over her head, hiding deep in the cloth. The trim of the hood nearly covered her eyes. She lifted the black bandana around her neck over her mouth and nose, hiding her true identity. Only her blue eyes were revealed to the world.

With a bob of her head, she signaled for the group to continue their journey. They ventured down the road, heading to the town.

"Out of curiosity," Charlie said, "I get the precautions, but wouldn't the unicorns be a dead giveaway to your identity?"

Nessa's eyes drifted toward the twisted, black horn bobbing up and down with the movement of her unicorn. She pulled back on the reins, commanding the unicorn to stop. The rest of the group followed suit.

"He's right," Nessa said. "The unicorns could give us away."

Lyra turned her horse to face the princess. "What do you propose, Your Highness?"

Thoughts pervaded her mind. They could stow the animals in the tree lines, but they would be at risk of the wild beasts that meandered through the woods. Worse, they could be discovered and stolen. Regardless of concealing her face, Nessa riding into the town on a unicorn would be a dead giveaway to her identity. The whole operation could be blown before they had a chance to make it to Gretel's Tavern.

Nessa focused on her trusted bodyguard, hoping she had an answer.

"I have an idea," Half-pint said.

All eyes focused on the wizard's apprentice.

"Alright, what do you got?" Charlie asked.

"What if Charlie and I take the animals to the barn? Then you two could walk in behind us, and we can meet up afterward," Half-pint said.

"What if they ask you where they came from?" Nessa asked.

Charlie turned to her and grinned. "I'll tell them I stole them from the princess."

Nessa shook her head. The plan was no good. What would stop anyone in the stables from absconding with her prized animals? She'd have no control, be at the mercy of whoever worked the stables. They'd be sold and gone by the time they returned. Or far worse . . .

"That plan won't work," Nessa said.

"Your Highness, what do you propose?" Lyra asked.

Nessa narrowed her eyes and focused on the town below. The multicolored roofs of the buildings stood out. A river ran through the middle of the town. Trees lined the streets. People came and went about their business. The town bustled with energy.

Nessa lowered her bandana. "They're coming with us," she said.

"So not in the stables?" Half-pint asked.

"No," Nessa replied. "We're riding right up to the tavern door with them."

The unicorns neighed and snorted. Nessa pulled on the reins to assert her authority.

"And you'll leave them on the streets?" Lyra asked. "I must protest, Your Highness."

Nessa turned to Lyra, locking eyes with her. "We won't abandon them. Besides, they'll be protected."

Lyra leaned forward in her saddle. "Your Highness, I can't abandon you to protect these animals."

Nessa smiled. "I would never ask you to abandon me." She pointed to Half-pint. "He's going to guard them."

Half-pint rose on the saddle of his pony. He placed a hand on his chest. "Me?"

They all turned to face the imp, smiling.

Nessa leaned forward, her hands resting on the saddle horn. Her eyes focused on his. "I'm decreeing you with the official title of honorary guard of the royal stable. You're hereby tasked with the guard and care of the royal horses."

"But . . . I . . . But . . ." Half-pint stumbled over his words.

Nessa raised her hand, mimicking touching the shoulders of Half-pint.

"It's official," Charlie said. "She knighted you."

"I . . ." Half-pint said. He straightened in the saddle, tugging at his jacket. He fixed his top hat. "I accept."

Lyra trotted closer to the newly knighted honorary guard of the royal stable. She leaned in, almost whispering. "You know what happens if you fail, right?"

Half-pint cleared his throat. "Umm . . . No. I mean . . . yes."

"Good," Lyra said. She smiled and winked at Nessa.

Nessa pulled the bandana back over her face. She rose high in the saddle and readjusted the reins. She clicked her tongue against the roof of her mouth and gave a slight tap against the unicorn with her heels. The beast took off, heading down the well-worn path.

The rest of the group followed. Lyra picked up the pace and took the lead, always in front, as was her duty. They rode single file, with Half-pint bringing up the rear. The horses kicked up small clouds of dust as they ventured deeper into the valley.

The town of Hollowreach bustled with activity. Children played in the streets. Vendors sold fruit, wood carved items, leather goods, and other wares. A small band of bards played their instruments, filling the air with their melodic tones. The town bristled with activity.

The group maneuvered through the cobblestone streets, careful to not trample any of the small children or spook the horses. A few stopped what they were doing and gawked at the sight of two unicorns walking through the town.

Nessa shifted her eyes back and forth, careful to spot anyone who might make a move on the unicorns. Her right hand let go of the reins, drifting toward the silver hilt on her side. The townsfolk murmured amongst themselves, never taking their eyes off the sight of two unicorns.

Nessa slowed her breathing. She drew out her inhale to soothe her nerves. Her head swiveled, shifting back and forth. Lyra did the same.

A few of the townsfolk moved toward the group. Nessa gripped the leather-wrapped handle of her silver blade. Her eyes focused on their movements. Three men followed along—one tall, one short, and one wide.

Nessa whistled a bird call. Lyra leaned her head back, slowing her horse. Nessa clicked her heels against the unicorn, picking up speed. She galloped next to Lyra.

The three men continued their approach. They maintained their distance, but only kept a few people between themselves and the group. Their eyes focused on Nessa's unicorn.

Nessa pointed to the men with her head, not wanting to make too sudden of a movement. Lyra dipped her head in agreement.

The crowded, cobblestone street was encased in two to three-story buildings. The buildings were made of stone on the ground level and wood encased in stucco on top. Street vendors peddled assorted items on both sides. A man guided a wheelbarrow full of melons, parting the crowd and blocking any immediate exits. People weaved in and out of the street—a perfect cover for an ambush.

"I think I know that song," Charlie said.

Nessa didn't reply.

"Why is that song so familiar?" he asked.

He galloped up toward Nessa, pulling up to her other side. "That band back there . . . I've heard that song before," Charlie said. "At least, it sort of sounded like it."

"I'll explain later," Nessa said in a low whisper. She tracked the three men following them.

"How did they know it?" Charlie asked.

"I'll tell you later," Nessa said in a raised tone, still trying not to speak too loudly.

"I don't see them any longer," Lyra said.

Nessa turned around, scanning the crowd. The three men were nowhere to be found.

"Thanks a lot, Charlie," Nessa said.

"What?" he asked, raising a hand.

"We were being followed," Lyra said in a hushed voice.

Charlie glanced over both shoulders. "Followed where?" he whispered.

"They're gone now," Nessa whispered. "Keep it down, and don't make it so obvious. We have to keep an eye out."

"The tavern is up ahead," Half-pint said. "If you take the next right, there's a shortcut, so we can get away from the crowds."

Without saying a word, Lyra pointed with two fingers, signaling for the group to follow into a seedy alleyway. Once again, they rode single file with Lyra in the lead. The alleyway was narrow and encased in shadows to cloak its dark secrets.

There were no children at play. No one sold any wares. People stood in doorways cloaked in shadows. Their clothes were tattered and dirty. Their eyes focused on any unsuspecting traveler who ventured down this road.

Nessa sat high in the saddle, her shoulders pulled back and head held high—a far cry from the beating of her heart. It raced as anxiety coursed through her veins. Her right hand was never far from the leather-wrapped handle.

"Up ahead and to the right," Half-pint said.

Nessa focused on a young girl leaning against the wall of a building. Her clothes were torn, and her hair was disheveled. The young girl's face was gaunt, sunken like the walking dead. She wore dirt for makeup and filth for perfume.

Nessa softened her eyes. This young girl could have easily been her. No place to go. No one who cared for her. Lost and trapped in a land full of abundance, yet also unforgiving. If not for the generosity of the king and queen, she easily could have been a beggar on the streets, unsure of where her next meal would come from.

Nessa pulled back on the reins, calling her unicorn to come to a stop.

"Why are we stopping?" Charlie asked.

Nessa never acknowledged Charlie's question. Her eyes focused on the young girl. "You girl . . . Do you have a home?"

The young girl cowered back into the corner of the building. She drew her arms in close, cupping her hands together. "Ah . . . no," she said in a sheepish voice. "No, ma'am. I'm tired and hungry and cold."

Lyra circled back on her horse. "We shouldn't be stopping."

Nessa ignored her advice. "How old are you?"

"Twelve," the girl answered.

"I was lost once as a little girl," Nessa said.

Her hand delved inside her cloak, scrounging inside a leather pouch. She withdrew a small, black leather coin purse, enough for a month or two of wages. Enough for the young girl to find comfort and food. Nessa tossed the bag to the young girl.

She reached out her hands to catch the bag. Her face beamed with a smile. "Thank you," she said. "Thank you so much."

Nessa grinned from ear to ear under her bandana. "If you ever make it to Glimmerfell, tell the royal guard you're a special envoy. He'll know what to do." Nessa clicked her tongue and poked the unicorn with her heels.

The group continued down the alleyway.

"Thank you," the young girl proclaimed. Her words echoed off the building walls. "Who are you?"

"A lost girl like you," she replied.

The quartet exited the alleyway into another bustling street filled with more vendors and musicians.

Charlie rode up next to Nessa. "That was nice what you did."

"I was a scared, lost little girl once," Nessa said. "I'm lucky I turned out the way I did."

"There it is," Half-pint said.

A wood sign hung over the door, brown with green and yellowish lettering—Gretel's Tavern. The words *Comfort For The Weary Traveler* were arched above two frothing pint glasses in mid-clink. At the bottom, in yellow letters, it said *All Are Welcome. None Turned Away.*

The building featured a pointed roof with brown wood shingles. Stone and wood were encased in stucco. A few steps led up into the tavern. The wood door swung open as people came and went. Glass was encased in iron in the center of the door.

They swung their legs over their animals and hopped down to the ground. They guided the animals to a hitching post, tying the reins around the worn wood.

"Mighty fine animals you have there," a man's voice said.

Lyra turned, her hand on her sword, ready to draw at a moment's notice.

Nessa raised her hand in front of Lyra to stop her. She turned to face the man.

The same three men who had been trailing them down the street stood a few feet from them. They brandished clubs. The short man wielded a crossbow.

"Someone could fetch a pretty penny for one of them horses there," the tall man said.

"They aren't for sale," Charlie said.

Lyra leaned over and whispered into Nessa's ear, "Say the word."

Nessa held her tongue. A street fight wouldn't occur on this day. She knew exactly what to say to scare off these men.

"Very unusual," the short man said.

"Some might call them royal," the wide man said.

The tall man poked his chest with his index finger. "I would call them royal."

"That's because they are," Nessa said.

"Seeing as you ain't royalty, then perhaps we should take them off your hands," the tall man said. "Return them to their rightful owners."

The short man pointed his crossbow at Nessa. "There might be a reward."

"Or keep them for ourselves," the wide man said.

All three burst into laughter.

Nessa shifted her eyes back and forth between the three men. She smiled under her bandana. She pointed at the tavern. "Do you know who's in there?"

"Lots of people are in there," the tall man said.

"In there is the rightful heir to Brightfell. The prince. He's a sea captain and a pirate," Nessa said. "Royalty."

"What's that got to do with them pretty horses there?" the tall man asked.

"Everything," Nessa said. "For we are members of his crew. And do you know the reputation of Captain Cyrus Blackstone?"

There was a pause. The men shifted in their stances, gazing back and forth at each other.

The tall man cleared his throat. "Perhaps we do," he said.

"Then you know how he once punished men like yourselves and tied them inside of crab fishing crates," Nessa said. She locked eyes with everyone, letting her gaze linger for a moment before moving on to the next one.

She continued, "The pirate prince placed them in high tide with their heads still above water for the slightest indiscretion. He left them there for the mermaids to drag them off into the murky depths."

She paused. "They begged and pleaded, but they found no mercy."

She pointed back to the tavern again. "Of course, if you did us a favor and helped guard our four-legged companions with the aid of our dapper friend here, we might see you handsomely rewarded."

The men huddled and conferred with each other.

After a moment, the tall man asked, "How do we know you're telling the truth?"

Nessa raised her gloved hands. "You could always take the risk."

"How handsomely?" the wide man asked.

Nessa's hand delved into her leather pouch once again, and she withdrew six gold coins. She tossed them on the ground in front of the men. They scrambled to collect them before someone else swooped in.

"That's to get you started," she said. "More when we leave."

"We'll guard them," the tall man said. "We'll take good care of them."

Charlie pointed to Half-pint. "He's in charge."

"Yeah," Half-pint said. "I'm in charge."

"Aye, aye," the short man said.

Nessa turned and climbed the steps to the tavern.

Charlie followed with Lyra bringing up the rear. She never took her eyes off the men.

"Good," Lyra said. "They better be untouched or else."

"No problem, ma'am," the tall man said.

Half-pint adjusted his top hat. "Now, there are a few ground rules for my crew. Number one, I'm in charge."

Darkness greeted Nessa as she opened the door to the tavern. The trio entered.

CHAPTER 14

THE PRINCESS AND
THE PIRATE

A dark haze permeated the room. Nessa's eyes failed to find their target. If he was here, he made a point to sequester himself in the shadows.

Candles flickered in lanterns attached to posts throughout the tavern. The posts were carved and painted with pastel flowers and decorative designs. Smoky-colored glass windows allowed only minimal light to seep into the clandestine walls. Their rays attempted to reach the dark corners of the tavern, only for the shadows to fight back.

The space brimmed with jovial activity. Raucous laughter and loud voices competed to be heard. Pint glasses clanged as the patrons regaled each other with tales of their daily exploits. A stone hearth, taking up a large portion of the back wall, crackled with a fiery blaze. A few people sat around the roaring fire, partaking in their drinks and telling tales.

A three-person band—composed of a concertina, clarinet, and tuba—played music on a raised stage near the hearth. People at long tables sang along as they ate and drank. Their arms locked together, swaying back and forth with the sound of the concertina playing a polka style song. The room was full of people who acted as if they had known each other for years. It was a festive atmosphere. A welcoming atmosphere.

"What was that all about outside?" Charlie asked.

Nessa turned to him, leaning in to be heard over the cacophony of sound. "A little diplomacy. My father taught me it's better to disarm a man with words than the point of a sword."

Lyra stepped in front of the princess, shielding her from the patrons as they came and went. "I'll be the judge of that."

"Any of it true?" Charlie asked.

"No," Nessa replied, shaking her head. "Well . . . a pirate does have a reputation to uphold." She winked at Charlie.

"This way, your . . ." Lyra said, stopping herself from completing the sentence. "Follow me." Lyra led the trio deep into the tavern.

They squeezed past the celebratory revelers. Nessa drew the hood of her cloak over her face. Tilting her head down, the tavern was barely visible under the hem of her hood. Lyra led them to an empty table in the corner of the room. They sat down, the walls to their backs and the activities to their fronts.

"What was the deal with the song out in the streets?" Charlie asked. "It sounded exactly like—"

"Because it was," Nessa interrupted. "Well, sort of. The king and queen wanted to provide me with a bit of comfort from home. My iPod only lasted so long before the charge ran out. Wynden couldn't figure out how to get it going again. They brought in musicians to help recreate my favorite songs from my memories. It sort of caught on, and other musicians started playing it as well."

Charlie chuckled. "We take their stories. They take our music. Seems like a fair trade. Speaking of which, where is she?"

"Where is who?" Nessa asked.

"Gretel," Charlie replied. "It's like meeting another celebrity. I already embarrassed you in front of the three queens and their kings. I can't wait to do the same in front of Gretel." He grinned at Nessa.

She rolled her eyes and shook her head, unable to stop herself from smiling, the smile hidden beneath her bandana. "Keep the embarrassment to a minimum, please," she said. "I have a reputation to uphold."

Charlie placed his forearms on the table and leaned in. "I promise I won't be on my worst behavior."

Nessa leaned back in her seat, scanning the room for the pirate prince. The room was far too dark to get a good peek at anyone sitting in the shadows, not wanting to be seen.

Lyra sat up straight. Her right hand was below the table, not too far from the hilt of her sword.

"Three more rounds for the table in the back," a woman's voice shouted as she placed a circular serving tray on the bar. Her light brown hair was pulled back into a bun. She wore a brown dress over a white long-sleeved shirt. A white apron was tied around her waist.

"Coming right up, Grets," a man said behind the bar. He was an older, bald gentleman. He had broad shoulders and a round belly that appeared to be the product of a few too many pints of ale. He filled three mugs and placed them on the serving tray.

"Thanks," the woman shouted, her voice nearly drowned out by the polka concert.

Nessa leaned over to Charlie. "I think your celebrity is right there. Don't go developing a crush on her." She winked at him.

Gretel lifted the serving tray above her head and maneuvered through the crowd. Masterful in her movements, she was able to hold the tray aloft with only one arm. She danced and weaved without spilling a drop.

"Do you think she can find your pirate?" Charlie asked.

Nessa shrugged.

Gretel stopped at a large table with a group of men and one woman seated not too far away from the trio. She lowered the tray and passed out the pints. It was a jovial, festive table filled with laughter. They raised their glasses and shouted a celebratory cheer.

"You still hanging around with these rapscallions?" Gretel asked the woman. She placed the tray under an arm and her other hand on her hip.

"Of course," the woman said. "Someone has to keep them in line."

The men broke out into a song of their own, swaying back and forth as they held their pints aloft. The woman joined in.

"Have fun," Gretel said as she turned away. She stopped and pointed at Nessa. "You!" Gretel yelled from across the room. "We have a strict no hood or mask policy here."

Nessa slunk in her chair. If she removed her hood and facial covering, then she'd be exposed. A princess of a kingdom out in the open would be easy for any assailants to attack . . . or worse.

Lyra rose, her hand on her sword.

The raucous crowd quieted. The band stopped. All eyes focused on the trio.

Gretel lowered the serving tray, holding one end with her hand. The other end of the tray pressed against the wood flooring. "Masks off or else you leave," she shouted. "You can stay as long as you like, but no masks."

"I'd like to see you come take it from her," Lyra shouted. She withdrew a small portion of the blade from its scabbard.

Charlie sprang to his feet. "No need for any of this. She'll take the mask off." Charlie leaned toward Nessa, speaking through his closed teeth. "Take it off."

"Don't take it off," Lyra said.

Nessa rose from her chair. Other patrons did the same. They armed themselves with forks and knives. They all turned to face the trio.

Lyra withdrew her sword, the blade held at the ready to strike.

"There will be no bloodshed in my tavern!" Gretel shouted.

Charlie leaned over to Nessa. "We didn't come this far to get into a bar fight. This is where one of your diplomacy things comes in handy."

"Put the sword away," Nessa commanded.

"But Your High—" Lyra said.

"Put the sword away," Nessa said. "It'll be okay."

Lyra sheathed her blade.

Nessa raised her hands, her open palms facing the crowd. "We mean you no offense and no harm. I'll take the mask off." Nessa lowered the bandana and pulled back on her hood.

Audible gasps erupted throughout the tavern.

Gretel bowed her head. "Your Highness, it's an honor for you to grace our small tavern."

Nessa bowed in return. "I thank you for your hospitality and meant you no disrespect."

Gretel snapped her fingers and pointed to the table. The bartender filled three pints and placed them on the bar top. A barmaid grabbed the pints and hurried them over to the trio.

"On the house," Gretel said.

Nessa smiled. "Thank you for the hospitality, but it's not necessary." She pulled out three coins from her leather pouch and gave them to the barmaid.

Nessa focused back on Gretel. "We're searching for someone. A friend."

"He's no friend of yours," a man's voice said from deep within the tavern.

The eyes of the patrons focused on the man beneath a set of stairs leading up to the second floor.

He slouched back; his face cloaked in shadows and darkness. Only a pair of black leather pants and boots were visible. His feet were crossed and propped up on a chair. "They should leave. Now!"

Gretel slumped her head and let out a sigh. "All are welcome, and none are turned away."

He uncrossed his feet and kicked away the chair. Its wooden feet screeched as the chair scraped across the wood floor. The force of the kick was enough to tip it over and send it crashing down. It bounced a few times before settling.

"They should leave. Now!" he yelled.

Gretel placed her free hand on her hip. "They're welcome in my tavern," she shouted back.

He leaped from his seat. His face emerged from the shadows. Black curly hair, slicked back. A billowing black shirt matched his hair. A beard a few days' old highlighted his high, protruding cheekbones. He was handsome, but rugged. His face was weathered from the sunbaked winds of the open seas—the face of the man Nessa had once loved. She still loved him, but only in the way someone had a fondness and nostalgia for the past.

He wasn't her true love.

"Traitors are unwelcome if I'm to be the head of your security," he said.

Nessa sighed, giving a quick tilt of her head before standing tall. "It's good to see you again, Cyrus."

A hush fell over the room, but his brown eyes spoke volumes. Piercing and narrowed, they found their target. Nessa.

"I wish I could say the same for you," Cyrus said.

Charlie leaned in and asked, "So, is this drunk the great swordsman you talked about?"

Cyrus pointed a gloved finger at Charlie. "Who is he?"

Nessa removed her gloves and placed them in her belt. "Cyrus . . . Cy, we need your help."

Cyrus laughed, a slow, sarcastic laugh drawn out to make a show of it and play to the crowd. "Of course. Of course. You only come crawling back when you want something. You only want things from me. Isn't that right, Your Highness?"

"Perhaps you two should take this into the back," Gretel said. "I'm sure no one else wants to hear your lovelorn bickering."

"I'm interested," the bartender said. He flicked a bar rag over his shoulder.

Gretel's eyebrows narrowed, and her lips pursed, throwing him a dirty glance.

The bartender raised his hands, backing away from the bar. He mimed the word, "What?"

Cy focused on Charlie. His gloved finger was heavy in the air like the duelist sword sheathed at his side. "Not until you tell me who he is and why he's here."

Nessa curled and bit her lip. She glared at a spot on the floor, cycling through all the ways to introduce Charlie that wouldn't threaten his life from the man they were seeking help from.

She took a deep breath, holding it for a moment before exhaling. "Cyrus—"

"You can't call me Cy, yet you come asking for my help," he said. "I thought I told you to go to hell when you first asked. I guess you needed to hear it from me in person."

Nessa closed her eyes. She sucked in her breath, a prolonged exhale after a short intake. She counted to three before opening her eyes once again.

"Cy, this is Charlie. He—" Nessa said before taking a brief pause. "We need your help."

Cy laughed, not a gleeful, happy laugh, but a sarcastic laugh. Short laughs came out before he gritted his teeth. He slapped his hands together. The smack of leather against leather echoed off the walls.

Cy moved through the tavern closer to the trio. All eyes focused on him. He bit his lips and let out a low grunt. He removed the glove from his right hand. "So," he said. "You're the famous Charlie."

Charlie shook his head. "I'm sorry. How do you know who I am?"

"Oh, I know you," Cy said. "I loathe you. I've dreamed of this day for so long. I want my satisfaction."

Cy slapped Charlie across the face with his glove. Charlie's head snapped to the side. His cheek turned red where the black leather glove met his bare skin.

"I want my restitution," Cy said.

Charlie stood motionless for a moment. He opened his jaw, rubbing his cheek. His eyes narrowed, focusing on the man once betrothed to Nessa.

"Cyrus!" Nessa said.

"Hey!" Gretel yelled. "I said no fighting in my tavern. Take this outside."

Cyrus slapped Charlie across the face again, striking the same cheek.

"Yes, let's take this outside," Cy said. "I've waited for this moment. Give me the satisfaction of running my blade through you." He swung the glove once more.

Charlie caught his wrist. The two men struggled in a test of strength, neither winning nor losing, locked in an eternal struggle.

"I didn't do anything to you," Charlie said.

"You did everything," Cy replied. "You took everything from me. You took her from me."

Their arms wobbled and wavered, but neither gave any ground. They glared at each other, grinding and gnashing their teeth in primal grunts.

Nessa's stomach fluttered as the two men fought over her. "Will you two knock it off?"

"I want my restitution," Cy said, never removing his eyes from Charlie's gaze.

"I didn't do anything," Charlie said. "We're coming to you for help because she said you would help us. I don't have time for this. My niece and nephew have been captured. If you're going to treat me like this, then to hell with you."

Cy snickered. "She never told you, did she?"

"Cy, don't," Nessa said. "Not here."

"Yes, let's take this someplace private," Lyra said.

Gretel rushed over to the two combatants locked in their stalemate. "Yes, please. Take this someplace private."

"No, no, no. Keep going," the bartender said.

They all glanced at the man behind the bar.

He raised his hands to his shoulders. "I'm invested. I want to know how this ends."

Cy turned back to Charlie. The two of them still locked in their arm-wrestling battle.

"Tell him," Cy said. "Tell him the real reason you left me the night before our wedding."

"The real reason?" Charlie asked. "She said she couldn't be the ruler of two kingdoms and got cold feet."

"That's not why," Cy said. "Not the real reason. Oh, she didn't tell you, did she?"

Charlie let go of Cyrus' arm. Both men dropped their arms to their sides.

"Cy, please," Nessa said.

He continued, "She didn't tell you the real reason she called off the marriage. It was supposed to be the union of two kingdoms. Her, the Princess of Glimmerfell. I, the Pirate Prince of Brightfell. Betrothed to each other. Uniting as one. But she got cold feet because her highness couldn't rule two kingdoms. At least, that's what she tells everyone publicly."

Cy turned to Nessa with a half-hearted grin on his face. His eyebrows narrowed. "But that's not the real reason. The reason she told me."

Charlie turned to Nessa. He shook his head. "What was the real reason you called it off?"

Nessa closed her eyes and buried her mouth in the palms of her hand. "Cyrus, please stop," Nessa said in a muffled voice.

"Ruling two kingdoms had nothing to do with calling off the marriage," Cy said. "She told me she couldn't go through with it because I wasn't you."

Nessa's fingers descended across her jaw. She opened her eyes and focused on Charlie. Their eyes met, his eyes beaming while hers narrowed. Charlie stumbled backward, catching himself on a chair.

"We had plans," Cy said. "We were going to sail the seas together. Our kingdoms would be united. We were in love . . . at least, I thought we were. I was in love. She lived a lie."

He turned to Nessa. "Now, you come crawling back to me. Asking me for help." Cy raised his hands to his shoulders, palms to the ceiling. "Is that all I am to you, Your Highness? Something to be used."

Nessa shook her head. A tear escaped her eye. A salty trail formed down her cheek. "I'm … I'm sorry, Cyrus. I'm so sorry."

"The name's Cy," he said. "You can't bring yourself to call me by my name."

"Hey," Charlie said. "I don't care about whatever happened between you two. As far as I'm concerned, you two can have each other. I need help rescuing my niece and nephew. They were taken to Castle Verafell."

"Castle Verafell?" Cy asked as he turned back to Charlie. "Well, I'm sorry for your loss."

"They're six years old. They're scared," Charlie said. "If you're the greatest swordsman in all of the realm—"

"I am," Cy interrupted.

"Then we need your help to rescue them," Charlie said. "We have two days. *Two days!* We'll rescue them, and then I'm gone. I'll never come back to this place. I'll never step foot in Everfell ever again."

Charlie glanced toward the floor. "This place has nothing to offer me any longer. I'm sad I came back. I'm sad I waited for twenty years." Charlie slapped the table with his palm. His voice raised. "I'm sad I waited twenty long years for that stupid mirror to start working again. And when it did, nothing was ever like I expected it. I wish it never started working again. I do." He pounded the table with his index finger.

He turned to Nessa. "I wish I never knew you were a princess. I wish I never knew you were so concerned with staying here that you were willing to abandon your previous life."

Charlie focused on Cyrus. "I wish she never had to leave you. I wish she never had to leave you because of me."

Charlie stormed around the table, flailing his arms, almost hitting the attentive patrons sitting at their tables. "I wish I never brought my niece and nephew here. This was supposed to be a fun week for them. They have enough to deal with at home. They have enough to deal with between a bickering father and a perfectionist mother."

He placed his hands on his hips and took in a deep breath. "What was I thinking that these *fairy tales* were remotely fun and safe? They're not. They never were. All they are is pain and suffering inflicted upon children."

Charlie stopped. He glanced toward the ceiling. "The king and queen protected us. They protected us from the real dangers of this place, and now they're gone. I put my niece and nephew in harm's way. I don't know if they're going to be alright. I don't know if they're still alive."

He pointed at Gretel, focusing his tear-filled eyes on her. She narrowed her eyes, taking a step back.

"You survived," Charlie said. "You survived with your wits and a little bit of luck. My niece and nephew may not be so lucky. They're only six-years-old."

Gretel shook her head. "You don't know that."

"Maybe I should go ask the bird on the juniper tree if they're going to be alright," Charlie shouted.

"Charlie!" Nessa said.

He spun around. Charlie slapped his hands to the sides of his legs. "What? There's nothing you can say that will help me. We came for him, and little did I know, because of you, he's angry at me for something I never did."

Nessa bit her lips. She glared at a spot on the floor. Emotions ran through her body. Her stomach churned, but her body surged with anger. Anger for how disastrous the meeting was going. Nessa couldn't convince the kingdoms to come to her aid, and now she couldn't convince her once betrothed to aid them in finding the lost children.

"I'm still going after those kids," Charlie said. "Even if I have to do it alone. When I find them, I'm getting them out of here. I'm never, ever coming back."

A silence fell over the tavern. Tears filled Nessa's eyes. This wasn't the reunion she wanted. Deep down, she knew coming to ask for the aid of the man she left would be confrontational, but she never thought she'd lose Charlie as well. Not again.

"I'm sorry, Charlie," Nessa said. "I'm sorry I didn't tell you. I'm sorry we didn't do enough to protect your niece and nephew. But mark my words, I'll help you get them back. I promise you. I'll be by your side the entire journey, just like when we were kids."

"I'll be by your side too," Lyra said. She pulled back her shoulders and raised her jaw, her hand on her sword.

"Me too," Half-pint said, his voice emanating from the door.

They all turned to see the imp standing in the entryway.

"What? I heard shouting and thought you needed help. The unicorns are fine, by the way. Those men are very scared of mermaids."

"Cy," Gretel said as she approached the pirate prince. She placed a hand on his shoulder.

Cyrus turned to face the owner of the tavern.

Gretel continued, "They need your help."

"Send your brother," Cy said.

"You know my brother is off in the dark woods somewhere," Gretel said. "Don't do it for her. Do it for the scared children."

Cyrus licked his lips. "It's getting late. I'll give you an answer in the morning." He stormed off, his leather boots echoing throughout the tavern as he climbed the stairs.

Gretel shook her head. "I'm sorry for the disruption, everyone. The next round is on me."

The crowd erupted in cheers as they raised their pint glasses. The band struck up a chord and started playing again, filling the air with their melodic tones. A jovial atmosphere replaced the somber attitude.

Nessa maneuvered through the tight corridors toward Gretel. "I'm sorry for the disruption. If there's any way I can repay you somehow . . ." She reached into her leather pouch and retrieved a few gold coins.

Gretel pushed her hand away. "It's alright. We've all been scared children. Sometimes it comes out when we're adults. The sign says, 'comfort for the weary traveler.' Here, you'll find comfort."

Nessa blinked a few times, wiping away the tears. "Thank you."

"Do you have a place to stay for the night?" Gretel asked.

"We were going to find lodging," Nessa said.

"Nonsense. I have rooms upstairs. I always keep them ready for any weary travelers in need. You're free to use them for the night."

"Thank you," Nessa said in a soft voice. "We have horses, including two unicorns."

Gretel held Nessa's hands. "I'll see to it that they're well cared for. You're tired. Get some rest."

CHAPTER 15
BEDTIME STORIES

The tavern was quiet. The boisterous voices had been long silenced as they retreated to their humble abodes for the evening. Chairs were turned up and placed on the tables. The dying embers of the fire glowed a bright red in the fireplace. A few candles flickered in their metal and glass lanterns hanging from the wooden posts. Their shadows danced along the wood and stucco walls.

Charlie rummaged behind the bar for a clean pint glass. He picked up a beer stein and flicked open the metal, pointed top. He turned the wooden tap on the beer cask, filling the stein with the frothy, dark liquid. The yellowish foamy head spilled over the edge. He shut off the tap and brought the stein to his lips, slurping up the liquid before any more spilled over.

The beer was fantastic, some of the best Charlie had ever tasted —a perfect mixture of hops and barley. He held the stein up to his mouth and took a longer drink. The malty flavor of liquid bread flooded his taste buds. He gulped down the entire stein in one go. He licked his lips to soak up any residual ale as he refilled the mug.

"I thought the bar was closed," Gretel said from the stairs.

Charlie shut off the tap and set the stein on the dark, polished wood bar top. "I'm sorry," he said. "I was thirsty and couldn't find anything else. I'll pay for it." He patted his pockets, remembering he carried no gold with him. "I guess, uh, Nessa will pay for it."

Gretel chuckled. "Don't worry about it. You're my guest. Feel free."

"Thanks." Charlie lifted the metal stein to take another sip. "Sorry about earlier. It's been a . . . it's been a rough couple of days."

Gretel pulled out a stool and took a seat, joining Charlie at the bar. She placed her forearms on the bar top, interlocking her fingers. The white, billowing sleeves of her night gown pulled taut under her forearms as she leaned forward.

"Don't worry about it," she said. "We've all had those moments where it feels like the world is crumbling around us."

Charlie's eyebrows shot up. "Tell me about it. This was supposed to be a fun week. My niece and nephew . . . They're going through a tough time right now. Their parents separated and are getting a divorce. I wanted to give them one week of being a kid before the weight of the world crushed their spirits. I couldn't give them that."

Gretel gazed into Charlie's eyes. "What does that mean to give them a week of being a kid?"

Charlie shuffled in his stance. "You know, no responsibilities and being protected from the harshness of an adult's life. Free from disappointment and pain."

"Everyone of all ages has disappointment and pain. But there's happiness too. It's all part of being alive."

"I know, but when you're young, you're supposed to be shielded from that stuff. You're not supposed to know the world is filled with monsters out to get you."

"Things were out to get me when I was a child," Gretel said. "I wasn't shielded from the harshness of life."

"Oh, I know," Charlie said before taking another sip. "I know of your story."

Gretel leaned back. One eyebrow arched upward. "How do you know of my story?"

"Ah . . . the brothers," Charlie said. "They wrote down your story. I read all about the gingerbread house and how you escaped."

"You know the brothers?" Gretel asked. "They were travelers from another realm. I met them once. How are they?"

"Umm . . ." Charlie pondered how to best explain the time difference. "They lived like two hundred years before me. I only know of them because they wrote the stories down in books."

"Two hundred years?" Gretel asked.

"I wish Wynden was here. He'd explain it better," Charlie said as he rubbed the back of his head. "It's something to do with how they traveled to get here versus how I did."

"Oh," Gretel said.

Charlie took another sip. "So, you met them. What were they like?"

"They were inquisitive," Gretel said. "They asked a lot of questions and constantly wrote in their books."

"I know of other stories from here as well, including the queens of the various kingdoms," Charlie said with a slight hint of glee in his voice.

"Do you?" Gretel leaned in closer. "Tell me, who's to blame for what happened in those woods?"

Charlie lifted the stein, holding it inches from his mouth. He paused for a moment, pondering the question. The obvious answer came to his mind, but no doubt this was some sort of trick question. "I feel like my answer is going to be the incorrect one."

"You could blame what happened on the witch in the gingerbread house. It's the obvious choice, but she isn't the real villain of my story."

"Then who is?" Charlie asked.

"My parents," Gretel said. "They were the ones who took us into those woods. They abandoned my brother and me."

Charlie placed his stein down on the bar top. He shifted in his stance, placing his free hand on the polished wood. He narrowed his eyebrows and leaned in closer.

Gretel continued, "I resented them for it. It took me a long time to get over it. Time is the biggest healer of wounds. It provided clarity and wisdom with age. We were starving and penniless. They couldn't provide for us any longer. My parents took us to the woods to set us free. It could have been worse for my brother and me, but our parents gave us what they thought was a fighting chance."

"That's ... that's rough," Charlie said.

"Tell me about it," Gretel said. "You can't hide from these events, but it's how we react to them that defines us. My brother, for example—he's off patrolling the woods with Red Riding Hood, hunting down monsters. He became the rescuer we never had."

She paused, glancing around the tavern. "I, on the other hand, opened this tavern. I wanted a place where people could come regardless of their situation. If they needed a meal, it would be on the house. If they needed a roof, I had rooms. All are welcome. None are turned away. I became the support we never had."

Charlie sighed. "I lost my best friend. We were inseparable. We spent almost every day together since we were four or five, until she disappeared. No one believed me about where she was. I tried to tell them, but they wouldn't believe me. I was alone, but I vowed to guard that mirror."

Charlie paused, taking a sip from his stein. "And I did. I waited twenty years for that mirror to work again. I dreamed of coming back here and taking her home . . . That we would be reunited, and it would be like old times again."

He took another sip. The malty liquid washed over his tongue. "After a while, I stopped checking every day," Charlie said. "I never fully gave up hope, but it defined me. It ruled my life. There was nothing but waiting for that mirror to work again."

Charlie curled his bottom lip inward and gingerly bit down. He paused for a moment, hesitating to finally admit the truth to himself. "Then I found out she's a princess and soon-to-be ruler of a kingdom. How could we ever go back to our old ways after that? I often wondered if I wasted my life waiting on her. She moved on. I didn't."

Gretel placed a hand on his. "You didn't waste it. You remained vigilant, and it paid off."

"Yeah," Charlie said. "But it's never going to be the way it was before."

"Of course not," Gretel said. "That's life. You can't go backward. You can only deal with the here and now."

"I keep thinking about those kids . . . how scared they must be."

"Oh, well, there isn't a way to sugarcoat that. I'm certain they're terrified. They're lost. Afraid."

Charlie closed his eyes and shook his head.

"But you know what?" Gretel asked.

Charlie opened his eyes, locking onto her brown eyes. "What?"

"They have each other, as my brother and I did. They'll be alright until you can get to them. Besides, they have you to count on, right?"

Charlie lifted his stein. "Thanks," he said before taking another drink. "They were about to go through hell with their parents. I—I wanted them to have one thing. One symbol of hope and joy and laughter . . . of innocence before their world crashed down around them."

Gretel patted his free hand. "They'll get it when you rescue them. Those children will know they can always count on you because you're their uncle."

Charlie huffed. "I wanted to be the cool uncle. I'm their *only* uncle, but still. I wanted them to know they're safe with me."

"What are their names?" Cy asked.

Charlie and Gretel turned to find the pirate prince emerging from the shadows beneath the stairs.

"How long have you been lurking over there and listening?" Gretel asked.

"I heard the whole thing," Cy said. "I couldn't sleep, so I decided to hang out under here. It's cozy under here. It could use a blanket or two. Maybe a small side table."

"Those could be arranged," Gretel said with a wink.

Cy pointed toward Charlie. "Then he came down and stole the ale."

"I wasn't stealing the ale," Charlie said. He glanced at Gretel. "I'll pay for the ale."

"I said it's okay," she said.

"For a moment, I thought about running him through for stealing," Cyrus said. "Only for a moment. Then I decided maybe he deserved a drink."

The steps creaked, drawing everyone's attention. Sitting atop the stairs, with only their two pairs of bare feet visible, were the inseparable pair from Glimmerfell.

Charlie shrugged his shoulders, rolling his eyes. "Has everyone been listening in on the conversation?"

The pair slid down a few steps, still seated on the staircase, but their faces now visible.

"We caught half of the conversation," Nessa said.

"It was the princess's idea," Lyra added.

"Traitor," Nessa said with a smile. "We couldn't sleep either."

"Well, everyone might as well join us down here for a round of drowning our misery," Charlie said.

Nessa and Lyra stood. They descended like a pair of sisters rushing down the steps on Christmas morning. The trains of their dark blue evening gowns flowed behind them. Cy waited for the two to join him before the three of them approached the bar. The pair pulled out barstools and took their seats. Cy swung a leg over his stool and plopped down.

"You never told me their names," Cy said as he retrieved his frothy mug.

"Ginny, short for Virginia, and Tyler," Charlie said.

"Ginny and Tyler," Cy said. "They sound like great kids."

Charlie sat upright. "They're great. Full of hope and optimism."

"Well, Mr. Bartender," Nessa said with a grin on her face. "Are you going to offer us any drinks?"

Charlie's eyes darted to Gretel, who gave the approval with a quick motion toward the keg. Charlie bent over, snatching up a few more beer steins. He filled them to the brim, their foam heads almost spilling over the sides. He snapped the metallic tops closed before the drink spilled over and passed them around.

Nessa raised her stein. "To messed up childhoods."

Everyone raised their steins into the air.

Charlie paused before raising his stein. "To messed up childhoods."

Everyone clanged their steins together and downed their drinks. Most only took a few sips before setting their steins back down. Cy, on the other hand, finished off the entire mug in one go, no doubt showing off in front of Nessa and showing up Charlie.

Cy slammed the stein down and let out an exasperated sigh. He wiped his lips clean before passing the stein back to Charlie. Cy pointed at the wooden tap, motioning for a refill.

Charlie rolled his eyes, but he still picked up the mug to refill it.

"I've been thinking," Cy said.

"That'd be a first," Gretel said. She winked at Cy.

"A direct assault into Shadowfell isn't going to work. There are too many obstacles and potential threats in the forest that will jump us before we catch the slightest glimpse of Castle Verafell," Cy said. "We'd need to take a different approach."

Charlie placed the refilled stein in front of Cyrus. "So, what's your plan, great pirate prince?"

Cy flipped open a metallic lid and dipped his fingers into the frothy brew. He drew out a liquid line across the bar top.

"Don't mess up my bar top," Gretel said.

"Don't worry," Cy replied. "The bartender will take care of it." He glared at Charlie and grinned, giving him a wink.

Charlie rolled his eyes.

"There's a river not too far from here. It runs the length of the border, close to Shadowfell." Cy drew out a river. He dipped his finger back into the drink, replenishing his liquid paint. "It splits right about here. It travels into the heart of Shadowfell, right up to Castle Verafell."

He circled a spot on the bar top, giving it two taps with his fingers. "I propose we go up the river," he said.

"Does this mean you'll help us?" Nessa asked.

"Help you? No," Cy replied. "Help those kids? Yes."

Gretel pushed against Cy with her shoulders. "I knew you weren't going to abandon those kids, you old softie."

Cy turned to Gretel and smiled. "Please, I have a reputation to uphold."

Gretel winked at him. "Your secret is safe with me."

"Okay," Charlie said. "We go up the river. Do you have a boat on this river?"

"No," Cy replied.

Charlie threw his hands in the air. "Great. What are we going to do? Swim?"

Cy sat up in his chair and crossed his arms. "Are you going to be like this the entire way or are you going to let me finish?"

Charlie rotated his hands in a flourish and bowed. "Please continue, Your Highness."

"That's better," Cy said. His lips curled into a half-smirk. "I know of a boat. It's captained by an old crew mate of mine—a riverboat, so it can move faster. He runs up and down this river, making deliveries. The captain is reliable. We called him Peg Leg because he used to wear a false wooden peg leg. He said it made him feel more like a pirate."

Cy pointed to a spot on his ale river. "He picks up shipments here —a place called Gruff's Landing. We can ask him to take us up the river."

Charlie stood up tall, with his shoulders pulled back and arms crossed. "Okay," he said. "Alright. That'll save us time. We can get there faster."

"Not to be a downer, but what if he doesn't want to?" Lyra asked.

Cyrus shrugged his shoulders. "He'll help. We're old crew mates.

Pirate code states you help a crew mate in distress as much as you can."

Cyrus leaned to his side, pushing against Nessa with his shoulders. "Besides, a little gold can convince most to travel into the heart of the dark forest."

Nessa rolled her eyes. "The kingdom will run out of gold before this trip is over."

"That's okay, Your Highness," Half-pint said. He appeared out of thin air, sitting cross-legged on the bar top. He took off his top hat and delved a hand into it, withdrawing a handful of gold. "I brought plenty with me."

"Have you been sitting there the entire time?" Gretel asked.

The gold fell from his hands and back into the top hat. Placing the hat back on his head, Half-pint tugged on the brim to secure it on his head. "Well," he said. "Since Charlie came down. I followed him. I don't need a lot of sleep, and I was bored."

"I'm coming with you," Gretel said.

Everyone focused on the tavern owner.

Cyrus shook his head. "I can't let you do that. This is dangerous."

Gretel shifted in her seat to face him. "I can't abandon those kids. I was like them once, scared and alone, hoping someone would come. I have a duty to rescue them." Gretel took a sip from her stein. "Besides, if my brother found out I abandoned kids in the woods, I'd never hear the end of it."

"Thank you," Charlie said.

Gretel raised her stein. "To the rescue mission."

"To the kids," Cy said, raising his stein.

Nessa raised her stein. "To childhoods."

Lyra followed suit, raising her metallic mug high. "To doing the right thing."

Charlie retrieved his stein, holding it aloft. He paused. Charlie struggled with the right words to say—the words he wanted to say. How he wanted to thank everyone for helping him. They were risking their lives to rescue the children. So many words crossed his mind, but only a single thought passed through his lips—a profession of thanks.

Charlie licked his lips before speaking. "I want to thank you all," he said. "Thank you for your kindness. Your generosity. For not abandoning those kids. For not giving up hope."

"To hope," Half-pint said as he held aloft an imaginary stein.

They all clinked their steins together and took a drink. Cyrus, of course, finished his off. He never broke eye contact with Charlie.

Returning the glare, Charlie finished his as well. The two men slammed their steins onto the bar top at the same time.

"Now, I think I'm ready for bed," Cy said as he stood. He swung his leg back over the barstool. "Better get some sleep. Pickup is at 9 a.m., and we've got an hour ride to get there."

Cy retreated to the steps. He paused for a moment, his hand on the newel post, before turning back to the group. "By the way, his crew is a little . . . eclectic."

CHAPTER 16
FULL STEAM AHEAD

The fog rolled in off the river. A ghostly, vaporous cloud rose from the rippling waters. It was eerily calm. Charlie shivered from the slight chill in the air. The sun's rays spilled over the peaks of the mountains off in the distance. The sun itself was still hidden behind the jagged, rocky teeth.

The horseshoes clomped against the wooden dock of Gruff's Landing. The saddled group, now six, waited patiently for the arrival of the riverboat. Charlie's unicorn neighed, swinging the twisted black horn wildly around. He bent down and patted the animal on its neck to calm it down.

"Easy, boy," Charlie said. "Easy."

The unicorn dug at the dock with its hoof. The metal horseshoe dug into the wood planks, leaving a trail of small scrapes. Noticeable to Charlie, but they blended into the weathered and scuffed up surface.

Charlie rose and turned to the man on the black stallion. "I thought you said he arrives at nine."

Cyrus shrugged. "He's supposed to arrive at nine. He's been known to run late."

"Perfect," Charlie said.

Cyrus raised one corner of his lips, smirking back at him. Charlie rolled his eyes before returning his focus to the river. He scanned up and down the waterway for any signs of the riverboat.

The river curved around a small cliff face in front of the dock. Charlie estimated it to be about fifteen feet in the air. The edge was lined with lush trees, steep and without any access to the water. It kept its secrets above and around the river bend.

The dock itself wasn't much—a small booth, manned by a humanoid black cat standing on two legs. He was as tall as Half-pint and had pointy ears on his head with round white eyes, white fur around his mouth, and a black nose. He scribbled a manifest for the riverboat. Crates and barrels littered the dock, awaiting the scheduled pickup. They were packed on square platforms with ropes to lift them up and onto the boat.

During the great awakening, when magic spilled forth through the realm many centuries ago, it transformed some of the wildlife. It gave them human mental and physical attributes with increased size and the power of speech. They became something more. New life-forms of their own.

Charlie glanced back at Nessa. She was shoulder to shoulder with Cyrus. Lyra was right behind her as her sworn guardian. Gretel was on Cyrus' other side. The pirate prince leaned in and whispered something to Nessa. The two of them laughed and giggled. Charlie squinted his eyes and drew his lips tight.

He had known Cyrus for about twelve hours, and to Charlie, that was twelve hours too long. Still, if they were to have any chance of rescuing the kids, he had to accept his help. He'd have to suffer with his annoyance until the kids were safe and sound. Charlie raised a hand and rubbed his cheek—the very spot Cyrus had slapped with the glove. Payback would come, but only after the children were secured.

Half-pint glanced back at the laughing pair and then at Charlie.

He sat up high in the saddle of his beige pony. "This reminds me of the time I waited for this delivery."

"Delivery?" Charlie asked.

"Yeah," Half-pint replied. "Some supplies. They were supposed to drop it off in the morning. I waited all day. *All day.* Well, it became the afternoon, and I was getting hungry. So, I went to get a bite to eat, and then when I got back, there was this note that said, 'Sorry. We missed you.' I was furious."

"I've had those too," Charlie said. "The worst is when the mail arrives. I was expecting a letter. It never arrived. Then when I told them about it, they said there was nothing they could do."

Half-pint shook his head. "That's the worst. The worst."

"Adulting," Charlie said. "It's for the birds."

Half-pint flashed a smile. "Right."

Charlie scanned up and down the river. "What time is it?"

Half-pint removed a silver pocket watch from his black vest. "Half past," he replied.

"We used to have this rule as kids," Charlie said. "If the school bus was fifteen minutes late, then we wouldn't have to go to school."

"What's a school bus?" Half-pint asked.

"Oh, right. Umm . . . It's a vehicle that picks up kids and takes them to school."

"Like this boat?" Half-pint asked.

Charlie shrugged. "Uh, sort of. But they were more on time. Never more than five minutes late."

The duo laughed.

Black smoke rose above the tree line to Charlie's left. Small, round puffs of billowing smoke popped into the air in rapid succession. The riverboat was here.

"That's them," Cyrus said.

The boat emerged from around the side of the cliff—a long, white hull with a red stripe and railing. A red paddlewheel, positioned behind the boat, propelled it through the water. A rope and pulley rig was on the back deck, no doubt to load the cargo. A two-story cabin was in the middle. Two smoke stacks rose up beside the bridge of the vessel. A whistle was positioned atop the white roof of the wheelhouse. A black pirate flag waved in the front—the image of a skull and crossbones except the skull had bent over dog ears.

Charlie sat back in his saddle. There was something oddly familiar about that flag.

The riverboat pulled past the front of the dock. The smoke stacks pulsated back and forth as they exhaled puffs of black smoke. The riverboat paused for a moment as the paddlewheel reversed its spin, and then backed up. The side of the hull was mere inches from the dock. The hook hung above their heads, perfectly positioned and awaiting its cargo. A white wooden loading ramp appeared over the edge and slid down the white railing to the dock below, wide enough for the animals to walk up.

A head popped up above the railing—white and fluffy, with elongated floppy ears—a humanoid, scruffy dog. He smiled with a wide grin across his white face, exposing his teeth. He had a protruding black nose and roundish white eyes with black pupils. His ears popped straight up to attention before flopping back down. He waved with his hand in the air to greet everyone. His arm waved back and forth as if it were made of rubber beneath his billowing blue shirt.

Cyrus leaped down from his black stallion, handing the reins to Gretel. He moved between Charlie and Half-pint toward the front of the dock. He ascended the ramp to greet the crewmate of the riverboat.

"I need to speak with Pierre," Cyrus said. "I'm an old friend."

The scruffy dog pointed toward the cabin. Cyrus gave a two-fingered salute with his gloved hand and continued deeper onto the boat. The dog turned his attention back to the group on the dock. He waved his arms, signaling for them to come aboard.

"Lead us up," Charlie said to Half-pint.

Half-pint clicked his tongue, and his pony tromped up the ramp. Its metallic shoes clomped against the white boards. Charlie soon followed behind. The ramp led up past the rail, with a small ramp leading down onto the deck of the riverboat. Once they were a safe distance away from the ramp, Charlie swung his legs over the saddle and hopped down, still holding onto the reins.

The scruffy dog, roughly the same size as the cat below, pointed to a wooden, fenced-in area toward the back of the stern. Charlie led the unicorn to the makeshift corral. Half-pint followed.

Nessa and Lyra soon emerged above the rail and onto the stern of the boat. Gretel led Cyrus' black stallion up the ramp. Charlie rushed over, taking the reins of Nessa's unicorn. She swung her leg over and hopped down.

"Thank you," Nessa said.

"Sure thing, Your Highness," Charlie said with a wink and a smile.

He took Lyra's reins as she dismounted her horse. Charlie led both animals over to the pen, with Gretel following. Once all the animals were secured, he closed the door. They rejoined the rest of the rescue party.

The scruffy dog clomped over to the cargo hook, his elongated feet flopping on the deck. His tail emerged from his tattered brown pants, wagging back and forth. He turned the crank on the pole, repositioning the hook over the crates below.

Charlie leaned in and whispered to Nessa, "A dog for a crewmate?"

Nessa shrugged her shoulders. "Cy said the crew was a little eclectic."

"Can't wait to meet the captain."

Lyra placed a hand on Nessa's shoulder as she walked past. "I'm going to inspect the boat to make sure it's safe." Lyra marched toward the front of the boat, one hand placed at the ready on her sword.

"I thought I told you no goofing off in the wheelhouse," a gruff voice said from the stairwell leading up to the bridge of the boat. "Now we're late."

Something ran down the stairs, nearly skipping steps—another dog with a round head and two floppy ears. It was diminutive, about the same height as the other one. Less scruffy in appearance, but still a mutt with tan fur. It had white, round eyes with black pupils. A protruding tan snout with a black nose. A tan tail with straggles of fur that waved in the breeze similar to the pirate flag. He wore black pants with a red billowing shirt. His feet were covered in a pair of black, rounded shoes.

Charlie stood frozen at the sight, his eyes unable to believe what stood before him. Charlie knew of his stories. He watched their cartoon adventures as a child—*The Voyages of the Salty Sea Dogs*. He turned to Nessa, who was gazing back at him. Their mouths were agape, and their eyebrows jutted up. They blinked at each other a few times.

"Well," Nessa said. "You wanted a sign. I think we found it."

Charlie smiled at the princess. He inhaled, holding himself back from bursting into joyous laughter at the sight of the salty sea dog standing in front of them. The mutt dusted himself off. He turned his attention back to Nessa and Charlie. He stuck out his fur covered hand. Like the other dog, his arm moved in rubbery, reverberating motions.

"The name's Mac," he said. "Welcome aboard."

Charlie shook his hand. "I'm Charlie." He let the handshake linger. His eyes were glued to the dog, unable to avert his gaze.

"I'm going to need that back," Mac said.

"Oh, uh, right," Charlie said as he let go.

Nessa presented her hand, palm down and fingers bent. "I'm Princess Nessa of Glimmerfell."

Mac wrapped his three fingers around hers, placed them into his palm, and secured them with his thumb. He shook her hand daintily a few times. "Nice to meet you, Your Majesty," he said as he released her hand. He bowed with a flourish. He placed his right hand on his stomach, and the left raised to the sky behind him as he bent over.

"There's no need for that," she said with a slight laugh.

"Well, it's a pleasure to meet you," he said as he rose. "I'm the first mate, and my friend over there is named Buster. He doesn't talk, but he's very helpful. Welcome aboard the Riverboat—"

"Salty Sea Dog," Charlie said.

Mac jolted back at his comment.

"I . . . uh . . ." Charlie said, stumbling to find the right words. "How do I explain this?" He ran his hand through his hair and paused for a moment. "Where I'm from, I know of your story . . . uh, stories. I've heard of you."

Mac pursed his lips and arched an eyebrow. "So, you've met the dreamers? Both of them? The ones who came here in their dreams."

Charlie froze. "Umm, not exactly, but they told tales of you."

Mac arched an eyebrow. "Tales of *me*?"

"Yeah," Charlie said. "It was called *The Voyages of the Salty Sea Dogs*. I used to watch your show every day before school. It was like . . . how do I explain this . . . it was like a moving picture show featuring you and the crew."

Mac squinted an eye and arched an eyebrow into a discerning glance toward Charlie.

"We need help with the crane," Half-pint said.

The dog pointed toward the crane. "I'm going to help load the cargo," he said before scampering off. He took up the position at the crank wheel.

"To the left," Half-pint yelled from below.

The mutt turned the crank.

"No. The other left," Half-pint shouted. "The other left. My left. Your left. Some left. Maybe right."

The dog reversed the direction of the hook.

"That's it," Half-pint said. "Now, bring it up."

Cyrus descended the stairs to the wheelhouse. He was followed by a large, bearish-sized bulldog, nearly as tall as Cyrus. He was covered in black fur with white around his jaw and mouth. Saliva dripped from his drooping jowls. A thick, black tail emerged from his blue coveralls. Only one strap connected over his shoulder. A sour expression was on his face, with narrowed eyebrows.

He adjusted his captain's hat. Flat on the top and round on the bottom, and a small black brim. Worn and tattered. The edges frayed.

"Pierre, we need your help," Cyrus said. "We need you to take us up the river into Shadowfell."

"Shadowfell?" Pierre asked in a gruff voice. "Why would you want to go there?"

"Something took these two kids," Cyrus said. "We're going there to get them back."

Pierre paused. He scowled at his former pirate captain. "And that's my problem how? You want me to risk my crew and boat going into Shadowfell? You have another think coming."

"Mister Peg Leg," Charlie said.

Pierre turned around and glared at Charlie. "Does it look like I have a peg leg?"

"Okay, Mr. Pierre," Charlie said. "We could use your help."

Cyrus raised a hand to Charlie. "I got this. Go help load crates or something."

"You got this?" Charlie asked in a raised voice.

"Yeah, the pirates are talking," Cyrus said, placing his hands on his hips. "Go make yourself useful or something."

Nessa wrapped her fingers around Charlie's arm and leaned in. "Let him go," she whispered. "He's trying to prove he's still captain."

Charlie huffed.

"Don't take it personally," Gretel said. "It's a pirate pride thing." She secured the black leather strap of her belt following the ride to the dock. Gretel had traded her barmaid's dress for something more accommodating for a pirate crew—black leather pants, a white shirt, and a black leather vest. She didn't carry a sword on her hip, but a small dagger the size of a kitchen knife.

Pierre crossed his arms and faced Cyrus. "What's in it for me?"

"Gold," Cyrus said.

Pierre arched an eyebrow. "Go on," he said. "How much gold?"

"I'm Princess Nessa of Glimmerfell. I can pay you five hundred gold coins," Nessa said. "Glimmerfell coins."

Pierre rubbed his white chin. "Glimmerfell, huh?" he asked. "Five hundred, you say?"

"Half now and half when we get back," Cyrus said. "You have the fastest boat on the river. We can get there in no time. In and out."

Pierre continued to rub his chin with his beefy hands. "I suppose you'll want me to fight alongside you?"

"Nope. We'll do the fighting. You can stay on the river. If we don't come back, you get our horses as well. Pirate rules."

Pierre narrowed his eyes, not in anger, but more like contemplation. He puckered his lips. "Let me see the coins."

Nessa flipped one side of the cloak over her shoulder and removed a black pouch from her waist. It jingled as the coins bounced off each other inside. She presented it to Pierre, dropping it into his awaiting hands. "Half, as promised," Nessa said.

"Hmm," Pierre said as he opened the pouch. He spilled out a few coins into his open hand.

"That has to be more gold than you'll make hauling cargo up the river," Cyrus said.

Pierre glanced at Cyrus. "Pirate rules?"

Cyrus pounded his fist against his chest. "Pirate rules."

"Put the cargo back, boys," Pierre yelled. "We're going up the river instead."

Buster and Half-pint stood atop the crates as Mac raised it onto the boat.

"Ah," Half-pint said. "We finally got the crane figured out. Actually, I finally got the crane figured out."

The dog reversed the crank, sending the cargo back down to the dock below. After a moment, Half-pint and Buster scampered up the ramp. The three of them pulled it back onto the boat.

Mac headed toward the wheelhouse. Pierre stopped him.

"Where do you think you're going?" Pierre said.

"To take us up the river," he responded.

"I'm the captain of the boat, thank you very much," Pierre said. He placed his arms under his rotund belly and lifted. His rubbery legs stretched high into the air. He let go, and his belly fell, bouncing a few times before settling back into place. He stomped up the stairwell to the wheelhouse.

Mac bowed his head, lips puckered and eyebrows narrowed. A sour, dejected expression appeared on his face. Buster flopped over and patted him on the back. He smiled at the other dog, trying to cheer him up.

The smokestacks puffed as the boat lurched forward. The paddlewheel rotated and splashed into the water. The riverboat took off from the dock, heading up the river toward the dark forest of Shadowfell.

TO FACE
THEIR
FEARS

CHAPTER 17
THE SILENT LESSON

"I want you to attack me," Cyrus said. He held out his sword with one foot forward and the other back to brace himself.

Charlie desperately desired to strike him. Attacking him would be sweet—to wipe his arrogant, smug smirk off his face. Ever since the incident in the tavern, he had been waiting for an excuse to deck him as hard as he could. But this wasn't the place or the time.

Cyrus had offered to teach Charlie a few moves, offensive and defensive moves that would become useful when they made landfall in Shadowfell.

"You want me to attack you?" Charlie asked.

"Yeah, I want to see what you can do," Cyrus said. A knowing smirk appeared on his face as if he were baiting Charlie into a trap.

Charlie drew his sword. He shrugged and rotated his shoulders. He raised the blade to face Cyrus. He put his lead foot out and turned his back foot to brace himself—a swordsman's pose.

"Good, good," Cyrus said. "You know a proper stance."

"You've got this, Charlie," Nessa said.

"Yeah, I believe in you," Half-pint added.

"I've got money on you, Cy," Gretel said. "Don't let me down."

Charlie turned to face his audience. Everyone gathered around the back of the boat as spectators for Charlie's training lesson. Everyone except Pierre, who was in the wheelhouse, navigating the boat.

Charlie smiled and slightly bowed.

Cyrus struck Charlie's sword, knocking it out of his hand. The metal blade bounced off the polished wooden deck.

"Rule number one," Cyrus said. "Never take your eyes off your opponent."

"I didn't know we'd started," Charlie said.

"We started the moment you drew your sword. Now pick it up," Cyrus commanded.

Charlie rolled his eyes and bent down to retrieve the blade.

Cyrus struck his sword again, knocking it out of his hand once more.

Charlie popped up, chest out. "Hey, let me pick it up first."

Cyrus poked Charlie in the chest with the tip of his blade, not hard enough to cut through the leather vest, but with enough pressure that Charlie knew the point was there.

"Are you already forgetting rule number one?" Cyrus asked. He slowly withdrew the blade. Cyrus returned to his fighting stance. "Pick it up."

Charlie squatted down, never taking his eyes off Cyrus. He spotted the blade out of the corner of his eye. His palm and fingers wrapped around the silver and leather-wrapped hilt. His body tensed and coiled for what was coming next.

With a flick of the wrist, Cyrus slashed at Charlie.

Charlie sprang up, stepping backward. He met Cyrus' blade with his own.

"Good," Cyrus said. "You're not some big, dumb oaf. You can learn."

Half-pint and Mac whistled and clapped. Buster joined in with the clapping.

Cyrus followed up with a quick strike. Charlie was prepared and blocked it. He drew on his rudimentary knowledge from his fencing classes and training as a child.

"You do have some training," Cyrus said. A grin crawled up his face.

"One year of fencing classes," Charlie said. "I may be out of practice, but it's there."

Cyrus struck at Charlie's left side. Charlie was quick to block it.

Cyrus swung around to Charlie's right, but he was ready for the attack. The swords clashed and clanked. Charlie's arm reverberated from the strike.

"Good. Good," Cyrus said. "You know the basics of defensive positions. What if I pressed the attack?"

Cyrus lunged forward, maneuvering around. Charlie shuffled his feet and bent his knees to match Cyrus' movement. Charlie brought the sword to his side to block the attack and then swung it around to block the secondary attack from his side.

"Time for rule number two," Cyrus said.

The sound of their swords striking together like two musical instruments filled the air with a symphony of steel.

"What's rule number two?" Charlie asked.

Cyrus flung his free hand toward Charlie, releasing a small cloud of dust.

Charlie flinched, shielding his eyes from the sneak attack. Cyrus' blade cut across his vest, leaving a small scratch in the black leather. Not cutting too deep, but it left a noticeable scar.

"Be ready for the unexpected," Cyrus said.

Charlie threw his blade onto the deck. He wiped the dirt from his eyes as his sight came back into focus. "What was that for?" Charlie yelled.

"I wanted to see if you were ready for a fight," Cyrus said. "Clearly, you're not."

He swiped at Charlie one more time, leaving another scratch in the worn leather. Neither cut was deep enough to break through, but enough for a mental reminder of their contest.

"I wasn't armed," Charlie said, throwing his arms into the sky. His heart raced and thumped against his chest. He gnashed his teeth together. Snarling, Charlie held back the urge to punch Cyrus right across his smug face.

"Rule number three. The enemy won't wait for you to be armed and ready," Cyrus said.

"Enough of this," Charlie said.

He bent down to retrieve the blade from the deck floor. With a flick, he sheathed the blade. The metal of the hilt smacked against the leather scabbard.

"Charlie," Nessa said. "He's trying to help teach you."

"Yeah, Charlie," Cyrus said, leaning against the railing. "Come on. I'll give you the children's lesson for sword fighting."

Gretel smacked Cyrus across the chest. "Will you stop? You should have taken it easy on him."

"What?" Cyrus asked. "He wanted me to teach him."

"You don't have to be so hard on him," Nessa said.

Charlie stormed off to the other side of the boat. He made his way to the bow. The black pirate flag flapped in the wind as the riverboat continued up the river. The dirt cliffs, long carved by erosion and the winding river, passed by on one side. The flatter shores were on the other side.

Charlie crossed his arms, buried his head into his chest, and leaned back against the rail. He seethed in his spot. The anger boiled within him. The pressure surged through his veins.

Charlie hated Cyrus.

No, hate wasn't a strong enough word. He loathed Cyrus. Detested Cyrus. Abhorred him.

That wasn't a lesson. That was humiliation. He did that on purpose. Yes. Cyrus wanted to humiliate him in front of Gretel, Lyra, and especially Nessa—with his stupid attacks and knocking the sword out of his hand.

It was all premeditated, designed to humiliate him in Nessa's eyes.

Charlie buried his face deep in his arms, letting out a low grunt. He needed to calm down. To soothe his nerves. Perhaps he should focus on the trees above. Yeah. The trees. Nice, soothing, calming trees.

Their green foliage whizzed by in a blur as the boat paddled down the river. It was dizzying to focus directly on the edge of the cliff, as his eyes struggled to follow a single tree. A little seasickness went to his stomach. Or sickness of something from the sea. Perhaps he needed to focus on a spot on the floor instead. He glanced down at the boat deck.

Laughter erupted from the back, no doubt directed toward him. His humiliation. His failure. Nessa was probably laughing at him right now. Praising *Mister I'm the greatest swordsman in the realm*. Charlie's fingers dug into his biceps.

The sound of footsteps tapped along the wooden deck.

"Go away," Charlie said.

The footsteps drew closer.

"I said go away," Charlie repeated, never raising his head. "I don't want to be around anyone."

A body brushed against his side, shoulder to shoulder, as the person leaned against the rail to join Charlie's pity party.

"What about an old friend?" Nessa asked.

Charlie raised his head to meet her blue eyes—the eyes he had sought for twenty years.

"I suppose you're all laughing at me back there?"

"No," Nessa said. "They're laughing at Cyrus. Gretel bet that Cyrus couldn't beat Lyra in a duel."

"Who won?" Charlie asked.

"Lyra, of course."

Charlie uncrossed his arms and joined Nessa, holding onto the rails. Their hands brushed up against each other. They both leaned against the rail in silence for a moment.

Nessa was the first to speak. "I should have told you the truth. The real reason I broke off the marriage."

Charlie shook his head. "Twenty years have passed. I half-expected you to be married by now."

"I expected you to be married too," Nessa said. "But here we are."

"Why not tell me the real reason?" Charlie asked. "You already told me you were engaged."

Nessa inhaled quickly, but she let the exhale linger. "I thought if you knew the real reason, you'd want to immediately take me back through the mirror," Nessa said.

Charlie narrowed his eyebrows. "Like kidnap you and take you back? What do you take me for? If you wanted to stay, I'd honor that."

"No, guilt trip me into going back. That I would allow you to convince me to go back," Nessa said. "There's no going back. Not now. An entire kingdom depends on me. I couldn't abandon them and go back with you. Your niece and nephew depend on you. I couldn't ask you to give them up and stay."

The idea of giving up his life back home never crossed his mind. Would he stay and give up his niece and nephew? His sister and parents? In the twenty years of waiting for the mirror to work again, he never contemplated staying, only bringing Nessa home.

"On lonely nights, I used to sit in front of that mirror," Nessa said. "I wished for it to work again. I wanted it to work so badly. As time went on, I stopped dreaming of going home. I only dreamed of one thing."

"What was that?" Charlie asked.

Nessa turned her head to face Charlie. "I dreamed that you came back. You came walking through the mirror, and we would go on our grand adventures again. After all, we made a promise."

"What promise?" Charlie asked.

Nessa smiled. "That when we turned thirteen, we'd make it official and be boyfriend and girlfriend. We missed it by a week."

Charlie laughed. "We practically were."

"Yeah, we had to wait, remember?"

"Because we thought being twelve and being in love was gross," Charlie said. "Instead, we had to wait until we were thirteen."

They laughed.

"I sat by that mirror most nights and dreamed," Nessa said. "Dreamed of home. Dreamed of you."

"I did too," Charlie said. "We probably sat and stared at each other without knowing it. On Friday nights, after school, my mom would get me a pizza from Blue Jay's Pizza, and I'd sit in front of the mirror waiting for you."

"Blue Jay's Pizza," Nessa said in a drawn-out tone. She shook her head. "I miss Blue Jay's Pizza so much."

"They make the best pizza, right?" Charlie asked.

"The best," Nessa said. "Is the cheese still extra stringy?"

"Oh, yeah," Charlie said. "It's still cut into squares. The bottom is the right amount of crispy."

"And the top of the crust is the perfect amount of doughy goodness," Nessa said as she leaned her head back. Her shoulders drooped, and she clutched her fists together before pulling them tight to her chest. "I would love to have a pizza from Blue Jay's right now."

"Maybe I'll bring one back sometime, and we can share it the way we used to on a Friday night."

"I'd love that," Nessa said.

They smiled at each other in silence.

After a moment, Charlie broke the silence. "I used to sit in front of the mirror, thinking about what you were up to. What new adventures you were on without me."

Charlie paused. He knew the next words he wanted to say. He gathered all of his strength and conviction to say them, risking it all. "I spent those years sitting in front of the mirror falling in love with the idea of you."

The smile faded from Nessa's face. Her eyes focused on the wooden deck of the boat.

Charlie's smile faded. He knew he said too much.

"I'm . . . I'm sorry," Charlie said. "That was too much."

"I sat in silence in front of the mirror, falling in love with the idea of you, Charlie," Nessa said. "Wondering what you were up to. If you still cared about me. I often questioned if you'd given up on me."

Nessa turned to face Charlie. "If you forgot about me."

Charlie met her gaze. "I'd never forget about you. After all, we made a promise when we were twelve."

They laughed.

"For what it's worth, you're a great leader," Charlie said.

Nessa sighed. "How so? I'm not half of what the king and queen were in the eyes of the citizens."

Charlie bumped into her arm and shoulder. "You're risking your own life to stop this threat instead of marching your citizens into the dark forest. I couldn't imagine a greater leader than one who would risk themselves over their own people. I know I'd be proud to call you my queen."

Nessa smiled.

Footsteps approached the pair. Standing in front of them, waving his hand back and forth, was Buster. The scruffy dog pointed to Charlie's sword and then to himself.

"Do you need me to help you?" Charlie asked.

Buster shook his head. He pointed to himself and then Charlie's sword. He mimicked the motion of sword fighting, waving his arm in the air.

"Yes, I know I'm not the best," Charlie said. "Did you come to rub it in my face?"

The scruffy dog shook his head. He pointed to himself, then to Charlie, and lastly to his sword.

Charlie furrowed his brow in confusion.

"I think he wants to give you a lesson," Nessa said.

Buster nodded. His lips stretched into a smile.

"You want to teach me?" Charlie asked.

The scruffy dog's grin exposed his white teeth.

"You're going to teach me?" Charlie asked, pointing to the scruffy dog.

The scruffy dog flailed his arm in the air, mimicking the skills of a sword fighter. He swung and attacked an unseen foe.

Charlie pushed off against the railing and stood. Charlie withdrew his sword. "Do you have a sword?"

Buster shrugged.

"You can use mine," Lyra said. She stood at the edge of the wheelhouse and withdrew her blade. She handed it to the excited scruffy dog.

Buster took the dueling sword, a grin on his face. He pointed toward the blade and then toward Charlie's. He poked the air a few times, indicating he wanted Charlie to practice with him.

Charlie followed the scruffy dog's motions. Up and down. Up and down. Left and right. Left and right. The blades clanged together. One fluid motion, back and forth, almost in a figure eight.

Buster reared back and lunged forward. Charlie blocked the attack, circling around, and thrust a retaliatory strike. Buster blocked the oncoming attack. On and on, they went. The scruffy dog smiled, raising his free hand to give a thumbs-up.

"Not bad," Lyra said.

"Thanks," Charlie said. "A little rusty, but I think I got it." Charlie lowered his blade. He bowed to the scruffy dog.

Buster placed a hand across his stomach and bowed in return.

"Thanks," Charlie said. "You're a far better teacher than the other guy."

Buster turned and handed the blade back to Lyra, hilt first.

"Thank you," she said as she sheathed the sword in her scabbard.

"What's happening over here?" Gretel asked.

"Uh . . . Buster here was teaching me a few sword fighting techniques," Charlie said.

The scruffy dog gave two thumbs-up, elbows up and one on each side of his smile.

"Teaching you, huh?" Gretel asked. "I'm sure he's far better than *Mister grumpy pirate* back there."

"He's a far better teacher," Charlie said.

Gretel shrugged her shoulders and crossed her arms. She leaned against the edge of the wheelhouse. "Don't worry about Cy. He's . . . he's showing off. He's a little salty right now."

"Salty about what?" Charlie asked.

Lyra smiled at Nessa. They held each other's gaze for a moment, as if having an unspoken conversation.

Lyra turned to Charlie. "There may be a new greatest swordswoman in the realm. I put him through a rigorous contest."

"Hopefully not too rigorous," Charlie said with a smile. "I should've trained with you instead."

Nessa smiled at Charlie. "You'll do fine. Don't worry."

Charlie shrugged his shoulders. "I hope so."

"Don't hope; know so," Lyra said. "Go in with confidence, and you'll be far better off than if you have doubt."

Charlie pounded a loose fist into his palm as he would to a baseball mitt. Not too hard, but it made a sound. He distracted himself from his nerves.

"I know. I . . . I'm worried about the kids," Charlie said.

"I'm sure they'll be fine," Nessa said.

"I'm worried I'm not going to be good enough for them," Charlie said. "Like they can't count on me."

Nessa placed a hand on Charlie's shoulder. He stopped smacking his palm.

"Charlie, you're braving the dangers of Castle Verafell to save them without giving it a second thought. I don't think they'll be disappointed in you," Nessa said.

"Thanks," he said.

"What are you talking about up here?" Cyrus asked. "When I'm going to get my rematch? The deck was slippery, you know."

Nessa turned to face the pirate prince. "We're talking about how that was a cheap shot with the dirt in the eyes."

Cyrus jolted back and raised his arms. "What?" he asked. "It's a valid training technique. It was used against me. You always have to be ready. You don't want to get caught off guard or fall into some trap."

"Everyone, be quiet," Pierre shouted from above. His voice bellowed out from the open windows of the wheelhouse. "We're coming up on the fork to Shadowfell."

Everyone turned their attention to the bow of the boat.

The cliffs descended toward the shoreline. The trees and brushes grew dense, filled with shadows and prying eyes. Leaves and branches swayed, no doubt from the creatures that lurked among them. A fork in the river appeared. A divergent path in the water led into the heart of Shadowfell and toward Castle Verafell.

The bow of the boat turned, following along the river path. Up the river it went, deeper into the heart of the lands of shadows.

A silence fell over the crew and passengers. Only the splash of the paddlewheel and the puff of the smokestacks remained.

The shadows crept over the river from the tall, overgrown trees. Vines interconnected them like webs. An eerie silence descended. No birds chirped. No animals called or howled. Nothing but an unsettling stillness.

Lyra and Cyrus moved toward the front of the boat with their hands on the hilts of their swords.

The riverboat paddled its way up the river. The rising smoke from the stacks signaled their arrival to any onlookers.

Charlie's throat tightened. A bead of sweat ran down the back of his neck. His hand wasn't far from the hilt of his sword. His eyes shifted along the tree line, searching for any signs of movement. He didn't know the monsters' form or appearance, but he was ready. Ready as he would ever be.

Nessa leaned over to Charlie. "Welcome to Shadowfell," she said. "Let's hope it's an easy trip."

CHAPTER 18
THE BAKER'S DOZEN

An eerie chill ran down Charlie's back as fog rolled across the still, dark waters. The tumbling vapor billowed out, shrouding what lurked below the surface. The riverboat glided down the river, surrounded by a forest of darkness. The thick canopy trees blocked out the sun above. Glimpses of the ruined citadel rose high above the trees.

Everyone was quiet. The forest was quiet with no signs of life. Only the sound of the paddlewheel splashing in the water and the puff from the smokestacks broke through the silence. All eyes were on the tree lines—monitoring, waiting for any signs of movement.

Lyra and Cyrus were stationed at the front of the boat. Lyra's hand was on her sword, ready to strike at a moment's notice. Cyrus turned and pointed to the wheelhouse. He motioned with his hand to a spot along the bank. The captain saluted with two fingers before turning the wheel toward the shore.

"We go by foot from here," Cyrus said as he moved toward the back of the boat.

The group followed.

Pierre slowed the boat to a near standstill. He reversed toward an opening along the bank. A small alcove was along the shoreline. A dirt path, carved into the cliffside bank, led up into the dark forest— a suitable spot to make landfall.

Mac and Buster lifted the ramp. Their rubber-like arms elongated and strained as they hoisted it over the side. Half-pint rushed to help lift it. It splooshed into the waterlogged embankment below.

Nessa and Lyra opened the animal pen.

"Leave them," Cyrus said.

"We'll need them," Nessa replied.

"They'll hold us back," Cyrus said. "We need to be quick on our feet. Besides, the forest is thick with overgrowth. They'll slow us down."

Nessa closed the pen, locking the door. The unicorns grunted in protest.

"I know. I know," Nessa said. "We'll be back. You'll be safe here."

Smoke billowed out of the pipe stack. Pierre trudged down the stairs from the wheelhouse.

"Thank you," Charlie said. "I can't thank you enough."

Pierre grunted. "Don't go tellin' everyone. It could ruin my reputation."

Charlie smiled.

Pierre glanced toward Cyrus. "Pirate rules?"

Cyrus pounded his fist against his chest twice. "Pirate rules."

They smacked each other on the forearms, clasping down. They shook each other's arms.

"You're looking good without the peg leg," Cyrus said.

Pierre laughed. "You're looking good without the silly hat you used to wear."

"Hey," Cyrus said, letting go of Pierre's arm. "I liked that hat."

"It was silly," Nessa said. "It was big and frizzy and wide. That feather was too much."

Pierre pointed to the princess with his thumb. "See, the princess agrees with me."

Gretel touched her hand to Cyrus' back. "If it matters, I love the hat," she said. "You should wear it more often."

"Thank you," Cyrus said in a low tone.

Pierre glanced over his shoulder, back down the river. "We'll be waiting for you right up the river."

Cyrus turned toward the ramp. One by one, they walked down the wooden ramp, splashing onto the shore below. Lyra led the way, hand on her hilt, followed by Cyrus and Gretel. Half-pint shook the hands of each crew member before disembarking behind Nessa. Charlie was the last one on the boat.

He rubbed the back of his head. "I . . . ah . . ." He struggled to find the words. "It's been an honor and a pleasure. Thank you."

"Go on," Mac said. "Get those kids. We'll be waiting."

Charlie proceeded down the ramp into the mud below. His leather boots sank into the soft earth. The dirt relented, giving up its newly trapped possession as he climbed up to higher ground. He bent over, crawling on all fours to make it up the steep embankment.

Charlie turned to face the boat. The ramp lifted above the edge. The smokestacks puffed in rapid succession. The paddlewheel rotated, and the riverboat glided back up the river. Buster popped his head over the railing, waving his rubbery arm back and forth.

Charlie waved back as the boat disappeared around the river bend. His heart skipped a beat. There was no more delaying the inevitable. The dark forest waited.

"We need to get moving," Cyrus said, taking lead of the group.

"What are pirate rules?" Charlie asked.

"If we don't return by sunset, they can leave and keep the horses in place of the gold," Nessa said.

Charlie glanced at her, his eyebrows narrowing in confusion.

Nessa shrugged. "What do you expect dealing with a former pirate? Come on."

"Don't worry," Gretel said. "We'll be back before supper time. Well . . . hopefully." She winked at Charlie.

The group trekked deeper into the forest. The trees were gnarled and twisted. A black, inky darkness pulsated between cracked fissures. Holes in the bark formed faces, screaming out in agony. Some trees were completely devoid of leaves. Others were so overgrown with vines and weeds that it was as if they were being hauled down into the earth.

Lyra and Cyrus drew their swords, hacking their way through the undergrowth.

"So, what's the plan?" Charlie asked. "We're going to march right in?"

"We'll figure that out when we get there," Cyrus said. "Anybody have ideas on what to expect?"

Nessa tripped. A brown vine twisted around her foot. She stumbled and fell into the soft earth below.

Cyrus and Lyra both stopped, turning back.

Charlie rushed in, grabbing her arms. "Are you okay?"

"I'm fine," she said.

He lifted her. Nessa dusted herself off. Splashes of mud covered her black leather vest.

Cyrus glared at him. Charlie glared back.

"You tripping the princess back there?" Cyrus asked.

"I tripped over a vine," Nessa said.

"Well, be careful. This place is full of things itching to grab you." Cyrus turned and continued forging a path through the underbrush.

Small glimpses of the castle became visible as they moved forward. Stone walls had fallen into disrepair and ruin. The land had reclaimed what was once a thriving kingdom. There were stone outlines of houses long gone. Only their foundations remained, claimed by the twisting, gnarled vines.

Charlie's heart raced and beat against his chest. There wasn't a sound. Nothing. It was eerily quiet. Too quiet for his liking. Not a bird or beast or the snap of a twig.

"Do you hear that?" Gretel asked.

"Hear what?" Cyrus replied.

"The voices," Gretel said. "I hear the voices."

The group paused. Each party member scanned their surroundings. No one said a word.

"I don't hear anything," Nessa said.

"The voices are soft. Childlike," Gretel said, a hint of panic in her voice. "I've heard them before."

Charlie turned around. The leaves blew in the slight breeze. Nothing else moved.

"I hear them," Half-pint said. "They're laughing. It's like children laughing."

"It's the dark forest," Cyrus said. "It's playing tricks on our minds."

Charlie's breathing became shallow. He couldn't hear anything.

"I hear it too," Lyra said. "Like chittering in the distance."

A twig snapped.

They all drew their weapons and turned toward the sound. A shadow moved behind a tree, about the size of Half-pint from Charlie's quick glimpse.

"What is it?" Charlie whispered.

"I don't know," Nessa replied.

"Oh, it can't be," Gretel said. Her chest rose and fell in rapid succession. "It can't be. Not again."

Charlie turned toward Gretel. "What is it?"

Her breathing became uncontrollable. Gretel hunched over, gasping for air. Nessa swooped in, placing a hand on her back.

"Gretel, what is it?" Nessa asked.

After a few more quick breaths, Gretel rose. Her eyes fixated on the trees. Her hand tightened around the end of her dagger. "It's gingerbread men," she said.

The chittering sounds grew louder, deeper. The forest growled beyond the trees. Small, cookie-like hands appeared from behind the trees. Circular, flat faces emerged with jagged white eyebrows over white dotted eyes. They had white lines for mouths that formed jagged teeth.

As tall as Half-pint, the gingerbread man appeared from behind the tree, brandishing a red-and-white striped candy cane for a weapon. The tip was sharpened to a point. Then another gingerbread man appeared, followed by another—all armed. More and more emerged, encircling the group.

The six members huddled up and circled around, shoulder to shoulder. Charlie gulped as the gingerbread men emerged from their hidden locations.

"How many are there?" Nessa asked.

"I count twelve," Lyra said.

The earth shook and tumbled as something approached. The trees shook with each stomp. Two trees were pushed aside as the gingerbread monstrosity appeared, twice the height of Charlie. It bellowed out a deafening scream.

Charlie's mouth dropped as his eyes traced up the monstrosity's body toward its gingerbread face. "Make it a baker's dozen."

"Half-pint," Cyrus said. "Teach that giant rule number two."

"Got it," he replied. The imp snapped his fingers and disappeared. A cloud of smoke was left behind. He reappeared, holding onto the giant's head.

"Glitterbomb," Half-pint said. He flung a metallic cloud at its white eyes.

The giant gingerbread man's eyes closed in a flat line. He swung an arm at his assailant. With a snap of his fingers, Half-pint disappeared into a cloud of smoke. The giant gingerbread man struck himself in the face. The earthy, brown cookie fell backward. It shook the earth as it crashed. The weight shattered it into pieces. Broken tree stumps pierced through its body.

"Now!" Cyrus said.

They rushed the army of cookies before them. Cyrus' sword ran through one of the gingerbread man's body. Still moving, Cyrus kicked the gingerbread man backward. Freeing his blade, he struck again, severing it in half.

Nessa and Lyra stood back-to-back. They hacked away at two

that approached them. They parried the attacks from the candy canes. Each blow chipped away at the minty weapons.

Gretel leaped onto the back of one. She drove her dagger into its body over and over. Chunks of gingerbread sprayed out. "You won't take me again!" she yelled out a war cry scream. A few more strikes of her dagger, and the gingerbread body crumpled in pieces.

"Grets," Cyrus said, parrying an oncoming attack. "You okay over there?"

Gretel huffed and puffed. An elated smile appeared on her face. "I believe it's called pent-up aggression."

Charlie swung his sword, engaging in combat. He parried the blows of the candy cane weapon. Shuffling his feet back and forth, Charlie positioned himself for an opening. The gingerbread man gave none. On and on, he went—metal against peppermint.

"Do you have one yet?" Cyrus called out.

"Working on it," Charlie said. He parried another, but the candy cane slid up the sword. The pointed end ripped his sleeve. It didn't cut him, but it was close. Charlie let out a sigh of relief, then struck.

"I'm already up to five," Cyrus said.

"Good for you," Charlie shouted. Remembering rule number two, Charlie rolled on the ground. He avoided a stabbing strike from the gingerbread man.

Charlie slashed across his body, striking the cookie's leg. The blade tore through the gingerbread with ease. It fell forward, smashing into the ground.

Charlie sprang to his feet. He drove the blade into the back of the gingerbread man's head. He continued chipping away at the soft cookie. The gingerbread man was no more.

"That's one," Charlie shouted.

"Great," Cyrus replied. "I'm up to six." With a flourish, Cyrus stretched out. His leg kicked back. He stabbed at the head of another. "Make that seven."

Charlie huffed. Under his breath, he muttered, "Show-off."

"Cy, behind you!" Gretel shouted.

A gingerbread man leaped from the tree. It landed on Cyrus' outstretched leg. Both feet crashed down on his left ankle. Cyrus let out a scream. He fell to the ground.

The gingerbread man stood over the pirate prince, holding his spiked candy cane high, ready to strike. It lurched forward.

A dagger flew into its body.

Gretel sprinted over, leaping into the air. She kicked the gingerbread man in the chest. It fell back, dropping its weapon. Gretel leaped on top of it.

Gretel retrieved the dagger. She slammed it down on the last remaining gingerbread man. It tried to swing up at her. Gretel was quick to block it with her arm. She pierced its head. With rapid succession, it crumbled into pieces.

Cyrus clutched his now free ankle. Rolling in the dirt, he screamed through his closed teeth.

"I think that's all of them," Lyra said.

Cyrus screamed in agony.

Gretel turned back to him and rushed to his side. "What's hurt? Anything broken?"

"I don't know," Cyrus said. "It's my ankle."

Nessa and Charlie rushed to his side.

"Can you put weight on it?" Nessa asked.

"I don't know," Cyrus said. "That little thing landed right on it. Help me up."

Charlie and Gretel each grabbed an arm and lifted him to his feet. He kept his right foot on the ground. His left foot dangled in the air.

"Let me see if I can walk on it," Cyrus said. He lowered the foot. He let out an agonizing yelp.

"Cyrus, you can't walk on this," Nessa said. "Let's take you back to the boat."

"No!" Cyrus was quick to answer. "I can do this." He took another step, moaning as his foot bore his weight.

"Cy, you've done enough. You don't have to show off," Charlie said.

"I'm not showing off," he said. "I want to get those kids back."

"We will," Charlie said. "Let's get you back to the boat first."

"No," Cyrus said. "Pirate rules. You do as your captain says."

"I'm not under pirate rules," Half-pint said, reappearing in a puff of smoke. "We're on land, not a boat."

They all glared at the imp.

"What?" Half-pint asked, shrugging his shoulders.

Gretel positioned herself under one of Cyrus' arms. "Let's at least sit you down on that log, and I'll examine your foot."

Charlie helped carry Cyrus as he hobbled over toward a felled tree log. The group gathered round. Lyra turned to face behind the group, sword at the ready. Cyrus sat down and raised his left leg. Gretel dropped to a knee and held his foot in her hands.

"Easy," Cyrus winced.

"I need to take it off," Gretel said.

Cyrus shifted his position on the log. He stretched out his leg, leaning back. "Do it. I can take the pain."

He grunted as Gretel removed the leather boot. She rolled up his pant leg and removed his white stocking. His ankle swelled to twice its normal size—a grotesque blend of purple, red, and blue.

"My stars," Nessa said.

"It's fine," Cyrus said as he attempted to stand.

Gretel pushed him back down on the log. "Sit back down, Captain."

He plopped back onto the log.

Gretel held his ankle in both hands. She pressed against the sides with her thumbs. "Does it hurt there?"

Cyrus grunted.

"I'll take that as a yes," Gretel replied. She repositioned her hands, placing her thumbs on the top of the foot. "Does it hurt here?"

Cyrus shook his head.

"Move it up and down for me," Gretel said.

Cyrus did as instructed, waving the foot back and forth. He bit his lip, chomping down with every movement of the foot.

"Hurt?" Gretel asked again.

"No," he replied. A slight moan revealed his lie.

"I can't let you go in there with a swollen ankle," Gretel said.

Cyrus leaned forward. His eyebrows narrowed, furrowing his brow in a deep scowl. "Patch it up or saw it off. Either way, I'm going in there."

"Cy, if you can't make it—" Nessa said.

"I said I'm going in there," Cyrus said. "So, patch it up or saw it off. Either way."

"Alright. Don't be so dramatic." Gretel turned her focus to Charlie, pointing off to the remnants of their battle. "Get me one of those candy canes. Break it in half equally."

Charlie sprinted toward a pile of crumbled cookies. He plucked up the candy cane weapon. Holding both ends, he kicked up his knee and snapped it like a twig. He rushed back.

"Two halves," Charlie said, handing them to Gretel.

"Place them on both sides of his ankle," Gretel said. "Anyone have cloth or something to wrap it with?"

Nessa untied her bandana and handed it to Gretel. "Here, take this."

Charlie placed the peppermint sticks on either side of Cyrus' foot, going up his leg. Gretel wrapped the bandana around the makeshift splints and the foot, securing it in place on his leg. She pulled the stocking back up his leg, securing everything in place.

Gretel focused on Cyrus. "I might have to cut the boot to get it on."

"Don't cut my boot," Cyrus said. "That's my lucky boot."

"My cousin twice removed on my mother's side is a shoemaker," Half-pint said. "We can always get you a new one."

Cyrus locked eyes with Gretel. "Don't cut my boot. Captain's orders."

Gretel's eyes softened and glistened. "This might hurt."

"It's okay. You won't hurt me." Cyrus picked up a stick lying on the log. "Shove my foot in there, but don't cut my boot." He shoved the stick into his mouth and bit down.

"Here we go." Gretel held onto both sides of the boot and shoved it onto his foot.

Cyrus bellowed out in agony, clamping down onto the wooden stick. The boot stretched and fought against the makeshift candy cane splint. Gretel wrapped her fingers around the top of the boot. She shoved a few more times, only meeting resistance.

Cyrus gnashed his teeth against the wooden stick.

"Almost there," Gretel said. With a final tug, the boot slipped into place. "All done."

Cyrus removed the stick. Teeth marks were etched into the broken branch.

"Can you walk on it?" Nessa asked.

"Let me see," Cyrus said. He pushed off the log and stood on his right leg. He placed the foot down, toes first and then the heel. Cyrus stepped forward with a limp. He gritted his teeth and took a few more wobbles forward. "I can manage."

"Are you sure?" Charlie said.

Cyrus snickered. "You think I'd let you show me up by not finishing?" He stumbled forward, hobbling and limping over to retrieve his sword. "Come on, we've got kids to rescue."

CHAPTER 19
OUT IN THE OPEN

The earth had attempted to reclaim the ruins of Castle Verafell. Vines covered the once mighty structure of the keep. Turrets, towers, and spires were missing chunks of stone, left in ruin and decay, as if some unseen force blew the top off the keep and scattered the remains. What remained cast a shadow over the land—cold, heartless, and unwelcoming to Charlie and his rescue party.

The group reached the edge of the tree line. The gaping maw of the entrance stood before them. An open drawbridge invited them inside. There were no guards. No watchmen. Only the twisted vines that wrapped around the citadel.

"This feels like a trap," Charlie said in a low voice.

"Of course it's a trap," Nessa replied. "Why else would he invite us here?"

The group scanned the area, searching for any other opening that could lead them into the castle.

"I'm not seeing any other way in," Cyrus said. He leaned against a tree as a crutch, with his ankle in the air.

"Maybe we should circle around the back," Lyra said. "There could be another way in."

"It would take too much time," Gretel said. "Besides, how's the ankle holding up?"

"It's fine. Thanks for asking," Cyrus said.

They smiled at each other.

"Thanks for taking care of it. The brace helps," Cyrus added.

"Don't mention it," Gretel said. "I need my head of security in tip-top shape."

Charlie scanned the area around the base of the castle. He searched for an opening or a grate that led underneath. "Perhaps we could go through a sewer or something."

"No, the sewer could be too dangerous," Nessa said. "Who knows what's down there?"

"There can't be much down there," Charlie said.

"One time, we found a colony of rats the size of dogs in our sewers," Nessa said.

Charlie glanced at the princess, one eye narrowed and the other arched in confusion. Charlie couldn't tell if she was telling a tall tale or the truth. "You serious?"

"Oh, yeah," she said.

"Our guards were terrified of going into the sewers for months," Lyra said.

"Little . . . little dogs or like big Saint Bernards?" Charlie asked.

Nessa locked eyes with Charlie. She let the pause linger before speaking. "The size of Half-pint."

"I wanted to name one Fluffy," Half-pint said.

Charlie drifted his attention back to the base of the castle. The thought of encountering massive rats cleared his mind of any tactical ideas. "Okay. No sewers," Charlie said. "What else do you have? I can't stop thinking about those rats."

"Too bad we couldn't fly up there," Half-pint said. "We could try to get in through one of those windows. Or the gaping holes."

Cyrus rubbed his chin. "I'm not exactly in the condition to climb. So that idea is ruled out."

Charlie pondered the various ways to get inside the castle. They couldn't climb because of an injured ankle. The sewer was too dangerous. They couldn't fly. But the front door was wide open and unguarded. There was no other way.

"Forget this," Charlie said. He stepped forward into the clearing before a hand snatched his arm and stopped him.

"What are you doing?" Cyrus whispered.

Charlie yanked his arm away from Cyrus' grasp and turned to the group. "He knows we're here," he said. "He's allowing us to come in. There are no guards out front. No signs of those pumpkin monsters that attacked the castle. No more gingerbread men. He wants us to go through the front door."

"Charlie, we need to think this through," Nessa said. "We can't wander right in. They could be waiting to ambush us."

"If it's an ambush, you want to march in and spring it?" Cyrus said.

"Do you have any better ideas?" Charlie asked. He raised his arms and swiftly smacked the side of his legs. "I'm all ears."

"I'm not sure about going through the front door," Gretel said. She shifted her eyes back and forth between the members of the rescue party. "That sort of turned out badly for me last time."

"I've been thinking this through," Charlie said. "We got attacked by a roving band of cookies. We have a pirate who can barely walk on a bum ankle."

"Hey!" Cyrus said. "I don't have a bum ankle."

Gretel shrugged. "You kind of do."

Charlie patted his chest. "If he can sense outsiders, I've got to be glowing like the sun to him. Rumple knew I was an outsider, and he had no idea about the mirror. This King of Verafell knew the moment we went up the river. Those gingerbread men were a test to see if he could take what he wants from us. Congratulations, we passed."

Lyra and Nessa glanced at each other, tilting their heads and arching their eyebrows.

Charlie turned back toward the castle, eyes focused on the open drawbridge. "There are no guards outside. He wants us to come through the front door. Well, I'm going to give him what he wants and walk through that front door."

Half-pint nudged Nessa. "He has a point."

Charlie lifted his sword and pointed at the castle with the blade. "I'm walking through these doors. You can go around or go up or go under if you want. I'm facing this head-on." He glanced back at the group. "Whatever it takes."

"Fine," Nessa said. "I'm going with you." She stepped into the clearing.

Lyra followed her. "If you're going, then I'm going."

"Oh, you've got to be kidding me," Cyrus said. "Can we at least think about this? You don't live long as a pirate by making foolish decisions."

"Well, it's a good thing I'm not a pirate, so I can make those foolish decisions," Charlie said.

The imp disappeared and reappeared next to the trio in the clearing.

Cyrus rolled his eyes. "Fantastic."

Gretel placed a hand on Cyrus' shoulder. "If it makes you feel better, I'm with you," she said with a smile.

Cyrus smiled back. "You always have my back, Grets."

"Someone needs to protect you," she said. With Cyrus' arm around her shoulders, Gretel helped Cyrus hobble into the clearing with the rest of the group.

Cyrus inhaled. He puckered his lips and lingered on the exhale, almost whistling. "Well, do you have a plan, Mister fool?"

Charlie ignored him. Cyrus was trying yet again to get under his skin. He had been trying ever since they met. He'd prefer to let it slide, but the constant one-upmanship and berating tore at his sanity. Like his sister. They both pushed and pushed and pushed.

Charlie gave his sister a longer leash, but not the pirate prince. He had a short plank over Charlie's sea of anger.

Charlie turned to face him, stepping right up to the pirate prince. "I do. I might be foolish, but I'm going to march right into this castle. I'm going to find him. Then, I'm going to stab him in his stupid pumpkin head. Now, you and your bum ankle can either come with me or turn chicken and run."

Cyrus pushed Charlie against his chest. "Who are you calling chicken?"

Charlie stumbled backward for a moment and then charged right back at him, bumping chest to chest.

Cyrus wobbled on his one good foot.

"I'm calling you chicken!" Charlie yelled.

"Boys. Boys," Nessa said, rushing in to separate them, pushing them away from each other. "Will you two knock it off?"

Cyrus pointed at Charlie over Nessa's shoulder, acting as if she was holding him back.

Charlie recognized his ruse. Cyrus could barely stand on one foot, let alone take on Charlie in another duel.

"You're lucky I came with you on this fool's errand," Cyrus said. "I don't need this. I don't need any of this. I'm leaving." Cyrus let go of Gretel, turned, and hobbled back toward the trees. He bounced on one leg a few times. He stumbled, nearly slipping to the ground. Cyrus groaned in pain as his bad foot planted on the ground.

"Cyrus!" Gretel said.

"Good. Go," Charlie said.

"Charlie!" Nessa said as she jogged after Cyrus. She ducked in front of him. "Cyrus, wait!"

"What?" Cyrus asked. "You got what you wanted."

Nessa placed her free hand on her hip, tilting her head. "And what's that?"

Cyrus turned and pointed his sword at Charlie. "Did you come back to rub it in my face?"

Nessa let out a sigh. "Cyrus, we need you," she said in a soothing voice, far lower in volume than the previous conversation.

"That's all you do. Need me," Cyrus said. "Use me."

"Hey, buddy, I don't know what your problem is with me, but I'll throw down right now," Charlie said. He took a fighting stance. "Come on. Let's settle this once and for all. Don't think I've forgotten about your little glove slap."

"You want to go?" Cyrus asked. He hobbled toward Charlie. "Let's go."

"Cyrus, stop!" Gretel said, moving in front of him to impede his progress.

Cyrus pointed the blade at Charlie. "I can take you on with one good ankle!" he shouted.

"Will you three shut up!" Lyra yelled.

Everyone stopped and turned their attention toward the normally reserved bodyguard.

"You're all acting like babies when children are in danger," Lyra said. "I've had enough of this."

Lyra pointed her sword toward Cyrus. "You!" she said. "Nessa is perfectly capable of making her own choices. If you don't agree with it, then that's on you. Don't think for a moment you can control her. She wants who she wants."

"I wasn't trying to control her," Cyrus said.

"Shut it!" Lyra said. "You're so blinded by your hatred for Charlie that you don't realize what you have. Someone standing right next to you. Someone who helped you. Cared for you. Took you in. Bandaged your ankle!"

Cyrus' eyes drifted to the woman in front of him. Gretel smiled back at him, her eyes beaming. Cyrus' lips curled, first into a half-smile and then ear to ear.

Lyra turned her blade toward Charlie. "You," she said.

Charlie took a step back, raising his free hand to his chest.

"You act as if Nessa was sitting by that mirror all this time, waiting for you to return," Lyra said. "I've got news for you. She was living an entirely separate life for those twenty years. She spent more of her life here than on the other side of that mirror. She had relationships. She has responsibilities. Nessa is the princess, the soon-to-be queen of a kingdom. If you still can't handle it, then that's on you."

"Thank you," Nessa said.

Lyra turned the blade toward Nessa. "And *you*! All you do is mope around the castle. Yes, running the kingdom is hard. Being a leader is hard. People aren't going to like you for your decisions. That comes with the job. Start acting like a leader."

Nessa lowered her head.

Lyra lowered the blade to her side. "You aren't King Aric or Queen Valeria. You're too obsessed with trying to be them. Stop comparing yourself to them. You're Princess Nessa. Do things your way, not theirs."

Nessa locked eyes with Lyra once again.

Lyra motioned toward the castle with her blade. "You stand in the shadow of Castle Verafell, braving the dark forest. They would have never done this. The King and Queen would have sent battalions of soldiers to rescue those children, while staying in the castle keep. Yet here you are." Lyra paused. "That's pretty . . . punk for a princess."

"She's right," Charlie said.

"Shut it," Lyra said. "I'm not finished."

Charlie covered his mouth with his free hand, averting his face from Lyra's gaze.

Lyra lowered her voice from a shout. "If you're afraid of doing it all by yourself, then look around you."

Nessa glanced from Lyra to Cyrus and Gretel. Her gaze then met Half-pint and Charlie before landing on Lyra.

"There are more people that care about you besides the King and Queen," Lyra said. "I've been by your side through thick and thin these past twenty years. We're all standing by your side now."

Lyra glanced at the ground, pausing for a moment. "Yes, you lost people. We all lose people, but there are still others there to help. People who deeply care. The King and Queen weren't beloved because they did it all themselves. They were beloved because they trusted in other people."

The group stood in stunned silence. Their eyes shifted to each other as if waiting to see who was brave enough to speak first. Charlie refused to be the person to speak first.

"I would like to point out that she didn't say your highness," Half-pint said, breaking the silence.

Everyone glowered at him.

He removed his hat, holding it in front of his chest like a shield.

Nessa turned back toward Lyra. "You're right. You're right. We lost sight of why we're here." She paused for a moment. "We were too caught up in the fear of our own personal baggage, and we forgot about the children. That includes me too."

Lyra lowered her sword. "I apologize, Your Highness. I was out of line."

Nessa shook her head. "Don't. That's how I want you to treat me from now on. Speak freely, and keep me in check. I've been so obsessed with trying to be like King Aric and Queen Valeria, I forgot who I was."

"And who's that?" Charlie asked.

Nessa smiled at him. "A rebellious pop-punk princess who does things on her own terms."

Nessa turned to the party. Her head raised upward, and her shoulders pulled back. She had an aura of confidence. "As Princess of Glimmerfell and leader of this rescue mission, I've taken everyone's concerns into consideration. After giving it some thought and considering the state of our party, I believe Charlie is right. We should go through the front door."

Charlie glanced toward the pirate prince. Cyrus bobbed his head, never taking his eyes off Gretel. She smiled back at him before resuming her position under his arm.

"Alright, Princess," Cyrus said. "Lead the way. Let's go get those kids."

"Charlie," Nessa said. "I want you and Lyra on point. You're the best two swordsmen we have right now."

"I would protest, but my ankle won't let me," Cyrus said.

Charlie cracked a half-smile. Swords by their sides, he and Lyra strode toward the downed drawbridge. The group followed as fast as Cyrus could move.

The boards creaked and moaned with every step, slick and covered in moss. The twisted vines that weaved in and out of the wooden planks of the drawbridge provided enough room to step comfortably. They also served as a warning to those who entered. Shadows enveloped the gaping maw of an entrance.

They proceeded inside the ruined castle, toward the awaiting monsters. Toward his niece and nephew.

CHAPTER 20
IN THE HALLS OF CASTLE VERAFELL

Darkness enveloped them. Charlie's eyes struggled to make out what laid in wait ahead of them. His sight was already strained from the shadows of the forest. The dark halls made it worse. The soles of his boots nearly slipped on the stone floor, wet with mildew. The twisting vines crawled up the entrance walls.

He breathed in and out. His heart raced. Each step brought him closer to his niece and nephew. The sword trembled in his hand. He closed his eyes and took a deep breath to still his mind. He focused on why he was in the castle.

Ginny. Tyler.

Their smiling, happy faces filled his mind. He was close. They were here. He needed to find them.

He opened his eyes. Multiple doorways led in different directions, carved in the stone walls. Tattered tapestries peeked through the crisscrossing vines. They begged to be free.

The ceiling stretched high in the cavernous halls. Small torches blazed with an eerie yellowish-green flame. They lit the path forward like a sickly trail of breadcrumbs. The torches stretched deeper into the hall of Castle Verafell.

This must be what Half-pint feels like.

"If you held kids for ransom, where would you hold them?" Nessa asked.

"The dungeon," Lyra answered. "We should go down."

"No," Cyrus said. "That's too obvious. Easy trap."

"Up high?" Half-pint said. "Like in one of the towers?"

Charlie scanned his memory of the various stories from this realm that he knew well. They all held a similar fate—kids under extreme duress, held prisoner by a monstrous force. They weren't locked away and hidden. They were with the monster themselves, forced to face their fears.

"He's got them with him," Charlie said. He focused down the dark hallway.

"How do you know?" Lyra asked.

Charlie shrugged. "A feeling."

"A feeling?" Cyrus asked. "You want us to follow a feeling?"

"Charlie's right," Gretel said. "I was held close when I was taken."

"See," Charlie said, pointing at Gretel. "In most of the stories of the dark woods, the children were held close. Better to keep an eye on them."

Cyrus leaned over to Gretel. "Are you certain?" he whispered.

Gretel locked eyes with him. "I'm positive."

Cyrus moved past the group. Gretel followed beside him. The pair trekked deeper into the castle.

"Alright. Let's go spring the trap and rescue these kids," Cyrus said.

"Hey," Charlie said.

Cyrus glanced back to face his one-time foe.

"I'm sorry about earlier," Charlie said. "I'm concerned for the children, and I acted out of anger."

"Save it," Cyrus said. "We'll both apologize when we're done."

Nessa leaned over to Charlie. She whispered, "Ah, you two made up."

"I still owe him a slap," Charlie whispered back. He winked at Nessa.

The group ventured deeper into the halls of Castle Verafell. The vines led the way, as if they were left as guides for the group to follow. They crawled and sprawled out on the floors and walls. Their heart-like leaves pointed the way, deeper into the castle.

Charlie's heart beat faster and faster the further they went. The sound of leather boots against stone echoed. Torches flickered. The sun's light at the entrance became a distant point. The darkness engulfed them the further they traveled.

Two large, black wooden doors greeted the group. They nearly reached to the height of the ceiling, at least two stories high. Towering and imposing, they invoked a sense of dread for what was held on the other side.

"Should we knock?" Cyrus asked in a hushed voice.

Charlie searched the area for any additional weapons they could use. The halls were barren. Only the torches and vines littered the landscape. Whatever treasures the castle once held were lost with time.

"We need a plan," Nessa whispered. "We can't waltz right in there."

Charlie glanced down at the imp. "That's exactly what we're going to do."

Cyrus sighed, tilting his head backward. "Why do I have a sinking feeling about this?"

"Half-pint, we need you to turn invisible," Charlie whispered.

"I can do that," he replied.

"What's that going to do?" Nessa asked in a low voice.

Charlie kneeled to the ground. "We'll enter and distract this King of Verafell," he said, drawing five circles on the stone floor. "Half-pint will circle around and free the kids from whatever he's keeping them in."

"What if it's locked?" Gretel asked. "What if they're chained up?"

"I can poof them out," Half-pint said. "No problem."

Charlie traced a line across his makeshift drawing. "Half-pint will poof them back to us. Then we make our escape," Charlie said as he stood. "We only have to outrun them."

"Outrun them?" Cyrus asked. "He has a whole forest of creatures and who knows what at his disposal. And I'm on a bum ankle."

"I'll poof you too," Half-pint said.

"No one is poofing me," Cyrus said.

"Do you have a better idea? Because now is the time to say it," Charlie said. He paused and raised his hands. "I ask with the utmost sincerity. I'm not trying to be condescending. Do you have anything?"

The pirate rubbed his chin. "What if . . . what if we pull a fast one on him? We give him something else. This thing he wants . . . he's never seen it. Right?"

"He'll figure it out," Charlie said.

"By that time, we'll be long gone," Cyrus said.

"What do you have in mind?" Charlie asked.

Cyrus reached into his pouch. "What does everyone have on them?"

"Besides you?" Gretel asked, winking at Cyrus. "Nothing of value. I traveled light."

"Gold," Nessa said.

"I had a few things, but they're in my saddlebags," Lyra said.

"More glitter," Half-pint said, delving his hands into his pockets. "I can glitterbomb them."

"I appreciate that, Half-pint, but I need you to focus on getting the kids out," Charlie said. "Nothing else."

"Gotcha," Half-pint said, withdrawing his hands from his pockets.

Charlie glanced at Cyrus. "I've got nothing," Charlie said, patting his chest and legs.

Cyrus retrieved a necklace hidden under his shirt—a shiny gold ring on the end of a thin band of black leather. He yanked on the necklace, breaking the ring free. "Take this," he said.

"A ring?" Charlie asked.

Cyrus glanced toward Nessa. "A wedding ring." He paused for a moment and then focused on Gretel. "I no longer need that one."

Nessa shied away, turning her back to the group. She breathed in deeply. After a moment, she straightened and faced the group. She nodded at Charlie. Charlie returned the gesture.

"Okay, we have something to bargain with," Charlie said as he placed the ring in his pants pocket. "We give him the ring. Half-pint gets the kids. We run like crazy."

"Everyone ready?" Nessa asked.

Half-pint turned invisible. Cyrus limped forward as Gretel held onto his shoulder. Lyra raised her sword, tip at the ready to strike.

"Here goes everything," Charlie said. He pounded on the black wooden doors.

Bang. Bang. Bang.

Both doors crept open inward. A yellowish-green light spilled into the hallway. The doors stopped midway. The gap was large enough for them to pass through.

"Lead the way, Charlie," Nessa whispered.

Charlie entered a cavernous hall. Columns of stone rose high and arched up to the ceiling. Torches lined the walls. Their yellowish-green hue bathed the area in a sickly, ghastly light. Two rows of pumpkin monstrosities lined a path leading toward a throne—a dozen pumpkin monsters in total.

A black throne, made of carved onyx stone, sat atop a dais. A pumpkin face, a jack-o'-lantern, rested on the seat of the throne. Teardrop eyes were carved into the rind. The mouth was full of jagged teeth. A flame roared inside.

"Uncle Charlie!" Ginny yelled.

"I knew you'd come rescue us," Tyler yelled.

Charlie's eyes found the children. They were locked in a cage to the side of the throne, large enough that the children could stand.

Twisted vines spiraled down from the ceiling, holding it aloft about a yard off the ground. Their faces pressed against the blackened metal bars. Ginny reached out for her uncle. Charlie held back every impulse to run to the children.

"Are you okay?" Charlie shouted. His voice cracked. "Are you hurt?"

"No," Tyler said. "I've been taking care of my sister."

"That's good," Charlie said. "You're a good brother."

"Help us, Uncle Charlie," Ginny said. Her arm stretched out between the bars.

"I'll be right there," he responded. "I need you two to stay put and be quiet for a moment."

The pumpkin monstrosities never moved. They were motionless and silent. Their carved eyes fixated on him. A flame burned bright behind their teardrop-shaped eyes.

Charlie glanced over his shoulder. The rest of his group was close behind. They formed a diamond-shaped pattern behind him, their swords held aloft. Gretel was side by side with Cyrus.

Charlie's heart raced. Adrenaline surged through his body. He needed to appear humble. His offering must be sincere. He sheathed his sword. Charlie couldn't give anything away.

Every ounce of his body told him to sprint to the children. To cut them down and free them from their prison. But the act must continue. Whoever this King of Verafell was needed to believe they were there to bargain.

There was no sign of a King of Verafell. Only the jack-o'-lantern on the throne. Was that the terrifying monster everyone was afraid of? A simple jack-o'-lantern?

Charlie scanned the chamber. If there was no King of Verafell, then how were these pumpkin monstrosities functioning? Why weren't they attacking? Something was off.

There was something else. Something hidden.

Charlie recalled his stories, searching for something deep within that could help explain what was happening or where his foe was hiding.

A jack-o'-lantern?

Charlie recalled the origin. Stingy Jack tricked a spirit and trapped him inside a jack-o'-lantern.

A spirit. The King of Verafell has to be a spirit.

Charlie snapped his attention toward the ceiling. Floating and circling above was a dark shade—a spirit. It had arms with dagger-like fingers and the floating torso of a man. A dark, billowing shadow enveloped his body. It roiled and turned, similar to a storm cloud. His legs were a trail of vapor.

He floated and circled above them. No doubt, he had studied their every move from the moment they entered through the double doors.

The King of Verafell wore a mask. No. A crown. A crown carved from the rind of a pumpkin and placed on his head. The crown gave his head form. Glowing, yellow eyes spilled forth through two carved openings in his crown. It stretched to what would be his nose.

This ghostly shade of darkness was the ruler of the castle. The terror of Shadowfell. The King of Verafell.

Charlie raised his arms into the air, palms facing the ceiling. "Your Highness, I've come to bargain," Charlie shouted.

The shade stopped. Though floating in the air, its shadow torso swirled like a storm cloud.

"There is no bargain," the shade yelled in a deep, unsettling voice —the voice of something otherworldly. "The way portal for the children."

"Yeah, well, I have it," Charlie said.

"Give it to me," the King of Verafell said, stretching out his shadow-like hand.

"The children first," Charlie said.

The shade floated down with grace and ease, a trail of vaporous smoke left behind. He floated above the rows of monsters. He tilted his head back and forth as if examining Charlie. Its eyes glowed a yellowish-green flame.

Charlie gulped. His stomach tightened in knots.

"I shall release them when I have the way portal in my possession," the King of Verafell growled.

Charlie shook his head, crossing his arms. He clicked his tongue against the roof of his mouth a few times. "No. No. No, that's not good enough," Charlie said. "The kids first."

"Go get him, Uncle Charlie," Ginny yelled. "Like the living room."

"We believe in you," Tyler said.

Charlie raised a finger to his lips, motioning for them to stay silent. The children buried their faces in between the bars of the cage. Their hands tightly wrapped around the darkened steel.

His companions were silent. Charlie glanced over his shoulder. Lyra, Cyrus, and Gretel fixated on the monsters before him. Nessa stared at the shade above him, her mouth agape. Her chest rose and fell as she quickly breathed in and out.

Charlie fixated on the jack-o'-lantern in front of him—the shade's source of power. Ending the shade might be easier than anticipated. If only he could tell Half-pint. He couldn't signal without giving it away. No, he'd have to be more tactful. Charlie would have to trick this spirit the same as Stingy Jack.

"Well, you see, I do have the way portal, as you call it," Charlie said. "How about an offer?"

"I take no offers," the King of Verafell said. "I only want the way portal."

"I want the children," Charlie replied. He pointed at the cage and then motioned to his side. "How about you bring them out? Bring them over here. Then we trade at the same time."

The shade floated, tilting its head back and forth, no doubt pondering his offer.

The cage rattled back and forth as if something moved atop it. Half-pint was in position.

Charlie smiled. He pulled back his shoulders and puffed out his chest. He stepped forward. "Bring the children to the center, and we'll exchange at the same time."

"Let me see the way portal," the King of Verafell said.

Charlie retrieved the ring from his pocket. He held it aloft between his thumb and index finger. "Here it is," Charlie said. "Now the kids."

"How does it work?" the King of Verafell asked. "How do you summon the portal to leave this realm?"

Charlie furled his eyebrows in confusion. "It's a . . . it's a ring. You put it on your finger, and then it will open the way portal."

The King of Verafell held out his hand.

"I showed you the way portal," Charlie said. "Now bring me the kids."

"Very well," the King of Verafell said. He snapped his fingers.

Charlie glanced toward the children. The cage door opened. Ginny and Tyler let go of the bars. The kids dangled a few feet from the ground.

Adrenaline surged and coursed through Charlie's veins. He held his breath, rotating his back foot toward the door. Charlie prepared to make a hasty exit.

Panic set in on the kids' faces. Their mouths were agape and their eyebrows arched wide. Charlie sensed their fear. They appeared unsure if they should jump. They hunched low, ready to jump down.

Charlie needed to act. He needed to give Half-pint the command. He gave a quick glance over his shoulder. Everyone was ready. Their bodies leaned toward the entrance.

"Half-pint, now!" Charlie yelled.

The imp appeared out of thin air. He reached into the cage. Grabbing the children's wrists, he vanished. They reappeared outside the double doors.

Charlie flung the ring toward the ceiling. "Here you go," Charlie yelled. He dashed for the door.

The King of Verafell screeched. It flew, snatching the ring mid-flight. He stopped, placing the ring on his finger. He waved it back and forth.

"It doesn't work," the King of Verafell shouted. "Seize them."

The group sprinted for the double doors. The kids and Half-pint were safely on the other side.

The vines sprouted from the walls. They grew, pushing the doors shut.

"Uncle Charlie!" Ginny yelled.

Charlie's heart dropped. They weren't going to make it. The doors were closing too fast.

"Get them out of here," Charlie yelled.

"We can't leave Uncle Charlie," Ginny cried.

Half-pint and the kids disappeared. The doors slammed shut. The echo reverberated through the halls.

Lyra and Nessa tugged on the door. The vines held the door shut tight.

"We're trapped," Nessa said. She glanced at Charlie, both immobilized with fear.

The footsteps of the pumpkin monsters closed in.

The entire group turned to face the pumpkin army. Charlie drew his sword. They held their weapons aloft, ready for their final stand.

CHAPTER 21
ALL TWISTED

The five of them stood with their backs to the door, swords out, ready to strike. Twelve pumpkin monsters fanned out and surrounded them. The shade screeched, circling above. Nessa never lost sight of the King of Verafell. She focused on his every movement. The billowing, vaporous trail spilled forth from his torso.

"This chicanery will not be tolerated," the King of Verafell said. "I want the way portal."

"We gave it to you," Nessa said. Her heart raced, thumping against her chest.

"Who speaks to me?" the King of Verafell asked.

Nessa stepped forward. "I'm Princess Nessa of Glimmerfell. You've attacked my kingdom and been a menace to my citizens. I'm here to defend my kingdom." She pointed her blade at the King of Verafell.

"Ah, the princess. We finally meet," the King of Verafell said. "My spies have told me a lot about you."

"Spies?" Nessa asked.

"The vines slowly engulfing your castle," the King of Verafell said. His voice was deep and unsettling, as if speaking from an unholy realm. "They listened to your words. They tracked your movements. They told me the way portal was open. That outsiders came to your kingdom. That I have my way home."

"Home?" Nessa asked.

"I'm not from this realm," the King of Verafell said. He shifted to the side of the group.

Nessa turned, following his movement.

Everyone else focused on the monstrosities before them.

"I seek to leave this land," the King of Verafell said. "The way portal reopened. It called out to me, as it did years ago."

"We gave it to you," Princess Nessa said. "It's yours to keep. Take it. We'll leave this castle."

The light of the King of Verafell dimmed. He removed the ring, throwing it down at her feet. "Put it on," the King of Verafell said. "Make it work."

Charlie bent down to retrieve the ring.

"No," the King of Verafell said, pointing to Nessa. "I want the princess."

Charlie straightened.

Nessa glanced at him, trying to think of anything that could help with the situation. Any potential solution. Any idea.

Charlie only blinked at her in return.

She gulped.

Cyrus, to her right, leaned in and whispered, "Now would be a good time if you have any ideas."

"Fresh out," she whispered back.

"Great plan," he whispered. "I love this crew. Rule number four: wing it."

Nessa sheathed her sword before bending over to retrieve the ring. Placed between her index finger and thumb, she rotated and examined it. A simple gold ring with an inscription on the inside.

For a Love Greater Than the Seas

Nessa closed her eyes. She couldn't bear to meet the eyes of her former betrothed as she placed the ring on her finger. His ring—his wedding ring.

Cyrus loved her, but she never truly loved him. Her heart always belonged to someone else—the one in the mirror. The one she spent years dreaming that he would one day return, and they'd be reunited. The man standing to her left. Her lifelong best friend. Charlie Grimm.

Nessa placed the ring on her right index finger. Designed for Cyrus, it was much too large for her. It didn't quite fit. It rolled around her finger, but it would do for now.

She took a deep breath and opened her eyes. Nessa held her hand aloft for the shade to see. "The problem is that you didn't say the magic words."

"The magic words?" the King of Verafell asked. "What words?"

"It's more of a hum than words," Charlie added.

Nessa glanced at Charlie. Her blue eyes met his brown eyes. An idea coursed through Nessa's mind. With a smile on her face, she bobbed her head from side to side. They need not speak a word. They knew what to do.

"Like a song," she said.

"Yeah, a song," Charlie said with a smile. "A song."

Nessa turned her focus back to the King of Verafell. Her eyes narrowed. A sly grin etched itself across half her face. "It goes like this . . ." Nessa started to hum.

Charlie joined in. They began to hum the tune from their childhood, the same song they had listened to over and over. Memories flooded her mind. She was no longer the Princess of Glimmerfell. In her mind, she was once again a pre-teen, dancing and bopping around in her room, with the song playing through her earbuds. She was at one end, and Charlie was at the other, both listening to the same song playing on her iPod.

"All the Small Things."

The two of them bopped up and down with the beat of the song.

As if from deep-rooted memory, the lyrics and rhythm spilled forth. Even though it was a song she hadn't heard in twenty years, it came back to her as if she had played it yesterday.

The two of them jumped around. Their bodies brushed against each other. Her eyes welled. Now, twenty years later, it was as if they were reliving that memory. She and Charlie, back in her bedroom, earbuds in, and bopping around. They stood shoulder to shoulder with smiles across their faces. She kicked and flared out her feet to the beat of the song. It was heaven.

They couldn't continue the song forever, no matter how much Nessa's soul longed for the two of them to keep going. She had to think of something, some excuse as to why nothing had happened. As they finished their musical concert, Nessa flailed her arms in the air.

"Ahhhh . . ." she said. Her voice trailed off. "I see the way portal. It opened for me, but I'm not going through. No, I choose to stay here." She pulled the ring off her finger.

"See, that's all you had to do," Charlie said. "Hum that tune, and the way portal will open."

"There was no portal," the King of Verafell said.

"Only I saw it because I wore the ring," Nessa said. "It appears before you, and you step through. You have to hum the right tune, though."

The flames in the King of Verafell's eyes dimmed. He glared at Nessa and then at Charlie. The throne room fell silent.

Her heart thumped against her chest. Their ruse fell apart with every passing moment lingering in the silence. A bead of sweat rolled down the back of her neck.

The flames in the King of Verafell's eyes roared with a fierce blaze. He pointed at both of them. "Charlatans," he said. "This will not stand."

Slithering vines wrapped around their feet and ankles. They yanked everyone up before they could react. Hoisted high in the air, the ground was now below Nessa's head. Nessa's sword fell from its scabbard. It clanged off the stone floor.

Gretel screamed. Cyrus let out a groan, no doubt from the strain on his ankle.

Lyra, Gretel, and Cyrus hacked away at their vines. They were quickly overcome. Their wrists were wrapped and pulled from their bodies. They struggled to free themselves. The vines gave no ground. They snaked up their arms. Their torsos, necks, and mouths were wrapped like a cocoon. Only their muffled voices could be heard as they struggled to free themselves.

Vines wrapped around Nessa's and Charlie's wrists and arms. Swinging herself, Nessa reached for Charlie as he reached for her.

The vines constricted her body. It was difficult to breathe. "Charlie!" Nessa shouted.

"Nessa!" he shouted back.

Their fingertips touched, trying to draw each other closer. The vines struggled and tightened to keep them separated. Nessa pushed with all her might. Their fingertips danced once more.

"I love you, Nessa," Charlie said.

"I love you too, Charlie," she replied. "I'm sorry. I'm sorry for everything."

"Don't—" The vines muffled his mouth, sealing it shut.

The vines coiled around her mouth, constricting like a snake. She tried to speak, but she couldn't. Horror and tears came to her eyes. Her blue eyes found Charlie's brown eyes—soft eyes, not furled eyebrows or eyebrows raised in fear. No. Reassuring eyes. Eyes that conveyed it was okay.

She pressed harder against the vines, reaching deeper into his hand. With all the strength she could muster, she stretched out once more. They dug their fingertips into each other's palms. They curled their fingers as if to pull their hands closer. They clasped their hands around each other.

If this was the end, then they would go out holding each other's hands.

"And now, princess, I shall tear you apart, limb by limb," the King of Verafell said. "I'll start with your friends as you listen to their anguished wails. Once I'm finished, I will then claim your kingdom. I will find the way portal myself."

Cyrus, Gretel, and Lyra's muffled screams pierced Nessa's ears as the vines pulled their wrists. Nessa screamed, only to be silenced by the vines. She tugged her arms to fight back. The more she struggled, the tighter the vines constricted and pinched her arms.

The end was at hand.

Bang.

A loud boom echoed in the halls from the doors, drawing Nessa's attention.

Bang. Bang. Bang.

A brief pause. The silence lingered.

Bang.

The doors blew open. The two unicorns stormed through the opening, with their riders holding long boat oars—the battering rams to open the door. Between them, atop Cyrus' stallion, was the bulldog captain of the riverboat with a cutlass held high.

"Charge!" Pierre bellowed. "Charge, you salty sea dogs." He rode forth.

The pair of unicorns followed Pierre. Buster and Mac were on one unicorn, with Half-pint and the kids on the other. Each held long oars for jousts under their arms. The unicorns grunted and roared as they charged in.

"Get them," the King of Verafell said.

Pierre rode by, striking at the pumpkin monsters, hacking away at their earthen bodies. Dirt and vines sprayed forth.

The unicorn riders charged. The horns buried deep into the earth bodies. They thrashed their heads, driving their horns deeper into the monstrosities. The riders struck the pumpkin monsters with the oars, freeing the horses. The two monsters tumbled to the ground.

The unicorns found their new targets and charged. Hitting with enough force, the monsters exploded into a clump of dirt. Their pumpkin heads shattered on impact. The light in their eyes was doused.

Buster and Mac circled back around and charged once again. Half-pint veered off and headed toward the captive audience.

"Uncle Charlie," Ginny said. "We're here to rescue you."

Half-pint hopped off the unicorn and retrieved one of the swords. He poofed into thin air, reappearing above Nessa. He sliced the vines, releasing her to the ground below. The cold stone floor was unforgiving as she slammed onto it. Nessa groaned, but she shrugged off the pain.

Half-pint vanished and reappeared by the ensnared group. He sliced at their restraints. One by one, the group plopped to the ground, now freed.

Nessa pulled and tugged at the vines, freeing her mouth. "Aim for the heads," she shouted.

The crew of the riverboat lined up the flattened wooden blades of their oars. They charged. The wood pierced into the pumpkin head. Off it popped in an explosion of orange rind and mush, leaving a mound of dirt and twisted vines behind. The unicorn circled around. The animal found its next target. It charged.

The King of Verafell screeched. He flew around the room toward his creations, too late to assist them. "No," he yelled. "My army. My children."

Half-pint poofed in front of her. "Your sword, m'lady." He handed the weapon to her.

Nessa took the blade and leaped to her feet, joining in the fight.

Everyone scrambled to their feet, blades in hand.

"Go for the jack-o'-lantern," Charlie yelled. "It has to be his source of power."

"How do you know?" Cyrus asked with one foot in the air and Gretel by his side.

The pair struck one of the remaining pumpkin monsters.

"The story of Stingy Jack," Charlie said. "He bound a spirit to a jack-o'-lantern."

The shade focused on Charlie. It flew toward him, its shadowy arms outstretched. The razor-like claws were ready to strike.

Charlie ducked out of the way, tumbling forward. He got back to his feet and sprinted for the pumpkin seated on the throne.

Nessa followed him, a few steps behind.

They bolted up the stairs toward the dais. They each raised their swords in the air and swung with great force. The blades pierced the orange rind. They hacked a few more times. The yellowish-green flame that spilled forth from the carved jack-o'-lantern grew dim.

The King of Verafell howled and screeched. His infernal screeches echoed through the hall. He closed in on the pair.

Charlie and Nessa hacked away. The blades reverberated off the black stone throne. Nessa's arm shook. With one final blow, the pumpkin was no more. The light was extinguished. Shattered and broken pieces were left on the vacant throne.

Nessa and Charlie turned to face the battle behind them.

The King of Verafell, a night shade, twisted and contorted as if it had lost its grasp on its form. The billowy, shadowy torso faded in and out of existence. It screamed in agony. Its cries filled the halls. Nessa covered her ears.

The King of Verafell's body collapsed in on itself and disappeared, poofing out of existence. Its pumpkin crown fell to the floor and split in half. The King of Verafell was no more.

"Did . . . did we do it?" Half-pint asked.

"Yeah," Charlie replied. "We did it."

"Uncle Charlie, we saved you," Ginny said from the back of the unicorn.

"You saved us, and then we saved you," Tyler said.

Nessa hunched over, laughing. "Yeah, you saved your Uncle Charlie."

Buster and Mac dropped their oars and stood atop the saddle. They clapped their hands together. The children joined in.

Charlie hunched over to catch his breath. "I didn't think babysitting a couple of six-year-olds would be such a workout," he said. He glanced up at Half-pint with his eyebrows furled. "What were you thinking bringing them back here?"

"What did you want me to do?" Half-pint asked in return. "Leave them alone on the boat?"

Charlie raised an index finger. "Fair point," he said. "That's a fair point."

"This is repayment for the name thing," Half-pint said.

Nessa and Charlie laughed, straightening back up.

"Anyone hurt?" Nessa asked.

"Does my ankle count?" Cyrus asked with a chuckle.

"Hey, Cyrus," Charlie said. "We all failed rule number three with those vines."

Cyrus gritted his teeth through his grin. "Good one."

"I thought you were prepared for things like this," Gretel said.

Cyrus rolled his eyes. "Can we go home now?"

"Yeah," Nessa said. "Let's go home."

CHAPTER 22
RULE FIVE

The riverboat paddled toward Gruff's Landing. The kids indulged in their youthful exuberance, entertained while playing with an excited Buster. He cartwheeled around as the children chased him. Charlie glanced over at Nessa by the animals. They caught each other's gaze and smiled.

"I'm never going to call them unicorns again," Charlie said.

"Oh," Nessa said as she combed her unicorn's hair.

"Nah, they're attack horses now," Charlie said.

"I like that. Attack horses," Nessa said. She stroked the brush a few more times. "I still prefer unicorns, though." She bumped Charlie with her shoulder.

He bumped her back. "Unicorn attack horses."

The unicorn attack horse grunted.

"We're playing," Charlie said. "We're only playing."

It grunted again.

Charlie threw his hands up into the air. "Alright, alright."

Charlie backed away, preferring to steer clear of the unicorn's bad side. His eyes caught Cyrus and Gretel leaning against the rail, engaged in conversation. He wandered over, sliding next to Cyrus. Charlie crossed his arms, bumping into Cyrus' shoulders.

"How's the ankle?" Charlie asked.

"It's been better," Cyrus said. "Still . . . with only one good foot, I'm the better swordsman." He winked at Charlie.

"I've got to give it to you," Charlie said. "You're pretty good."

"Yes . . . he is pretty good-looking," Gretel said, smiling at Cyrus.

He smiled back. "Good?" Cyrus asked with a hint of sarcasm in his voice. "I was great. What was it? Five or six gingerbread men felled by my blade?"

"It wasn't a competition," Charlie said with a smile.

"Oh, right. *Seven*," Cyrus replied with a cheeky grin. "To what . . . your one?"

Charlie sighed. "Do you want me to admit you're the best?"

"I want you to want to admit I'm the best," Cyrus said.

Charlie shook his head. He licked his lips. "I admit that we couldn't have done it without you."

"Close enough," Cyrus said. He smacked the back of Charlie's shoulder. A friendly gesture, yet with enough force that the sting of his palm lingered. "I have to admit you did great yourself today."

"Coming from you, that's high praise," Charlie said. He rotated his shoulder to alleviate the sting of the shoulder he had landed on in the castle.

"I mean it. You faced incredible odds and never gave in or gave up," Cyrus said. "You'd make a good pirate."

Charlie turned to face his one-time rival. The corners of his lips curved into a knowing grin. "I appreciate that," he said. "Maybe one day I'll take you up on it."

"Not too soon," Cyrus said. He motioned to the approaching princess. "I think you have another priority."

"What are you two fighting about now?" Nessa said as she joined the trio against the rails.

"Boys being boys," Gretel said. "Arguing over who is the better pirate."

"Which is me," Cyrus said.

"Thank you, Cyrus," Nessa said. "We couldn't have done it without you."

"You're welcome, Your Highness," he said. "I would like to officially rescind my declined invitation to the council of the realm."

"It will be duly noted," Nessa said.

Cyrus stood, hobbling on one leg. He straightened his posture, chest puffed out. One hand was on his hip, and the other was on the rail for balance. His voice boomed for all to hear. "Let it be known throughout the realm that when the kingdom of Glimmerfell called for aid, only the kingdom of Brightfell answered their call."

Half-pint turned to face the pirate prince. One eyebrow arched, while the other narrowed. "Do you want me to write that down or something?" Half-pint asked.

"Spread the word," Cyrus said. He turned to Nessa. "Anytime Glimmerfell calls for aid, Brightfell will answer. I mean that."

"Thank you," Nessa said. "I appreciate that our two kingdoms could form an alliance. I'll keep that in mind for next time."

"I especially want King Christopher to know," Cyrus said. "Him and his smug little face."

"What did King Christopher do to you?" Gretel asked.

"That man owes me money," Cyrus said. He slumped back onto the rails. He crossed his arms. "He stiffed me on a shipment."

Gretel and Nessa laughed.

Charlie curled his lower lip inward, gently biting down. "Hey, Cyrus," he said.

"Yeah?" the pirate prince replied.

Charlie swung his hand upward, slapping him across the face.

The pirate prince recoiled, unfurling his arms and touching his cheek.

Charlie turned to him and smiled. "We're even," Charlie said. "I told you I'd slap you back."

"If rule four is wing it . . ." Nessa said. "Then is rule five 'expect payback'?"

Cyrus rubbed his cheek in circles. "Funny."

"The landing is up ahead," Lyra said as she came around from the front of the boat.

The wooden dock for Gruff's Landing emerged from around the bend of the river. Another set of crates was ready to be picked up. The boat had never dropped off the first shipment to begin with; instead, it had diverted into the dangers of the dark forest.

The riverboat slowed as it passed. It paused for a moment and then reversed, ready to make landing on the dock below.

Mac and Pierre descended the steps to the wheelhouse.

"Mighty fine docking, Mac," Pierre said. "Mighty fine."

"Does this mean I can finally captain the boat full-time?" Mac asked.

"Let's not get ahead of ourselves," Pierre said. "I'm still captain of this here riverboat. Maybe you can co-captain a time or two."

Mac joined Buster and Half-pint in lifting the ramp up and over the side. Their rubbery arms strained and elongated as they lifted the wooden plank and shoved it over. It landed with a thud on the dock below, bouncing a few times.

Nessa flipped open her saddle bag and retrieved another pouch of gold. She held it in both hands and brought it to Pierre. "I want to thank you for your help. As promised, here's the other half."

Buster and Mac glanced at Pierre, both shaking their heads back and forth. Buster held his hands together, palm to palm, as if begging Pierre to reject the money.

Pierre rubbed his white, protruding chin. "I've been doin' some thinkin'. Maybe we'll call it even. After all, it was for the children."

Buster shifted to one foot, lifting his other with the heel on the ground. He gave two thumbs up and grinned from ear to ear. His white teeth shone. Mac whistled and hooted.

Nessa handed the black pouch to Pierre. "Take it anyway. Get something nice for the boat."

"Maybe . . . maybe I'll give them a pay raise or something," Pierre said.

Buster and Mac glanced at each other. They clapped. Nessa turned and bowed to the pair. Buster returned the gesture.

Lyra opened the gate to the pen and grabbed her horse by the reins, leading it out and down the ramp.

Gretel helped Cyrus over toward the riverboat captain.

"Pierre, it was good to see you again," Cyrus said as he clamped onto the bulldog's forearm.

"You as well, Captain," Pierre said as they shook. They released their hold. "You know, if you need a peg leg to help you walk, I have it below deck."

"Why do I need a peg leg when I have her?" Cyrus said, pointing at Gretel. "Thanks for the offer. It's better on you, anyway. Until next time, Pierre."

"May the wind be in your sails . . ." Pierre said.

"And the seas be calm," Cyrus finished.

They closed in, embracing in a hug and patting each other on the back twice.

"Don't go spoilin' my reputation, you old softie," Pierre said.

"Don't go spoiling mine," Cyrus said. "You big softie."

They released their embrace. With a quick nod, Cyrus and Pierre parted ways. Cyrus took the reins of his stallion and Gretel's horse. Gretel and Cyrus exited down the ramp with their horses following.

Half-pint shook Buster's and Mac's hands at the same time. "It's been a pleasure," he said.

"Ours too," Mac said.

Buster nodded in agreement. He pointed to himself, then Mac, and then Half-pint.

Half-pint hopped onto the saddle of his pony. With a click of the tongue and tap of his heel, Half-pint rode down the ramp toward the dock below.

Ginny and Tyler approached Buster and Mac.

"Thank you for rescuing us," Ginny said.

"Yeah, I can't wait to tell everyone what happened," Tyler said. "They'll never believe us."

The kids hugged both Buster and Mac. The two dogs patted the kids on their backs. They released their embrace, and the kids headed for the ramp.

"See ya later," Ginny said, waving back to the duo.

"You too," Mac said. "Take care."

The pair waved to the kids as they descended the ramp.

Charlie and Nessa retrieved their unicorn attack horses. They guided them toward the ramp.

Charlie stopped. "Thank you," he said, extending his hand toward the dog.

Mac shook his hand. "You're welcome."

Buster scampered over to Nessa, took her hand, and gave it a kiss.

"A gentleman," Nessa said. "You'd make a great knight." She raised her hand and tapped both shoulders of Buster. "I dub thee Sir Buster of Glimmerfell."

He shifted his head to the side, fluttering his eyes, and stomped his foot.

Charlie saluted Buster, who saluted back. Nessa and Charlie led their unicorns down the ramp.

Once everyone was on the dock, the ramp lifted back into the boat.

"Okay, Mr. Mutt," Pierre said. "Take us home."

Mac emerged in the window of the wheelhouse with his hands on the helm. The smokestacks puffed their black clouds in rapid succession. The red paddlewheel turned, splashing in the water. The riverboat powered forward, picking up speed.

Buster popped up behind the railing, waving one final time as the boat disappeared around the corner of the cliff.

A happy sadness fell over Charlie. One half of his lips smiled, while the other half frowned. He was happy the kids were safe and sound and relieved they all made it out and made new friends. A rush of sadness filled his heart—sadness for their departure and the thought that he might not see his new friends for a while. But he had the memories and a new story to tell back home.

"Uncle Charlie," Tyler said. "I'm hungry."

"Yeah, I'm hungry too," Ginny said.

"I know the place to get the best apple pie in the entire realm," Cyrus said as he climbed onto his horse. He winked at Gretel as she mounted her steed.

Charlie lifted the young boy up onto his unicorn. "Come on, young pirate."

"I want to ride on a unicorn," Ginny said.

Nessa lifted Ginny onto her saddle. "It's a unicorn attack horse."

"A unicorn attack horse," Ginny repeated.

Charlie smiled. "I'm hungry too."

With Cyrus and Gretel in the lead, they took off toward Hollowreach.

CHAPTER 23
TAVERN TALES

"The best pie in all the realm," Gretel said as she placed an entire pie plate in front of the children. "Eat up."

"Not too much," Charlie said. "Your mom would be furious at me if she found out."

"She's not here, so she doesn't need to know," Gretel said with a wink. She slid onto the bench next to Cyrus.

Charlie and Nessa sat across from the pair. Lyra was on Nessa's other side. Tyler and Ginny were on opposite sides of the elongated table. Half-pint sat cross-legged at the end of the table. Steins of ale and empty plates of stew sat before them.

Ginny and Tyler picked up their spoons and scooped up large portions of the pie. The filling dripped over the edge of the spoon and onto the table. They shoveled the heaping helping into their mouths.

"Slow down," Charlie said. "Not so much at one time."

"Oh, let them have some fun," Nessa said. "Besides, they must be starving."

With a gulp, the kids both downed their mouthful of pie.

"*Starving*," Tyler said.

"They only gave us berries and rotten apples to eat," Ginny said.

"And not the good kind," Tyler said. "It was bitter and nasty. Not like the pie at all."

The band played on the makeshift stage in the corner. The mixture of concertina, flute, and drums filled the dimly lit air. The place was packed, every table filled with nightly revelers. Voices talked over each other. A pleasant cacophony of sound and a joyous atmosphere.

"So," the bartender said as he approached the group. "These are the children."

"Ginny. Tyler. This is Liam," Gretel said. "Liam, this is Charlie's niece and nephew."

"Nice to meet you," Tyler said through a muffled mouth.

Liam wiped his hands with a towel. He threw the towel over a shoulder. "So, were you two scared?"

"Oh, yeah," Ginny said. "Very scared."

"I protected my sister," Tyler said.

"And I protected my brother," Ginny said.

The bartender stood with his hands on his hips. "That sounds like a lot," he said. "Then what happened?"

"And then Uncle Charlie came to get us," Tyler said.

"Yeah, Uncle Charlie is the greatest uncle ever," Ginny said.

Charlie grinned at his niece and nephew—a proud uncle as the two children faced their fears and never gave up. His fears of disappointing them had washed away in a moment. "Well, it wasn't only me."

"Don't forget the princess," Nessa said.

Cyrus leaned back and kicked a boot up onto the table. "And a one-legged pirate."

Without a glance, Gretel said, "Boot off the table."

"Yes, ma'am," Cyrus said as he removed his footwear from the table.

"And a tavern owner," Gretel said.

"Don't forget a Half-pint," the imp said.

"And a bodyguard," Lyra said.

"Yeah," Ginny said. "They all came to save us."

"Then Uncle Charlie was going to give this ring to the flying pumpkin monster. And the monster opened up the cage," Tyler said as he scooped up more pie.

"But then Mister Half-pint appeared and poofed us out of there," Ginny said, throwing her fingers into the air.

"Poofed?" Liam asked.

Ginny flared out her fingers, mimicking a puff of smoke. "Yeah. We poofed and were outside the room. Then we poofed more times and before we knew it, we were on a boat."

"And there were these two small dogs and this huge dog," Tyler said. The small child stood on the bench. He pointed his spoon toward everyone around the table. "We jumped on horses and went back to save Uncle Charlie, and Princess Nessa, and the pirate, and the nice lady who gave us pie."

Ginny swung her spoon through the air as if she were swinging a sword. "We rode on the unicorns, and we attacked all the pumpkin monsters. It was awesome."

Tyler plopped down and scooped up another mouthful of apple pie. "Yeah. Awesome."

"Don't talk with your mouth full," Charlie said.

"This has been the best vacation ever!" Ginny said.

"The best," Tyler added.

"Uncle Charlie is the coolest uncle ever," Ginny said.

They both scooped up more apple pie and chomped down on it.

Charlie smiled. That was all he wanted from this week—for the children to have a great time and know they could count on him. His eyes glistened. He closed his eyelids a few times, not letting himself shed a happy tear—not in front of Cyrus, at least.

Charlie wrapped an arm around Nessa's shoulders. Her head rested against his. Charlie's heart was full.

Charlie lifted his stein and took a drink.

Gretel turned to Charlie. "I don't think you have to worry about them."

"No," Charlie said. "No, I don't think so."

"I told you," Gretel said. "They know they can count on each other, and now they know they can count on their uncle."

Charlie smiled. He saluted her with his stein.

She smiled and returned the gesture. They both took a sip.

A large creature squeezed between the legs of the table. Covered in reddish fur, it stood on hoofed legs. It had human arms, four-inch horns on its head, and the eyes and snout of a bull.

Tyler's mouth dropped open as he focused on the creature.

Ginny's eyebrows popped up. She leaned in and whispered to Charlie. "Uncle Charlie, that's a Goredellum."

"Oh, hello," the Goredellum said in a soft voice. It waved as it passed by. "How are you?"

The children cowered in their seats, slouching under the edge of the table.

"My name is Bob," he said. "What's yours?"

The children glanced at their uncle.

He nodded back, a signal that it was okay to talk to him.

"I'm Tyler, and this is my sister Ginny," the boy said.

"Well, it's a pleasure to meet you," Bob said with a slight bow.

Liam pointed to Bob with his thumb. "He may appear mean and scary, but he's got a big heart."

The children sat up in their seats.

"Wow," Ginny said. "We got to meet a Goredellum too."

They raised their spoons in the air.

"Best week ever!" they both said.

Everyone at the table laughed. Charlie's laugh unlocked something deep within his soul, something long forgotten and locked away. He was happy. Whole. Charlie was home.

∾

THE TAVERN WAS QUIET, the patrons long since gone. The joyous revelry had been silenced. The children and guests were asleep upstairs. The concertina and other instruments rested on the makeshift stage in the corner. Candlelight flickered from the lanterns hanging from the wall posts and ceiling.

Cyrus finished off his mug of ale. He licked his lips to mop up any remains of the frothy liquid. He leaned over the bar to refill his drink, not quite reaching the tap of the wooden cask.

He stewed for a moment, thinking he could hop all the way around to the end of the bar. His ankle still throbbed in pain. But he was a pirate and a prince—a pirate prince. He was going to refill his mug his way, distance or no.

Cyrus hopped up from his stool. He placed both hands on the bar rail and leaped into the air. He lifted a knee and placed it on the bar top. Cyrus snatched up his mug and leaned over the divide. The space behind the bar was too far for him to reach comfortably. He braced himself against the wooden cask with one hand. He placed the mug under the tap with the other. He needed a third hand.

His thumb rose to release the liquid held in the barrel. It slipped off the slick wooden tap. He scooted closer. He caught himself, pulling back up. He nearly fell over the ledge. At least no one was around to see him almost crash to the floor below.

Cyrus was unable to let go of the wooden cask. It was the only thing holding him upright. He repositioned himself to get a better angle on the tap. His thumb pressed against the wood. Cyrus sucked in his bottom lip, his upper teeth clamping down, with determination in his eyes. He wouldn't be defeated in his quest.

Cyrus pressed the tap again. It budged, but only slightly. He repositioned his hand once more. It slipped, but Cyrus caught himself. He almost had it. A few more attempts, and the frothy liquid ale would be his, despite his bum ankle.

"What are you doing?" Gretel asked as she approached the bar.

"I'm trying to refill my cup," Cyrus replied.

"Are you attempting to hurt yourself further?" she asked.

Cyrus tried to release the liquid two more times. Both times his thumb slipped off the tap. It wouldn't budge.

"I didn't want to walk around," he said. "I can do this."

"You're stubborn," she said. "Let me help you."

Gretel turned around, her back facing the bar. She placed her hands on the rails and lifted herself. She swung her legs around and hopped down. "Give me that," she said, pulling the mug from his hand.

Cyrus pushed himself off the cask and slid across the bar top. He hopped down onto one foot. He plopped back onto his stool. "I almost had it."

"Sure, you did." Gretel placed the replenished mug in front of him. "Want something to eat? I can get you a bowl of the perpetual stew."

Cyrus took a sip. "No. I'm good. I'm thinking."

Gretel leaned on the bar, inches from his face. An unseen tension pulled Cyrus toward her, as if he wanted to move closer.

"Thinking about what?" Gretel gazed at Cyrus through the soft flutter of her eyelids.

Cyrus smirked. "Thinking about how much time I spent competing against someone I never met for someone who never wanted me."

Gretel's smile faded.

Cyrus continued, "Then I got to thinking about the past few years. Being here. How you welcomed me in when I said I didn't want to return home. That disappointed a lot of people."

Gretel shrugged, tilting her head and closing her eyes. "Not everyone." She opened her brown eyes and locked her gaze onto Cyrus.

"Saving those kids got me thinking."

"Because deep down you're not a ruthless pirate, but a big old softie?" Gretel asked.

"Come on now. I have a reputation to uphold." Cyrus took another sip. "I've been thinking about a lot of things."

"Like what?" Gretel asked.

"How a certain tavern owner helped me hobble around in the dark forest. How I wouldn't have been there to help those kids without her."

"She sounds great," Gretel said. "Stupendous. Amazing."

A grin crept across Cyrus' face. "I've been thinking about returning home. Sailing the seas again."

Gretel's face turned solemn. Her eyes dropped with sadness, and the smile faded. "Oh."

The mug clanked against the wood as Cyrus set it down. He slouched back, crossing his arms. His eyes never left Gretel's gaze.

"I was thinking that the seas are a big place. Don't necessarily want to sail them alone." He paused for a moment. "Besides, if I hurt my ankle again, I thought about who I'd want by my side to help me hobble around. I thought maybe you—"

"Yes," Gretel said. The smile returned, beaming more than ever.

"You don't know what I was going to ask."

"Please continue." She flashed a teasing gaze. "My answer is still yes."

Cyrus leaned in. That unmistakable force drew him closer, pulling him toward her.

"Would you like to sail the seas with me? I figured you can let Liam run this place while you're gone."

"I already said yes."

Cyrus beamed back at her. He lifted his mug. "To the seas," he said. "May the winds be in your sails and the tides high."

Gretel raised an imaginary mug. "To the seas."

"I can wear my hat again," Cyrus said. He retrieved the wide black hat from the stool next to him. Flat and narrow on one side, it rose from the ends into a hump. Frilly white lace lined the hat. He set it on his head. The flat end faced Gretel. "Do you like my hat?"

"I love your hat," Gretel said. She twisted the hat on his head so the tip pointed forward. "I think I like it that way better."

Cyrus glanced up to the tip of the hat hanging over his head. "I think that's a problem."

"How so?"

"What if I wanted to kiss you?" he asked. "The hat would be in the way."

"We can always try." Gretel winked at Cyrus.

"Do you want me to try?" he asked.

"No time like the present," she said.

Cyrus and Gretel leaned toward each other. The tip of the hat bumped against Gretel's forehead. She recoiled.

"Maybe it's better this way," she said, twisting the hat back to its original position. "Much better."

They leaned in, their lips meeting for the first time—teasing, soft glances before the tender embrace of passion. There, in the darkened tavern, a pirate prince fell in love with a tavern owner.

CHAPTER 24

THE POP-PUNK PRINCESS OF GLIMMERFELL

The sun's golden rays gave way to a mixture of orange, red, and purplish hues as it descended for its nightly slumber. The castle glowed and gleamed in the dying light of the sun. The citizens of Glimmerfell wrapped up their activities for the day. They packed away their goods in their stands. They swept the landings to their stores. Children played in the streets as adults carried their boxes and packages home.

Nessa entered through the front gates, atop her unicorn attack horse, weary from the events of the past few days. Her mind was set on a good night's rest in her bed. She could have taken the secluded path that led to the royal stables, but not for this. The kingdom was under attack. Towns had been endangered. They needed to see their conquering hero . . . *no* . . . their leader return with news of the King of Verafell's defeat.

The jaws of the citizens dropped. They murmured amongst themselves. Whispers gave way to audible conversations. They gathered around as their princess, their leader, returned on her mount with her royal guard, companions, and two children.

Nessa followed the path toward the castle's fountain square. The streets parted, giving way to the royal group. Nessa pulled back on the reins of her unicorn, coming to a stop. The fountain, in all of its splendor, was to her back. It bubbled and poured crystal-clear water. It spilled forth down the marble carved hands of former leaders into the massive basin. The crowd pushed in.

Lyra scowled, narrowing her eyebrows as the crowd circled the fountain square. She signaled for guards stationed at various guard posts along the castle walls to come down and join them.

Nessa waved her hand, calling off her guard. "My fellow citizens of Glimmerfell, I bring good tidings," she shouted.

The crowd murmured and then hushed.

"Three nights ago, we were attacked," Nessa said. Her eyes scanned to meet the worried faces of her citizens. "Attacked by forces not of this realm. Forces attacked our border towns. An army was conjured from a powerful shade, who took up residence in Castle Verafell."

The crowd gasped. Whispers of the forbidden castle spread through the fountain square.

"On the night of the attack, they took these two children back to the castle." Nessa said. "They demanded a ransom for their return."

Nessa paused. The concerned eyes of the citizenry focused on her, hanging on her every word. She inhaled, puffing out her chest. Her nose pointed toward the sky. "I couldn't allow any of you to march to the castle if I wasn't willing to do it myself."

The princess pointed to Lyra, Half-pint, and then Charlie. "My personal guard, my royal advisor, and my—"

Nessa paused. She didn't know what to call Charlie. Her friend? Charlie had always been her friend.

Her companion? No, that sounded too formal. She needed something else. Something appropriate.

"My boyfriend," Nessa said.

Charlie smiled at her. He flashed his eyebrows up in excitement.

The crowd buzzed at the mention of a boyfriend. The whispers spread like wildfire.

"Boyfriend?" Charlie whispered.

"Would you prefer another title?" Nessa asked.

"No," Charlie said in a raised voice. "Boyfriend sounds really good to me."

The Princess of Glimmerfell glanced at Tyler, seated on Charlie's unicorn. She patted the head of Ginny seated before her. "We embarked on a secret mission to rescue these children. A dangerous mission."

She turned to face the crowd. They hung on her every word. Their eyes focused on her, not muttering a word.

"Aided by the kingdom of Brightfell and Prince Cyrus Blackstone and a tavern owner in Hollowreach, we ventured deep into the heart of Shadowfell. I'm happy to report that the King of Verafell is no more," Nessa said. "We've brought the children home. The threat from Castle Verafell is gone."

The crowd erupted into cheers. They threw flowers and an assortment of ribbons into the air.

"Three cheers for Princess Nessa, leader of Glimmerfell," Charlie yelled. "Hip, hip, hooray!"

The crowd repeated the phrase.

"Hip, hip, hooray!" Charlie said again.

The crowd answered back.

"Hip, hip, hooray!" Charlie said a final time.

The crowd responded once more. They rushed toward the princess, giving her flowers, breads, and fruits.

Lyra pushed her horse through the crowd to create space for the princess. "Stay back. Stay back," Lyra said. "Give the princess some room."

"It's okay," Nessa said as she leaped off her unicorn attack horse. "You can stand down."

Lyra did as commanded. She pulled back on her horse, allowing the crowds to greet their conquering hero.

"Thank you," the Princess of Glimmerfell said. Nessa received every member of the crowd—her citizens. She accepted their gifts and shook their hands. "You're too kind. Thank you."

After the crowds quieted down and dispersed, Nessa took in her kingdom. The colorful sky gave way to stars, gleaming and shining down on the kingdom of Glimmerfell. Nessa was no longer the Princess of Glimmerfell. She was, as the stone statues behind her were, a leader of Glimmerfell.

CHARLIE LEANED back in Half-pint's high-back chair, stretching out his leg. His body hurt, and his shoulder throbbed. Although the adventuring was fun, the bumps and bruises had caught up to him. Having a day to relax before heading home did nothing to alleviate his aches and pains. His shoulder clicked when he rotated it, no doubt from his fall in the twisted vines.

"Fascinating," Wynden said. He flipped through a book. "And it disappeared when the pumpkin was smashed?"

"Yep," Charlie said, rotating his shoulder. "Do you have any ice? Of course you don't have any ice. Do you have anything to fix my shoulder?"

"I can make you a potion to help with it," Wynden replied. He tossed the book aside and grabbed a new one.

"A potion sounds good," Charlie said.

"It will take me some time to make it," the wizard said, turning his attention back to his research.

Charlie shrugged his shoulders. "Well, have it ready when I get back."

"There is nothing in my books about a shade from another realm," he said. "First, those who could travel through books, dreams, and water. Then the mirror. Now a shade who appeared from nowhere." Wynden slammed the book shut.

"What does that mean?" Nessa asked.

Wynden shook his head. "I don't know. Maybe the magic of the realm is opening holes to other places. What exactly happened when it disappeared?"

"The whole shade sort of faded in and out, and then it was gone," Nessa said. "It screamed in agony, but it was gone when Charlie and I destroyed the pumpkin." She sat on the arm of the high-back chair.

Wynden stroked his beard, deep in thought. "Hmm . . . fascinating. It bound itself using unknown magic. I wonder where it came from."

"I'm glad it's gone," Half-pint said, reappearing out of thin air. He sat atop Wynden's stack of books. "And those pumpkin monsters too."

The kids rumbled into Half-pint's private study. They ran around and around in circles.

"We don't want to leave, Uncle Charlie," Ginny said. "Miss Lyra took us down to the dungeons and then the armory. This place is amazing."

"We got to swing swords around," Tyler said. He mimicked his motions with an invisible blade.

Charlie raised an eyebrow. "Swords?"

Nessa smacked him on the arm—his bad shoulder. "We were playing with swords at their age. They're fine."

"That's my bad shoulder, thank you," Charlie said. The palm of his hand circled around. He played up the motion to feign that it hurt.

Lyra sprinted into the room. Hands on her hips, she breathed loudly from sprinting. "They move fast up those steps."

"I told you," Charlie said. "You've got to keep an eye on them."

"Can we stay forever?" Tyler asked.

"I want to stay forever, and ride the unicorns, and play with Mister Half-pint," Ginny said.

"No," Charlie said. "We stayed for an extra day, and you got your time to explore the castle. Now, we have to head back. Your mom will be home tomorrow. We can come back another time."

"Aww," they protested in unison. "But we like it here."

Nessa turned to Charlie. "What about you? When will you be back?"

He smiled a sly grin. "I'll be back soon," Charlie said. "I have to make sure their mom picks them up. The mirror is working again. I'm not going to stay away as long this time."

Nessa smiled. "You better not."

"What about you?" Charlie asked. "Are you curious what life's like back there? Do you want to know what your parents are up to or meet your sister?"

Nessa narrowed her eyebrows and tightened her lips. She glanced at the mirror and then at Lyra. "I can't," she said. "I mean, I would love to see them again. Let them know I'm okay. That their daughter is okay. Be held in my mom's arms one more time. Hear my dad's voice. I wish . . . I wish I could." Nessa paused, bowing her head.

"I didn't mean to upset you," Charlie said. "I—I thought . . ." He failed to find the words to finish his sentence, not wanting to make the situation worse.

She glanced at Charlie, smiling and shaking her head. "No, it's okay," Nessa said. "I thought about it. I did. I thought about going, so I could hear their voices over the phone."

She glanced at the swirling vortex. "I went through the mirror once, and it closed on me. I can't take that risk again. I can't, no matter how much I want to. The majority of my life has been devoted to Glimmerfell. I have a kingdom to run. I'm going to do things my way, but I have to think of the kingdom first. Besides, I'm sort of a big hero now."

"A hero punk princess," Charlie said.

Nessa smiled.

Charlie stood, clapping his hands together. "You kids ready to go?"

"No," they said in unison.

"Too bad," Charlie said. "You two hold hands and go through together."

The twins took each other's hands.

"So long, everyone," Tyler said as he waved with his free hand. "Thank you for rescuing us."

Lyra waved back. "My pleasure. Take care and see you later."

"Nice to meet all of you," Ginny said as the pair moved toward the mirror.

The twins pushed through and disappeared into the swirling glass.

Charlie paused before going through the mirror. He turned back to the group. "I won't be gone long. Thank you again. See you soon." He moved toward the mirror.

"Charlie, wait," Nessa said.

He turned around. Nessa hugged him, burying her head into his chest. He wrapped his arms around her and held her tight.

"Thank you," she said. "Thanks for coming back."

"Thanks for waiting for me," he said. "I'll be back. I promise. I'm good on my promises."

They gave one final squeeze and let go. Charlie wiped away Nessa's tear. Without saying anything further, Charlie turned and entered the mirror, leaving behind the realm of Everfell once again.

"Your dinner, Your Highness," Lyra said as she placed a plate and a chalice in front of Nessa.

Nessa removed the napkin from its place setting on the table. She carefully unfolded the deep blue colored linen and placed it on her lap. She examined the plate—a beef roast with vegetables exquisitely prepared by the finest chefs in all of the kingdom. The juices glistened on the meat. An intoxicating aroma filled her nose.

Nessa lifted her two-pronged fork and knife, one utensil in each hand. She paused, glancing down the elongated table. Her eyes caught the empty seats filling each side. The gold candelabras held their golden candlesticks. The lights of the wall sconces flickered, and their shadows danced off the stone walls. Royal tapestries draped the walls for decorations. All provided light for a party of one.

"If there won't be anything else, Your Highness, I'll retire and leave you to your meal," Lyra said.

Nessa had eaten many meals in this room. She had entertained dignitaries from other kingdoms. Dinners with her adopted parents. Meals with good food, good company, and lively conversations. Since their passing, Nessa found herself eating alone. Only the golden candles kept her company.

Charlie had been gone for a day, but his absence might have been another twenty years. The worry that the mirror would stop working coursed through her mind, a worry that overtook her mind and made sleep elusive.

He would travel back and forth through the mirror. He wasn't always going to be here. She needed to fight through her emotions. She needed someone. Nessa needed to correct a wrong.

She glanced at Lyra. "Where are you taking your meal?"

Lyra stood at attention, shoulders pulled back and arms to her sides. "I'll be eating with the other guards, as per usual."

Nessa set her knife and fork down beside her plate. "Go to the kitchen and ask them to fix you a plate, then come back and join me."

Lyra shifted in her stance. "Decorum states that guards aren't supposed to eat with the heads of the kingdom," Lyra said. "It would be uncouth."

Nessa interlocked her fingers and placed her hands on the table. Her arms went to her sides. "Well, what about instead of having dinner as princess and bodyguard, we have dinner as sisters?"

A grin broke Lyra's stern, pursed lips. "Sisters?"

Nessa leaned back in her seat. "Charlie was right. We've grown up together. We're around each other all the time. You're my closest confidant, and you protect me. You're more of a sister than a bodyguard. You always have been."

Nessa glanced at the empty seat next to her. "I want you to join me. Tonight and every night. Right here." Nessa tapped the table, pointing to the empty spot next to her. "We'll have dinner as a family."

Lyra's eyes glistened, holding back tears. Her smile curved as she beamed from ear to ear. "I'd very much like that." She giggled, unable to maintain a stoic posture.

"Go. Get something to eat. I'll wait for you," Nessa said.

Lyra pivoted on her foot and marched toward the door. She picked up speed until she passed through the door, bolting down the hall.

Nessa smiled. "I have a sister. I've *always* had a sister."

CHAPTER 25
A FAIRY TALE WEEK

The doorbell rang.

"Kids, your mom is here," Charlie yelled up the stairs. He opened the door and smiled at his sister.

"You wouldn't believe the week I had," she said, entering Charlie's townhouse.

Charlie shut the door and paused for a moment, carefully choosing his next words. "Good or bad?"

Julie turned around. Her face beamed with excitement. "It was great. Relaxing. I was able to get away and not think about anything," she said. "Except I did call one night, and you didn't answer. I thought maybe something was wrong. What were you doing?"

Charlie ran his hand through his hair and scratched the back of his head. His phone. His mind cycled through a list of plausible answers—something, anything that would get her to not question why he didn't answer his phone for the week besides the truth.

"Umm . . . Besides telling you I wasn't going to answer?"

"I still called. I thought you would answer," she said.

"The truth is . . . my phone doesn't work," he said. "My phone didn't work all week. I can't get a new one until payday, so I'm kind of out of luck until then."

Charlie dove his left hand into his pants pocket. His thumb glided across the silicon edge of the case to find the switch to silence the device.

Julie swung her purse around and rummaged through the contents. "Here. Let me help you."

Charlie stuck out his arm, shaking his head. "Oh, that's not necessary."

Julie withdrew a handful of cash. "No, I insist," she said, handing him the money. "Besides, you helped me out in a pinch. It's the least I can do."

Charlie's hand hovered over the dollar bills for a moment. He didn't need to take the money, but he also didn't want to embarrass his sister. He accepted the money. Charlie pulled out his wallet and placed the money inside.

"Thank you," Charlie said.

"One of the kids didn't break it, did they?" Julie asked.

Charlie shook his head. "Nope. It was all me."

"Were they well-behaved?"

"The best. I think they had a great week."

"Mom!" Ginny shouted from upstairs. She bounded down the steps, dragging her suitcase. The black wheeled suitcase bounced and slammed against every step on the way down. She dropped the handle and sprinted to her mother, wrapping her arms around her waist. "We missed you."

Julie patted Ginny on the back. She bent down and gave her daughter a hug. "I missed you too," Julie said. "Did you have a good time?"

"Oh, yeah! We had a wonderful adventure."

Tyler stomped down the staircase, dragging his suitcase. It banged against the steps. The neighbor next door pounded three times on the wall, signaling his annoyance with the commotion in the house.

"Mom!" Tyler said. "We met a funny imp and Gretel, and we rode on a boat, and Uncle Charlie met these princesses." He jolted over to hug his mother.

She hugged him back. "A boat and princesses?" she asked as she glanced up at Charlie. Her eyebrows furled in an inquisitive, *please explain* gesture.

"Oh, you know, we were playing," Charlie said, shrugging his shoulders. He waved his hands back and forth in the air. "You know. My stories."

He maneuvered behind his sister. His eyebrows popped up, and he gritted his teeth in a half-smile. Charlie raised his right hand to his neck, shaking it back and forth, hoping the kids would take the cue to stop talking.

"And we were kidnapped by a pumpkin monster and taken to this castle," Ginny said.

Charlie squinted his eyes closed and buried his head into his palm.

"And Uncle Charlie came and rescued us with a princess and a pirate," Tyler added.

Charlie lifted his eyes from his palm, still covering his mouth.

"A princess and a pirate?" Julie said, turning to Charlie. "It sounds like you had a great time."

Charlie smiled, not saying a word.

"And we ate a whole apple pie," Tyler said.

Julie frowned at Charlie. "A whole pie?"

Charlie shrugged. "Shared a pie."

"Ah," she said, turning back to her kids. "It sounds like you had a busy, fun week."

"We did," Tyler said. "Uncle Charlie is a cool uncle."

"Can we come back next weekend?" Ginny asked. "I want to go back to the castle."

"Yeah, we want to come back and stay with Uncle Charlie," Tyler said.

Julie patted her children on the head. "We'll see," she said as she stood and turned toward Charlie. She gave him a hug. "Thank you. Thank you taking care of them and giving them a good time."

"You're welcome," he said as he patted her back. "Anytime. Anything for you. I'm glad you had a relaxing week. You needed it."

Julie let go of Charlie and turned to her kids. "Have your stuff?"

"Yep," they said in unison.

"Let's get going. I'm sure Uncle Charlie wants some time to himself," Julie said.

"He's probably going to spend time with his princess girlfriend," Tyler said through a giggle.

Ginny giggled as well. "Yeah, his princess girlfriend."

Julie turned to Charlie. Her eyebrows pushed down, portraying a state of shock. "You have a girlfriend?"

Charlie raised his hands to his shoulders. "Someone I see every now and then."

"Well, maybe I'll meet her someday," Julie said, not giving up her shocked expression.

"Yeah," Charlie said, scratching the back of his head "Someday."

"Gather up your stuff, and let's take it out to the car," Julie said.

The kids retrieved their suitcases as Charlie opened the door. One by one, they filed out. They opened the car doors, leaving their suitcases near the trunk, and climbed inside.

Julie paused at the doorway. She turned back to Charlie. "Thanks again," she said.

Charlie leaned into the doorframe. "Anytime."

Julie strode to her waiting children. The heels of her shoes clacked against the stone walkway. She lifted the bags and placed them into the trunk. She closed the kids' door, opened hers, and entered. The car roared to life and backed up. Julie and the kids waved at Charlie. He returned the gesture as the car sped off. He closed the door behind him, locking it.

The townhouse was quiet. Playtime was over. The cheers and raucous activity had been silenced. A half-grin filled Charlie's face. He inhaled, holding it for a moment before exhaling.

Charlie did it. He gave the kids a week to remember—a time filled with joy and laughter, regardless if it was slightly scary. But that was life—two sides of the same coin. The kids couldn't have one without the other, but they should be better equipped to face the dangers life would throw at them.

Besides, his niece and nephew now knew they could always come to their uncle to help in times of danger. The cool uncle.

"Ohh . . . Charlie has a girlfriend," an impish voice said. Half-pint appeared out of thin air, grinning from ear to ear.

Charlie glared at the imp sitting cross-legged on his white end table. A white pizza box from Blue Jay's Pizza was on his lap. He held a squarish, flat piece of pepperoni and extra cheese in his hand with a bite taken from the corner.

"I do, don't I?" Charlie asked.

Half-pint took another bite. "This is amazing," Half-pint said. "Far better than anything the royal kitchen makes."

"Save some for the princess," Charlie said. He glanced at the basement door. "Last one through the mirror is a rotten egg."

Half-pint disappeared in a cloud of sparkly, purple magical dust, only to reappear at the basement door with the pizza box in hand. He snapped his fingers, flinging the door open and disappearing once more.

Charlie sprinted after him. "No fair!" he yelled. "You can't use your powers. And don't drop that pizza." Charlie followed down the steps, shutting the door behind him.

THERE WAS a knock at the bedroom door. Nessa sat in a chair close to the roaring fire in the hearth.

"Enter," Nessa said.

The hinges creaked as the wooden door opened. Charlie stood in the entryway. It had been a day since they were last together. Their personal lives kept them apart for now. She had a kingdom to rule. He had a day job to pay the rent. They agreed to spend their evenings together when they could.

A deep anxiety built inside her every time he had to travel back through the mirror. It was torturous. Her mind was a tempest of fears, quelled every time he returned. They were together again, as they were when they were kids.

Her stomach fluttered. She tried to hold in the smile, but her face betrayed her.

Charlie leaned against the door frame, grinning back. His eyes portrayed an aura of devious thoughts running through his mind.

"I brought something," Charlie said.

"Oh," she said. "More Blue Jay's Pizza?"

"No, something better," he said.

Nessa leaned her head to the side. A half-grin formed across her face, and her eyebrows arched high. "Oh! Care to share what you brought me?"

Charlie smiled back. "You have to play a game. Twenty questions."

Nessa sat up and pouted her lips. "As your princess, I command you tell me." She winked at Charlie.

Charlie winked back. "As your boyfriend, I'm not telling you unless you play the game."

"Very well," Nessa said as she shifted in her seat. "Can it fit in your hand?"

"Yes," Charlie replied.

"Is it white?"

Charlie's grin faded. One eyebrow popped up. "Yes."

"Does it run on power?"

"Maybe."

"Does it have earbuds?"

Charlie's eyebrows narrowed. He pushed off from the door frame and stood up straight. "How did you know?"

Nessa giggled. "Half-pint told me you took the iPod to charge it."

He shook his head as the smile once again beamed from ear to ear. "That little traitor."

"Did it work?"

"Charged and ready to go," Charlie said as he presented the device to her. Its white, plastic sheen had faded. The earbuds dangled from his hand. "I brought a couple charging packs for you, in case it runs out before I can get it charged again."

"How very thoughtful." She stood and joined Charlie. The ruffles of her dress swayed back and forth as she approached.

"I thought we could listen, you know, for old time's sake." He placed one earbud into his ear and handed the other to her. "I added some new songs as well."

Nessa placed it into her ear. "Are we dancing around together like we used to?"

Charlie rolled his eyes. "I don't know if I can bounce around like when we were kids. How about a slow dance? Hand in hand. Arms around each other."

"Deal," she said. "On one condition."

Charlie narrowed his eyebrows. "What's that?"

Nessa's blue eyes found Charlie's. She had waited for this moment for twenty years. Now, it had finally arrived. "You have to kiss me at the end."

Charlie's lips stretched across his face, smiling from ear to ear. "You don't have to ask me twice."

Charlie pushed play on the iPod. He took her hand and wrapped the other behind her back, pulling her closer. They danced in circles, cheek to cheek, holding each other tightly. After years of waiting, wondering if she would ever see her best friend again, they were finally reunited, dancing together and moving as one. Their ears filled with the melodic music of their joy-filled youth as their favorite song serenaded their dance.

As the music came to a crescendo, they paused. Both leaned in closer. Their lips finally met, fulfilling a promise they made to each other twenty years ago. Finally, officially, they were boyfriend and girlfriend.

They were together once again. The girl who vanished and the boy who waited.

AND THEY LIVED HAPPILY EVER...

AFTER IN THE VOID

The void. The endless void. Darkness encircled and ensnared him. No light. No ground. Only endless weightlessness. A loss of self and everything he once was. Memories of his past life taken away. Locked away. As if he was frozen. The man he once was. A king.

A ruler of pumpkins. A king of a castle. A ruler of a foreign realm. A strange, fantastical place he was thrust upon after his first time in the void.

Yes. The first time in the void.

The endless swirl of madness from being locked away. His true form . . . his true self. Lost. Screaming out for him. A desire to reconnect. Reform. To be whole and renewed. It called to him, but he was lost. Spinning out of control. An unending prison unfit for a king.

A king? He was a king, but not always a king. No. He *became* a king. A castle he called his own while he reformed. But he was something else. Not a king. Something more. Who was he?

He searched his mind, but the answer didn't come. His true form screamed for him. He was locked in a prison of madness.

But why?

He couldn't remember. He couldn't remember the events that led him here. There were flashes. Memories seeped through a crack in the void. Flashes of brilliance.

A flash. Yes, there was a flash. The first time in the void, there was a flash, and he found himself in the ruined castle. Overcome with vines. Wild plants grew. Pumpkins. Wild pumpkins.

He was formless. Shapeless. A dark, shadowy cloud. Yet, something deep within instinctively knew how to rectify the situation. How to give himself form.

He reached for a pumpkin, but he couldn't grasp it. His dark hands passed through it. No. Not in his phantasmal form.

He called upon something mystical. Something magical. An innate power deep within. Something familiar. A power in his phantasmic state, he could call upon to wield as a tool. To fashion himself a new form.

He plucked a pumpkin from the vine with unseen hands. He uttered a phrase. He did not know the origin or where he first learned it. The phrase poured out of his very being. His soul.

Shapes formed in the pumpkin. The orange rind peeled away as if carved by spiritual hands. Eyes. Teardrop eyes, as if the pumpkin cried out. A mouth of jagged teeth stretched across the bottom. A face took shape.

And then a flame formed to light the lantern. Uttering a phrase of clandestine origins, an eerie yellowish-green flame emanated from within. The light spilled out of the eyes and mouth. Not welcoming, inviting light, nor filled with warmth. A sickly, ghastly light to warn everyone of its presence. This carved head served as an anchor, a token for his new corporeal form.

Fingers formed from shadows, long and pointy. Hands and then arms. A torso. Finally, a head and face. He floated there. No legs. Nothing to stand on the ground, yet he could freely float across the room, covered in billowing shadow. He glided as if wading through water.

He picked up a stone and threw it across the room. He had form once again, although incomplete. He had to view himself, hoping for the slightest remembrance of who he was.

He roamed the castle, searching for anything. The castle was long since abandoned, overcome with vines and leaves. Darkness enveloped the halls. No signs of life. No signs of anything.

He stumbled into a bedroom. The bed was long ago reclaimed by nature. Cracks in the wall allowed bluish-white moonbeams to spill inside. The rays illuminated objects buried beneath the twisted vines. The shine caught his view.

A mirror. A mirror trapped on a nightstand. He plucked the silver-plated hand mirror from the nest of vines. They struggled, almost if they tightened around the handle the more he pulled. Not wanting to give up their precious item, but the vines were no match for his determination.

He glanced at his new form, hoping it would give him clues as to who he was in his previous life. His head was formed in shadow. His eyes glowed a yellowish-green light. His nose and mouth were still trapped in their shadowy cocoon. This would not do.

A thought pervaded his mind. He'd wear a mask. Yes, a mask. No. Not a mask, but a crown.

He'd become a king. This would be his castle. The vines and their fruits would become his army. If he could not find his way out of here, he'd rule this place instead.

But he had to leave. He had to return home. There was someone waiting for him. He couldn't remember. The life he once lived tore through his sanity. It was there. He could see flashes, yet they made no sense. Images. A person.

Then he found himself in the void once again. His anchor was destroyed. His corporeal form returned to the shadowy depths of this despair. Floating endlessly. Time lost all meaning. Eternity meant nothing. He struggled to restore his sanity, but only found madness. Madness of the emptiness of his prison.

The flashes of memories drove him mad. He couldn't make out

the images. A blur. A blur in his mind he sought to give form and shape. A winged creature. A bird. Some sort of bird.

Black feathers and a black beak. It stood on something. A perch maybe. The faint calls formed in his mind. A caw. Deep and gravelly. A caw from a bird. Its long beak took form and shaped into an image.

He recognized this bird. It was a pet. A family pet. His, but not his. Something that was a symbol. A symbol of who he once was. The word flooded his memory.

Raven.

Yes. A raven. The symbol of someone he once knew.

A face formed in his memory. A woman's face. Blurry, but distinct. Her soft cheekbones. Her slight smile. He had seen her face a million times, but he begged and pleaded for one more view. A clue as to his true form. His true essence. Who he was.

Her hair pulled back into a knot. He still couldn't see her face. Her eyes. A washed-out painting being erased from existence. It lingered in his memory. He focused, trying to give it form and shape. It slowly dissolved, only returning to a blob of colors.

No, he thought. *Stay with it. Who are you? Who am I?*

The image faded from his mind. Despair rushed to fill the void. He wouldn't give up. He focused on the image. The knot. The porcelain like face. His memory scanned for anything. Any hint of who it was.

"Raven. Raven. Raven," he chanted.

The raven brought on the image of the woman. Perhaps it could restore it again.

"Raven. Raven. Raven," he said over and over.

A flash in the void.

"Raven. Raven. Rav—"

The flash blinded him with brilliant white light for a moment. Not the image of the woman, but a name. A name he hadn't heard in an eternity, but it provided clarity. An anchor. The name echoed over and over in his mind. The madness quelled.

He was surround by the darkness of the void, but he had a new light. Every time he shouted the name, a light appeared. A new sense of hope in the darkness. A single name. *Madeline*. A name he chanted over and over in hopes of restoring his true self.

"Madeline," he called out. A flash of light. "Madeline. Madeline. Madeline."

Acknowledgements

The author would like to acknowledge the following public domain works and characters used in this novel.

The original creators and The Walt Disney Company are not affiliated with and did not produce, endorse, or sponsor this book. Characters appear only as they are depicted in their original public domain versions, not as later adapted by The Walt Disney Company or any other company or person. Any trademarks are the property of their respective owners.

No commercial affiliation is claimed or implied.

Listed in order of appearance

"Cinderella, or the Little Glass Slipper" by Charles Perrault (1637)

"Cinderella" The Brothers Grimm (1812)

"Snow White" by The Brothers Grimm (1812)

"Sleeping Beauty" by Charles Perrault (1697)

"Little Briar Rose" by The Brothers Grimm (1812)

"Rumpelstiltskin" by The Brothers Grimm (1812)

"Hansel and Gretel" by The Brothers Grimm (1812)

NOTE FROM THE AUTHOR

DEAR READER,

Thank you for taking the time to read this beginning entry in the world of *Everfell*. I truly appreciate your time and commitment. I hope you enjoyed the adventures of Charlie and Nessa as much as I enjoyed writing them. If so, please post a review online for *Once Upon A Mirror*.

Posting reviews online is one of the best ways to help and support authors. Please consider leaving an honest review on the website where you purchased the book and/or other book review sites, such as Goodreads.

If this is your first entry to my works, please check out my other novels and stories. There are more stories to come, and you don't want to miss out. I can't wait to share these stories with you in the near future.

Thank you for reading!

C. M. MASON

ALSO BY C. M. MASON

GOTHIC OHIO FAIRY TALES

THE NEIGHBORHOOD SERIES

"The Lovers' Kiss" Trilogy

The Neighborhood Witch

The Neighborhood Vampire

The Neighborhood Ghost

The Sinclair Saga

The Neighborhood Werewolf

STAND-ALONE NOVELS

The Cowboy and The Witch

EVERFELL FAIRY TALES

Once Upon A Mirror

SUBSCRIBE TO MY NEWSLETTER

The world of *Everfell* is rich with wonderful stories, and there are more stories to come. I can't wait to share with everyone. If you would like to know more, please consider signing up for my newsletter. There you will find:

- Upcoming works in progress and book releases
- Exclusive book related art and other content
- Behind the scenes notes
- Upcoming appearances
- Exclusive giveaways
- And more!

Subscribe to my newsletter at **cmmason.com.**

ABOUT THE AUTHOR

C. M. Mason is an award-winning, international bestselling author fueled by a lifelong passion for fairy tales, gothic, and paranormal stories. In 2023, readers were introduced to a magical and intriguing world in the award-winning debut novel, *The Neighborhood Witch*.

A graduate of Wright State University, C. M. Mason studied the art of storytelling. Holding the belief that stories are a source of light amidst the darkness, allowing the ordinary to escape into extraordinary adventures. New characters and imaginative adventures are created by the flickering of candlelight in the dark of the night.

cmmason.com

www.ingramcontent.com/pod-product-compliance
Lightning Source LLC
Chambersburg PA
CBHW050033120726
47903CB00006B/2024